NAKED UNDER CAPRICORN

AUSTRALIAN CLASSICS

NAKED
UNDER CAPRICORN
Olaf Ruhen

ANGUS
& ROBERTSON
PUBLISHERS

ANGUS & ROBERTSON PUBLISHERS

Unit 4, Eden Park, 31 Waterloo Road,
North Ryde, NSW, Australia 2113, and
16 Golden Square, London W1R 4BN,
United Kingdom

First published 1958
This Australian Classics edition first published in Australia
by Angus & Robertson Publishers in 1982
Reprinted 1987

Copyright © Olaf Ruhen 1957, 1958

National Library of Australia
Cataloguing-in-publication data.

Ruhen, Olaf, 1911-.
  Naked under Capricorn.

  First published: London: MacDonald, 1958.
  ISBN 0 207 14423 0.

  I. Title. (Series: Australian classics (Angus &
  Robertson)).

A823'.3

Printed in Singapore

To BILL HARNEY

. . . good bushman,
. . . good thinker,
. . . good friend.

FOREWORD

The tracks of the camels, a broad line of prints shuffled into the red receptive sand, led off directly enough into the distance. They were alone and distinct, not to be confused with the casual pads of lesser animals—the patterned print of the dingo, the deep claw-marks of the kangaroo, the pattering circumambulations of the porcupine, the clear prints of birds and the feather-light scamperings of lizards. Only the camel-tracks had direction. Only they led into the desert distance with the passivity of obedience. They were the only mark that man had ever made in this Australian solitude. No one had followed this lead; no one ever would. They traced the beginning of a journey and no one could ever say how it had ended, though to guess might be easy enough. But they marked the end of a journey too, a journey that had begun half a century before and half a continent away in the North; a journey that began and ended under the stars of Capricorn.

1

The harsh desert air, hot and brooding, seemed to shiver delicately as though under the onslaught of distant bells, and the man by the billabong, sprawled uncomfortably on the rock in the inadequate shade of a river gum, lifted his head and looked about him. The rich red overtones of Australian earth were here muted, overwhelmed by the greys and greens of the trees plentifully surrounding the water hole; and by the blue of the water hole itself, a half-mile stretch of wide stream bed filled to a considerable depth with the remnant of last season's rain. The sky too, as it was disclosed through the desert-sparse foliage of the trees, was brazen blue; and the brilliance of light dazzled where it struck the white bark of ghost gum and coolibah, and the young branches of the river gums.

The man was naked. His arms and neck were bronze-tanned; the rest of his lean body would soon be uncomfortably burned. As he watched, intent on recapturing the impact of the sound that had so delicately fractured the silence, four emus came to drink, poised heads following in wary rhythm the movements of the legs, bright eyes searching against the mischance of an enemy's presence, heavy bodies threading the shrubbery, the boronias and turkey bushes, the desert fuchsias and the stunted acacias that crowded near the end of the hole, where an outcropping of red conglomerate had dammed the waters.

The emus came steadily on, waded into the water and drank deeply, and the man sat up, disclosing the tattered and filthy remnants of an old red shirt with which he had

9

been protecting his back from the rock. He sat up and listened, and the expected was resolved into sound, the tinny distant tinkle of a horse-bell.

In some excitement he climbed the bank behind him, catching up the shirt from the rock and tying it by the sleeves about his waist so that it formed a loose, flapping apron that emphasized as much as it hid his nakedness. From the top of the bank the plain stretched, level and wide, in every direction. No mountains broke the symmetry of its horizons; the frequent bushes and small trees, grouped or solitary, hid from him the source of the tinkling of the bells.

A man more accustomed to the plains would instantly have fixed upon the skyline to the east, where a rising column of dust announced the imminent arrival of horses with the finality of vision; but this man was not aware of its significance, or, indeed, of its presence.

Disconsolately he returned to the shade upon his rock, stood hesitantly for a moment, then waded into the water. Soon he was swimming in its depths, almost carefree, as though he were washing away his worries in the water that struck, now warm, now icy cold, upon his skin. The emus lifted their heads and, one behind the other, climbed the bank and struck out over the plain, breaking into an ungainly heavy run, water-filled and reluctant to move fast.

The man shook the water from his eyes and started up the length of the water hole, swimming steadily though not powerfully with a sideways kicking stroke. He covered a couple of hundred yards and returned. Suddenly he stopped. There were horses massed above the bank of the water hole. He stared at them for a second and then swam quickly to the edge, picked up his shirt and, hastily adjusting it as before, hurried to the top of the bank. The horses wheeled and reared away from him, and a man's voice was raised in curses.

In a moment he appeared, a big, bearded fellow, square-shouldered, free-striding, a stockman dressed in the uniform of his trade: a wide-brimmed felt hat, a shirt open at the throat, narrow-legged trousers, high-heeled, elastic-sided boots, and a plaited belt adorned with cartridges and with half-a-dozen pouches—for matches, tobacco, castrating knife.

He slapped at the haunch of a young horse, pushing it out of his road as he shouldered his way into the open.

"What the hell?" he said. "What in God's name are you doing here?"

The man in the shirt said nothing. His mouth worked as though he were trying to speak, but no sound came. The newcomer watched him searchingly for a moment and then spoke as though he had received a full reply.

"All right," he said. "Sit down for a minute until I get these packs off."

He turned back to the herd, where four pack horses milled among the others, four stockily built beasts, heavy in the body. One at a time he led them to the shelter of a bloodwood tree where three saddles already stood on edge, their blankets draped over them to dry. Only one carried its stirrups. Here, working with the utmost precision, a precise conservation of energy, he off-loaded the packs. The man in the shirt went forward to help; but the earth on the plain was plentifully covered with a variety of angular and needle-sharp seeds; and after a few steps (dancing painfully among the grass clumps) he retreated to the top of the bank. When the pack horses had been off-loaded the herd wheeled and whinnied, and raced to the water, like schoolboys new-released from the restrictions of the day.

The drover stood for a moment watching them, then walked back to the man, holding out his hand.

"Jeff Edrington," he introduced himself. "I'm headed south. You got stranded, is that it? Someone left you here? Stole your gear and left you?"

The man in the shirt nodded. He looked grateful, as though relieved that his story was half-accepted before it had been told.

"Davis Marriner, that's my name," he said. "All I've got is what you see." He fingered the filthy shirt. "It wasn't even mine. It's all they left me with."

"They? Who's 'they'?"

"A fellow called Simmons, Bob Simmons," Marriner began, and Edrington nodded.

"I've heard of him. Hang on. We'll put the billy on and talk over a pot of tea."

Still with the same economy of motion he set his fire near the saddles grouped under the bloodwood tree, looking up to grin as Marriner hobbled painfully over the thorned seeds on the ground.

"You'd better put that shirt on your shoulders, before the sun does any more damage." He half unrolled a canvas-wrapped pile of blankets and threw over a pair of coarse denim trousers and a pair of elastic-sided boots that looked new.

"Try them for size," he said; and went back to his fire, seemingly indifferent.

"Simmons had a big mob with him then," he suggested over his shoulder. "I cut tracks a day from here. They'd have been his."

"There were three others besides Simmons, and six blacks."

"And he took you?"

"He . . . ?"

"You had some money?"

"A little. Not much. But all I owned."

"How much?"

"Four hundred quid."

"That was enough. Well, what was the story? How come you're here? Did he sell you a gold mine?"

"Not exactly. Oh, I was a fool. It was rubies, he said. I met him in Darwin. . . ."

"Start before that. Start with yourself. Where did you come from? Sydney? You're not from the bush."

Marriner moved uncomfortably.

"I kept a store in Brisbane, a little corner shop out in South Brisbane, across the river. It belonged to my parents when they were alive. I helped my mother after my dad died, and that lasted five years. Then I had it to myself. It started going downhill. I gave it away, sold up, and set out to see the world."

"Got restless, eh? No kith nor kin?"

"No. I had nobody. And yes, I got restless. It started when the soldiers came back from fighting the Boers, with their talk of Africa and the sea. I seemed to have a skinful of slicing bars of soap and weighing out tea. And I thought I'd take a look at the East; I've always wanted to see the East. And I came to Cairns and Cooktown, and Thursday Island, and then to Darwin."

"And fell in with Bob Simmons, and swallowed some yarn about rubies."

"I didn't listen to him straightaway. Though he was such a likeable fellow, I thought. He was talking about this valley out to the south and west; and a stream running through it, and rubies studding the gravel in the bed. But he had no thought of taking me. 'Twas me that begged him. 'Rubies,' I said. 'I'd surely like to see that.' In my mind's eye I could see them piled up in leather sacks like potatoes in a bag, and the light making a fire of them. And I begged and begged him and at last he said I could come. And on that he had trouble with the others. They were against me coming. They said I was a new-chum; I'd be in the road. I'd make their share smaller. But he argued for me; and one night he fought for me and then it was agreed I could come. It would be the others—Rankin,

13

Randall and Sears; it would have been them that robbed me."

"And left you to die. You'd have been dead, come the week end." Edrington shook his head. "No, it was Simmons. He's done it before. Four hundred, he got? It's a good haul. It's his trade, you might say."

"I'll follow him. I'll follow him till I find him and take it back."

Edrington looked him over. Marriner had pulled on the trousers and the boots, and now stood awkwardly, stamping his feet into the loose red earth, the shirt hanging outside the trousers, the trousers too short for the leg, leaving a strip of bare skin above the ankle-hugging boot tops. In spite of the comic effect Marriner seemed a good stamp of a man. He was straight enough, taller than average. He was fairheaded and had good features, but the jaw was a little slack, the mouth a little uncontrolled and the blue eyes a little dull.

"You'll kiss it good-bye," said Edrington. "If you know what's good for you, you will." He spread out a square of canvas near the fire, and poured a little pile of flour on it.

"Simmons is bad medicine. He's unhealthy." At the top of the cone of flour he made a depression with his thumb and then restored the symmetry of the peak with a fine dribbling of baking-powder. Then, grasping the corners of the canvas to make a rough bag, he shook all up together. "Anyway, how do you propose to follow him? Are you going to walk? He's headed east; I'm going south. Are you going to come with me or wait for the next man to happen along? Next man might be six months, a year."

Marriner looked at him steadily enough, but his lower lip trembled.

"I could sell you a horse—but I doubt that shirt of yours

14

would buy it," Edrington went on, a precise neat man, marshalling his tidy arguments as now, with precise additions of water from a quart pot, he worked the flour into a dough.

"And judging by the tracks I cut he'd be a couple of days ahead of you, or three."

"Four," said Marriner.

"You've had nothing to eat then, for four days?"

"Just water." Marriner nodded.

The intelligence seemed to make little impression on Edrington. He continued to work at his dough, occasionally dusting the canvas square with flour.

"You'd better throw in with me. I'm going through to South Australia, and I can use a man. I want to have a look at some country south of the Macdonnell Ranges—I may take it up. Once we get down there we'll see how we get on. It should be easy enough then for you to pick up with someone going through to Port Augusta."

"Thank God you came. You've saved my life," Marriner said, belatedly enough, and the other man nodded.

"Probably," he admitted. "But you don't have to thank me. You can work it out instead. You've got a couple of hard months ahead of you."

It was his only reference to the possible trials of the fourteen-hundred-mile desert journey that lay ahead. Abandoning, for the moment, his roll of worked dough he took a billy of boiling water from the fire and made tea. He set a pannikin beside the new-chum.

"Sugar in the packs," he said, nodding towards the accumulation of saddles and gear under the bloodwood. "We'll have some tucker later on. I've got nothing ready." For himself he poured out a substantial measure of the tea into the lid of the billy.

Marriner gulped at the strong black tea. Immediately the sweat started through his pores so that he was bathed in it; and immediately he felt the coolness of its evaporation. He sat there enjoying it, long after Edrington had finished his tea and—methodically, efficiently—stacked the fire high with wood. The horses, replete with their own refreshment of water, had returned to the bank, some standing with their heads plunged into the shade of the small whitewood and blackheart trees; some rolling in the loose red earth; some, young and mischievous, nipping and wheeling, trying to start an argument in the ranks of their elders. As soon as the fire was to his satisfaction Edrington moved to the herd, taking a pair of rawhide hobbles from the neck-strap of each horse and adjusting it about the fetlocks. After a moment's thought Marriner went to help him, but the horses wheeled away from him, and would not stand.

"I'll get round to them," Edrington called. "But stay where you are. Let them get used to you. See if you can handle a few of them."

He hobbled the whole herd with remarkable speed. When all were secure he walked back to the fire, now all glowing embers, lifted his bread dough into the base of a covered pot, and with a shovel dug a hole at a little distance from the fire, a hole of a few inches greater diameter than the pot, and double its depth. Then with the shovel he half-filled the hole with live embers from the fire and settled the pot upon them. That done he covered the pot with the remaining embers and buried everything at last in hot sand from under the fire.

He set the shovel back in its place with the packs, dusted off his square of canvas and repacked it, and returned the flour bag to its place. Without a pause he unpacked a towel and a square bar of soap from somewhere in his blanket-roll and walked to the lagoon. Every movement he made seemed to have been planned far in advance, to fall into a pattern thoroughly practised, to produce effortlessly the desired effect. From the top of the bank Marriner watched

him walk directly to the rock bar, where a few pools held
water made hot by the sun-baked rocks. Here he stripped,
washed shirt and socks in one pool, then wallowed in
another, washing from head to toes in a strict order. When
he was clean and rinsed he lay in the warm water of yet a
third pool. He stopped there half an hour, completely
relaxed, before he emerged, towelled himself dry, and
dressed again in the still-damp clothes which he had spread
upon bushes by the bank.

He walked back to where Marriner awaited him. Halfway
he stopped, and, above the rock where the naked Marriner
had lain, he peered into the trees for a moment.

"This is a good camp," he said. Back at the fire he took
the shovel and dug up the covered pot, setting it aside to
cool. Then he took an axe.

"Come down, I want to show you something," he said to
Marriner, and led him back to his familiar rock. Above it
a slim branch of the river gum towered high towards the
sky.

"See where the dead branch has broken off? See anything
there?" Marriner couldn't.

"If you watch awhile you'll see a little fly, a little black
fly, coming or going."

There was indeed a little traffic of flies going and coming
at an almost invisible hole in the dead wood. Marriner
had seen them, but thought them not worth noting. Edrington said no more. He put his ear against the lower half of
the branch, moving his head up and down, listening. He
selected a spot well down, stepped back and chopped it with
the axe. The branch here was about ten inches in diameter;
but after the first inch the axe bit into the black sponginess
of rotted wood, and with half-a-dozen strokes the branch
came down. A little crowd of black flies congregated near
the dead wood, and here Edrington cut again. Then with
an economy of strokes he split the branch.

17

It was hollow, and for eight feet of its length it was filled with a honeyed hive: breeding cells at one end, honey and comb in the centre, and a pollen store at the top. Tiny black bewildered bees made no attempt to fly away, nor did they make any attack upon the intruders.

"Take no notice of the bees. They have no stings," said Edrington. He took a lump of the pollen and dipped it in the flowing honey, flung his head back and filled his mouth. Half-a-dozen bees went in with the honey. Timidly, Marriner broke off a fragment of the pollen, dipped it in the sweetness and popped it in his mouth.

The fragment yellow pollen blended well with the sweet remembered honey. It carried an acidity that made a new and attractive flavour for Marriner. And when the mouthful was ingested there was a residue of honeycomb on which he chewed. That there was also a fragment of dead wood and another foreign body which he suspected may have been one of the fly-like bees was something from which he turned his mind away. He was starving, and he took another mouthful.

Meanwhile, Edrington with the axe had cut away a broad section of bark from one of the near-by trees and with a small stick was transferring the hive from the hollow in the tree to its sap-moist surface, mixing the honey, the pollen and the comb all together, leaving only the breeding cells in position.

"A good hive," he said. "Enough honey to keep you alive for a fortnight. It would have kept you filled for a couple of days." He looked at Marriner meaningfully. "You have to learn this country to live in it."

"I had no idea there was food at hand," Marriner admitted, admiringly. Edrington represented something new in his experience, and was already humbling him. But a latent self-conceit came to his protection.

"Of course, I had no axe."

Edrington nodded. "True enough," he said. "But there's a wealth of sharp-edged stones by the reef there that you might have been able to do something with. You had enough time at your hand. And where there's a will there's a way."

For the next hour or two Edrington overhauled one of his saddles, using a small, but remarkably adequate kit that had its own leather pouch, and that included a small lump of lead for an anvil, an even smaller vice, an assortment of punches, bradawls and needles, a supply of threads and beeswax and copper rivets, pliers and knives and palms. With these he attacked defects which Marriner would have dismissed as too trivial; but finally the saddle and a bridle were satisfactory to his eye, and he set them back under the tree and replaced the half-blanket with them.

"Right, there's your gear," he said. "That saddlecloth will have to double as a sleeping blanket; especially if we get south a bit; I haven't too many spares. But there's maybe enough for now while the nights are hot. In the south we may have to sleep between fires. It gets cold on the desert."

He shook up the fire, refuelled it, and began making a pile of the dead branches that lay plentifully about the trees near by. Marriner jumped up to help; and when the stack was satisfactory Edrington took a rifle.

"Stay here," he said. "I'll see if I can get a 'roo."

The white cockatoos had returned from their day's foraging to the water hole, and now each pair stood like neighbourhood gossips by the entrance to their home in a hollow branch, screaming abuse and retaliation to the world or breaking off to make short flights of braggadocio about the avian settlement. A colony of divers was disposed about the branches of a tall tree near the camp; and on the opposite side of the water hole a thousand galahs, grey and rose, had stripped the leaves entirely from a group of three river

19

gums, so that they could perch in safety, as they were now beginning to do, and enjoy at the same time an unrestricted view of their surroundings. The trees were rose coloured where the beams from the setting sun caught the breast feathers of the assembly, and when, as now and again happened, a flight of the parrots left the tree and circled overhead, there was a breathtaking glimpse of a deeper rose beneath their wings. The budgerigars were making their last swift dispositions for the day, flying in glittering green flocks above the water, changing direction and velocity with a speed and a unanimity which the human mind could only imagine must come from the expressed command of some martinet in the ranks.

A shot rang out, and all the noisy parrot world was momentarily silent—the budgerigars, the galahs, the cockatoos, the grass-parrots, the bluebonnets and the quariens; then the clamour transcended anything that had gone before. The cockatoos rose and swept into a flock, traversing the length of the water hole, screaming like demented spirits. And shortly Edrington returned, carrying over his shoulders the limp body of a small kangaroo.

"Just the right size," he said. "Dinner and breakfast, and not too much waste."

He skinned the animal and roasted the ribs and the saddle on the embers of the fire, without benefit of any utensil whatsoever. The damper he had cooked earlier turned out to be a success; a bread that was lightly browned as to the crust, heavy and even-textured. Marriner, with a thick slice in one hand and the grill in the other, ate ravenously; and when the flavour of the meat palled he followed Edrington's example, toasting slices of the damper over the fire and spreading it thickly with the remainder of the bush honey. The meal, washed down with three large pannikins of black and heavily sugared tea, was a substantial one; Marriner ate heartily and with obvious enjoyment. He had to ignore the grit

which had invaded the skirts of the meat, the tiny bees
drowned in the honey-morass of their own making, the
unreasonable heat of the metal pannikin; but it was as
though these things did not exist for him. When at last he
was satisfied, his contentment seemed sincere.

They sat over the dying fire for a little while, but Marriner's head was nodding, and he was pleased when Edrington showed signs of laying out his bedroll for sleep.

When, precisely at three in the morning, the planet Venus
showed its bright lamp over the edge of the eastern sky,
Edrington was awake in an instant. Immediately he began
dressing; or rather, completing his attire, for he had slept
in his shirt. He pulled on trousers and high-heeled boots,
adjusted short leggings, added spurs, pulled a scarf about
his throat and put on a hat.

There were small whimpering noises coming from the
dark figure of Marriner lying wrapped in his blankets.
Edrington walked up close and looked down. The moonlight picked out a trail of moisture on the still-young cheeks
as though the man had been crying in his sleep. As Edrington looked at him the whimpers were repeated twice more,
but the sleep was undisturbed. Edrington grinned, and,
hooking a bridle over his arm, walked off to the plains where,
in the distance, the muted tinkling of the horse-bell adver-
tised the whereabouts of the herd.

When he returned, perhaps three hours later, riding on the
back of the old, belled mare and driving the herd before him,
the sun was rising, and Marriner had lit a fire and had the
billy boiling. They ate the damper and the cold meat from
the previous night's meal, then Edrington turned to the bed-
rolls and the utensils, folding and wrapping them, putting
them into packs, working, apparently, to a long-practised
formula. When all was tidied he brought the pack horses,
one at a time, to the bloodwood tree, and fitted their
saddles.

Marriner watched him rather helplessly. Then he walked over from the fire and said, "If ever I can repay you some-day . . ."

"You could start," said Edrington, "by getting some of these hobbles off."

2

So swiftly did Edrington impose the discipline of his personality upon the days, and so exactly did he keep to his routine that soon it was as though the journey had always been a ceaseless unchanging rhythm of movement, of which the integral variations were predictable and expected, of which the constant change was itself changeless. At each dawn they were packed and ready to move, hobbles all jangling at the neck-straps, the water canisters freshened and filled, hooked to the saddle of the heaviest pack horse and fastened with a surcingle of leather ten inches broad, the camp left tidy, the fire safe, Edrington's rifle in a saddle holster at his knee and the Australian plain stretching illimitably before them.

When they moved off at a mile-consuming gait that varied between a slow jog and a fast walk the little cavalcade stretched out to take up a pattern of march, a pattern that, however it varied throughout the day, fell always into similar variations. There was a skewbald gelding who ran always at the tail of a skewbald mare, the pack horse with the water canisters inevitably dropped back to the unpopular position at the rear, four mares jostled always for the lead, each enjoying her triumph for a brief passage. The friendships and rivalries of the herd were reflected always in the line of march.

When the trail led them over the sandy ridges covered with spinifex the cleverer horses dropped back and left the lead to the stupid, fearing with reason the harassment of the needle-sharp blades of the grass upon fetlocks and

23

coronets and lightly protected cannon-bones. When their way led through the stands of mulga, the adventurous pushed forward, thrusting through the grey foliage. Infrequently, when they traversed a range of granite hills, still another pattern was impressed upon the herd.

Edrington rode in silence for the most part, his eye forever ranging the horizon like a sailor's. In general their route lay south, but sometimes, in midmorning say, there would be a change of direction. Edrington would canter along the flank of the cavalcade and turn the leaders, east or west; and always, within an hour or two of noon, they would make camp alongside some water hole; usually a stretch of river bed, or one of the billabongs which formed a subsidiary channel in the infrequent floodtime; but once a small rock pool among granite boulders, and another time a dry river where no water showed upon the surface at all.

Marriner, remembering perhaps the stories of men made mad and perishing through lack of water, was shocked at this dearth. He reined in at the bank, looking down at the river of dry sand and wondering how they would manage. But already the horses were streaming past him; clattering down the banks and heading for the bend that lay ahead, where a drift of rock ran from bank to bank. Here they gathered in little groups, scratching and pawing at the sand; and at a little depth the water appeared at the bottom of the holes they made.

"Water's getting scarce," he said to Edrington, who shook his head.

"There'll be plenty at a soak like this for months to come," he argued. "That rock bar holds it here, and there's little evaporation under the sand. I've never seen so much water in this part of the country as we've passed; and that's a fact. It's been a good season."

Each noon they lunched upon the remnants of their meal

24

of the night before, and of their breakfast. In the afternoons Edrington was always busy, handling a young horse,
mending harness which he kept up to a standard of peak
efficiency, making the rawhide hobbles which the horses
were forever losing, sharpening his knives and tools, check-
ing and sometimes doctoring his stock, washing his clothes
and mending them, and finally, on each day, securing the
food for the evening. At this, his prowess seemed almost
magical.

One noon, an exceptionally hot noon, when the red earth
sent up a shimmering stream of heat to the brazen sky, two
emus moved away from the water hole they were approaching.
Edrington immediately pulled his tired horse into a gallop
and raced after them. The birds, water-filled and stupid
under the sun, lumbered away, displaying nothing of the
speed for which they were renowned. Edrington quickly
overhauled the nearer one, slipping his off stirrup-leather
away from its anchorage as he raced, and brought the bird
down with a smart clip over the head with the iron.

It was a good display of horsemanship; Edrington obviously
regarded it as nothing more than the occasional duty of an
efficient commissary. He filled the belly of the bird with
heated stones before he cooked it on the fire, and Marriner
thought the meal delicious.

Fowl of one sort or another was frequently on the menu,
mostly in the form of the big turkey bustards, fearless and
inquisitive, that roamed the plains. But often enough the
meal was of a sort that Marriner would once have scorned—
the grilled tails of goanna lizards each more than filled a
man's stomach; the porcupine-like echidna made a meal as
homely as grilled pig.

In none of these hunting activities did Edrington require or
much appreciate the little co-operation that Marriner could
give, and the afternoons seemed to hang heavy on Marriner's hands. Sometimes he moved among the horses, as

though he longed for the company of any living things; once or twice he sat down with Edrington's only book: a battered copy of More's *Utopia* bound in a homemade cover of rawhide that was still adorned with a few red and white hairs. Often he sat still, or swam if the opportunity presented itself; or wandered through the trees surrounding the water hole looking for "sugar-bag," the hive of the wild bees. In this he was singularly unsuccessful. The signs, so obvious to Edrington, evaded his senses.

Yet he was not unhappy. The constant riding, the discipline imposed on him was toughening him, making him healthy. The weather, hot in the day, cold at night, was uniformly good; bracing during the period of their greatest activity and delightful for their evening repose. Game was never scarce; water and fuel were there for their collection; and there was an abiding satisfaction about their life as though they had left the world and discovered reality.

They had maintained this unbalanced partnership for ten days when Marriner discovered, not without some consternation, that the country they traversed was as new to Edrington as to himself.

"Never saw it before," Edrington said, as casually as he made any other commonplace conversation. "I've been right over the Island a couple of times, in the north-south line, but both times further east, over in the Channel country. There's country for you," he added. "Good fattening country."

"Then how do you know where to find water? I thought you must know all the camps."

"Plenty of water—so far," said Edrington. He reined in his horse. "Look here. Over east—see the line of trees? That's the river. Water holes all along her. We'd get there in an hour, but we have three or four hours in hand. See yonder, straight ahead. Looks like the trees swing back there. Well, we'll make for them, somewhere near the bend.

Could be that a rock ridge there turned the water in the first place, and if that's so there'll be a water hole or a soak behind it. Anyway, we'll get an idea as we go up. And when we get near, the horses will pick it up and lead us in."

"They smell it?"

"So they say. They smell it, or they smell the vegetation that grows near it. Can't say I could put a name to the smell of water, but there's times I've sensed it myself. And then, of course, the game trails lead in, and the horses know about them. Watch the flock pigeons; they'll give you a good sign. Emus in the afternoon are working away from water; in the morning they're working in. 'Roos drink at night. You'll get water always against the hills. There's a thousand signs to tell you—the way the parrots fly; the galahs will always lead you, the white cockatoos. Up in this country it's no problem. It'll get tougher as we go down. Anyway, the water canisters will always carry us over a dry camp; we have five or six hours in hand every day; the horses have plenty of condition yet, and where's your worry?"

"Oh, I'm not worried," Marriner said. And indeed his worries were limited to an appreciation of his own newly discovered ineptitude.

The country was, however, changing. The open plains stretched ever wider; the small humped mountains, mere hillocks of boulder-capped granite or flat-topped conglomerate, loomed up less often. The spinifex ridges spread their monotonous rippled pattern more and more frequently and ever wider over the landscape; and the patches of dried polygonum swamp, ringed by stands of mulga, grew smaller. The game, however, seemed to congregate in greater numbers than before. The river courses, marked by trees of considerably greater development than those which studded the plains, were easier to distinguish and far less frequent.

These changes were so gradual as not to be apparent to Marriner, to whom it seemed that the pattern of days was undisturbed. He did not notice, for example, that the horses looked for their feed less and less upon the ground, and more and more on the bushes, nibbling at whitewood and blackheart and mulga; and feeding greedily on clumps of supplejack, a vine that was adapting itself, over the centuries, to arboreal form. Sometimes they nosed among the spinifex for parakeelia, a lush succulent that, as Edrington demonstrated, was palatable enough as it grew to keep a man alive; or upon another succulent, munyeroo.

None of this seemed significant. The first incident that provided a break in the pattern came after they had been on their road for nearly two weeks. Marriner had fallen behind the herd for twenty minutes or so and was cantering to catch up when he saw Edrington, reined in, looking back and waiting for him.

"We've got company," he announced, as Marriner drew up.

He pointed ahead, far ahead on the plain where five small figures, people on foot, threaded the scattered trees to intersect the line of march. They seemed in no hurry.

"You'll find these desert natives a different kettle of fish from the ones up north," Edrington observed. "They look different, for a start. Uglier, for one thing. And a lot of them are blondes, even though they're black. You've got to take them with a grain of salt. Anything they tell you will be the truth, but it won't be all the truth."

"That's if they tell you anything, I suppose," said Marriner.

"Oh, they'll answer our questions."

When, after twenty minutes, the riders came up with the party, the leader came forward. He was a man of medium height with a good chest and arms, but with thin shanks and delicate ankles that made his feet seem big. He wore his hair in a bun caught up with some textile at the back of his head, and he carried an assortment of weapons.

In his left hand, by his hip, were three spears and a woomera, the simple implement which, by doubling the length of the throwing arm, gave tremendously increased impetus to the thrown spear. There was also a throwing stick, like a boomerang with one arm three times the length of the other. Tucked into a bracelet on his arm was a knife flaked from a white stone that looked like a jasper, a knife furnished with a black handle of spinifex gum. In his right hand, and leaning against his right shoulder, was another throwing stick, a thin ribbed club-like artifact, stone-carved from end to end with a simple pattern—a pattern that approximated the one inscribed upon the woomera and the curved stick. When the two white men reined in he set his weapons carefully on the ground and came up to the horses, without any outward sign of fear or hesitancy.

He was stark naked, but he had the dignity of a man in his own country, and he took in the appearance of the two riders without visible signs of surprise or curiosity, or any emotion other than such interest as might be considered polite.

"Which way to water?" asked Edrington, and to Marriner's surprise the man understood the question and answered immediately, swinging and jerking his chin in the direction from which he had come.

Behind him the rest of his party stood motionless where he had left them. There were two women, each, as Marriner judged, a great deal younger than the man, and each as naked as Eve. There was a boy of about twelve years, carrying spears and a woomera of his own, and a younger girl, of perhaps five.

The hair of all of them was blonde, matted locks of uneven length making a ragged aureole that caught the light of the sun in a drift of colours. One of the women carried at the curve of her elbow a coolamon, a sheet of bark with upturned edges between which lay, in untroubled sleep, a tiny baby. The other, a younger woman, stared calmly at the horseman, and Marriner, staring back, realized with a shock that her face was almost beautiful. It was a beauty of infinite pathos. Its most prominent adjuncts were the eyes, large deep brown pools, bordered by whites that were white only by suggestion, being caught in veined nets of a misty brown. She was slender, thin rather, but not thin to emaciation. Her breasts were small and well separated, and between them four parallel ridges of raised scars testified to some tribal ceremony. She stood loosely, quietly, looking straight in front of her; and her face bore an expression of such poignancy that it seemed to establish a communication.

Her companion was older and plumper, with similarly marked breasts that were two pendulous dugs.

"Water this way?" Edrington was asking, pointing directly in the path he had been following.

The native shook his head.

"No more," he said.

"Where's your tribe?" Edrington asked, but the native did not answer, not understanding, perhaps. Edrington tried again.

"Some man belonging you, some other man?" he asked.

There was an indefinite gesture of the chin.

"Long way. One, two, t'ree, days."

"They camp along water here?" Edrington pointed.

"No more, boss. Maybe some man."

"Are there cattle ahead?"

"No more. Nothing."

"All right."

Edrington lifted his reins, and immediately the younger of the women, she of the beautiful eyes, started forward.

"'Bacca," she said and held out her hand.

Her man stood still, looking at Edrington.

"All right," he said again, and searched in his saddle pouch. He produced a stick of a dark, moist-looking tobacco and the native took it.

"Plour," said the woman, but Edrington shook his head.

"No flour," he said, and then grinned. "No more. Nothing."

They moved on, leaving the little family standing, looking after them, in the desert.

"They're not afraid anyway," observed Marriner.

"They're not afraid, and they're not unfriendly. You could trust them. You could trust any of them if only you knew what the fellow ahead of you had been doing to them."

"They'll spear cattle, though."

"Yes, they'll spear them. Don't forget, they live by the spear. But it's in the cattle country that they'll spear white men and you have to watch them. Because there they've been hunted and shot; they've had their wells poisoned. They've been ridden down. They've been spread-eagled, tied up in the hot sun and left to die. And they're men. And men will fight back."

"You reckon it's the white that causes the bother?"

"Look at the record. And look from the other angle. Look at the explorers. Giles tried to cross this country, east to west. He had good equipment, and he had camels. He took a pot shot, just for luck at the abos he saw; he treated them all as potential enemies, and he failed. Couldn't find water. Came back with his tail between his legs. Warburton had the best expedition ever seen round here—camels too, the lot. He shot some blacks, mistrusted the rest. And he failed. Forrest starts in West Australia with a ragtime expedition, mediocre horses; and wishing he could have got camels. But there just weren't any in the West. He had to find water just five times as often as the others. He took a couple of blacks with him, made friends with those he met, and came through without trouble. In the same season as the other two. They all crossed one another's tracks."

"Maybe he was lucky," Marriner said diffidently, and Edrington considered this.

"Maybe he was lucky," he said, "but he was consistently lucky, and in my book luck isn't consistent. Some say he was lucky. And some say he did it because he wasn't English. He was Australian born, and he wasn't a superior bastard like the others. But when I'm in the desert I take a leaf out of his book and I'm friendly with the blacks. I haven't come to grief yet. And when you get to know them they're better than they look."

"That slim girl was almost good-looking," Marriner said.

"Yes?"

"She was a little wild thing, but she had beautiful eyes. Did you see?"

"Well, if you want her, go back for her. I'll give you tobacco—that'll buy her. But don't bring her into camp. And do your bargaining with her man. I don't want arguments."

Marriner was shocked.

"I didn't mean . . . I didn't think of her that way. I just meant—she was beautiful to look at, just like any wild thing. I've never seen a woman naked before."

"They're all naked round here. Till you get to the missions and the cattle stations. Then they stink."

Marriner wrinkled his nose.

"How could a white man mate with them? I couldn't understand that."

Edrington looked at him as they jogged along.

"They'll look whiter the oftener you see them. Sometime, if you're on your own, you may feel different. There's a lot of understanding in a couple of months of loneliness."

When they had ridden on perhaps two miles Edrington looked back, and grunted. A thin column of smoke was rising to the zenith.

"That fellow wasn't telling all the truth," he said. "Plenty more of his tribe around somewhere."

"Is that a signal fire, then?" Marriner asked, and his companion nodded.

"He's telling his friends that we're a strong party, that he has met us but come to no harm. That's all."

"But it looks just like an ordinary fire."

Edrington laughed.

"That's all it is. What they can read into it, though, is amazing, sometimes. But it's all based on a foreknowledge. His friends know he is out here in this country. They can tell there's a new element come in. He's put up a smoke behind us, so they know he's met us. He hasn't changed his plans or he'd put up two smokes or three in a line in the direction he is now travelling. If they rose a long way apart in a short time they'd know he was travelling fast. There's only one smoke, so he's still doing what he was before and the inference is that he is untroubled by our presence, that we are friendly. There's another inference too, that he found us in no need of help from him. In fact, you'd be amazed what you can read into that smoke. But there's no special way of reading it. There's no words in it, no special formation. Just the fact that it's there is enough."

"Well, how do they know we're in the picture at all?"

"Dust. From here you can't see it; but travelling horses raise a dust you can see ten miles or more. Cattle don't— not the way the country is now. But everyone for miles around knows there's a party here with horses; and they know exactly where we are. They've been watching us since first thing in the morning, probably."

"Then that fellow met us on purpose?"

"That's right. He came and looked us over for the benefit of his countrymen."

"He's not timid then."

"No. He's got plenty of guts. With a good-looking gin like that in tow, especially. There's many a man would have carted the gin off at the end of a rope, and shot the buck if he objected. Oh, he'd know that. But as it is, the tribe can have an easy mind. But he told us the tribe was a long way away; and if they had been he wouldn't have bothered to light the fire."

"They might be waiting for us then. Or perhaps there's no water where he's sent us."

"No, there'll be water. But the tribe won't be there. They don't want to meet us. Some corroboree business, maybe."

They found the water at the foot of a low range, in the line that the native had indicated. There was a sandy pass between two cliffs and here, touching both rocks, a pool not more than twenty feet across lay in the shade. Edrington pointed to a series of scrapes nearby, shallow holes, water filled, that had been dug in the sand.

"There must have been a big tribe of them camped here. They make their own scrapes, see, when they can. They get the water purer that way, and colder than it is in the big water hole. It's funny. Sometimes, at a rock hole, where the parrots flock, they'll drink stinking water, thick and soupy, if there's no other. But they're mighty particular whenever they have a choice."

Marriner slept uneasily by the water hole that night. Several times he got up and walked about the camp, leaving Edrington, a silent inert bundle at the foot of a tree, while he trudged back through the river sand that spewed out from the pass between the low bluffs. There was a bird singing insistently, a willie wagtail repeating his call-sign over and over: "Sweet pretty creature, sweet pretty creature"—in the purest notes that ever issued from a feathered throat. There was half a moon well down on the western sky, and the galaxies seemed to hang low, close to the earth.

Partly his restlessness was born of the temperature, for the nights had grown colder as they thrust southward and the desert enclosed them; partly it was an inheritance of the morning's meeting. He imagined a disposition of warriors squatting behind the clustered rocks on the cliffs, spear-armed, threatening the sleeping camp. He imagined fearful and shapeless dangers behind them. But the last time he crawled again into the rumpled pile of his blankets he slept until Edrington, barebacked upon a big roan gelding, ran the horses into the camp in the half-dark that forecast the dawn.

It was the roan that Edrington saddled for himself that day, a fine, deep-chested weight carrier with round, heavily muscled haunches well coupled to the body, a tall upstanding horse that could not be tired, and of which the only fault was that he was a little unresponsive to the rider's signals. He was a young horse, a favourite of Edrington's.

He was a good choice for the day, for their path lay through the scattered ramifications of a granite range, over and round a series of short shoulders and spurs, and then for seven miles along a barren ridge, strewed with round and weather-rotted boulders. Eastward of them lay a wilderness of ridges and valleys stretching into the blue haze of the far distance, and to the west a lesser system promised no ease from the rock travelling. There was no shortage of water. Nearly every valley to either side carried the traces of its presence. But there was an anxiety nevertheless, which the horses seemed to share with the men, to return to the easier travelling of the plain.

At last they came to a place where the ridge they were following swung to the southwest, and the change of direction disclosed a new illimitability of flat country ahead, a huge prairie dotted thinly with bushes, and traversed by a winding snake of heavily foliaged trees that followed the line of what must have been, in every wet season, a substantial river.

Edrington's eyes brightened when he saw it.

"We'll make an early camp," he said. "There should be water near the first bend. A couple of days of comfortable travelling and then we hit the true desert. It must be somewhere in these latitudes. We want to rest up the horses all we can; though they've kept fit enough till now."

"How long will we be in the desert?"

"At this end I wouldn't know. Not more than one day without water, if we're lucky. If we're not—well. This season looks as though we may be lucky."

The watercourse, as they approached it, was beautiful. Scattered among the trees on the bank were some covered with a brick-red mantle of flowers in the midst of which the green leaves were just beginning to show. The water they could glimpse between the heavy trunks was populated by a variety of fowl, among which white pelicans cruised like overlords. At the point for which they were heading, a series of scrubby tangles of heavy growth stretched out into the plain as though to mark an earlier course of the river; and at this point, just as they came close, two hesitant emus beat a cautious retreat while they eyed the advancing herd.

Immediately Edrington pulled the big roan into action and thundered after them. The birds veered right, then left, then plunged heavily towards the thicker growth. Edrington was rapidly overtaking them when they all disappeared among the bushes, and in the next moment there was a crash, an instant of silence, and then the panic screaming of a horse in agony.

Marriner's instant of shock was curtailed by the abrupt rearing of his own mount, a microcosm of the shock transmitted immediately to the herd. He established control in a second and ran the mare without delay to the spot where Edrington had disappeared.

The big roan lay floundering and screaming on the ground, threshing about like a freshly landed fish. It was easy to see what had happened. At full gallop he had put both legs in a hole, hardly a foot in diameter, which went vertically into the ground. Both legs had snapped. The rifle had come adrift from its holster and lay nearby. Marriner took it, worked a shell into the breech and shot the roan neatly in the centre of the forehead. Only then did he think of looking for Edrington. He found him in the thick scrub about six yards in front of the dead horse.

The fall had been disastrous. He was lying twisted, his shirt and trousers bloody. He was unconscious. Marriner turned him, as gently as he could, on his back, and was horrified at what he saw.

In the scrub, the broken, jagged fork of a mulga tree, hard as iron, had stood a foot above the ground as though in league with the hole to trap the flying figure of the horseman. It had crushed his chest, broken several ribs on his right side. But more than that, its razor edge had ripped through shirt and skin to flay the lower ribs and the belly. There were other wounds—a torn cheek and forearm—and these were bleeding.

Marriner stood for a moment aghast. He walked round to Edrington's head, and back to his feet. He dropped to his knees beside the still body. Then he put his hand inside the shirt and felt the heartbeats. At that, Edrington opened his eyes, his face contorted, and he closed them again. His shoulders twisted as though he were about to roll over, and, as the horse had done, he screamed. It was an arrested scream, quickly suppressed. Marriner caught him by the shoulders, holding him still against the earth. Edrington's knees drew up. He kicked, and his mouth made sounds, though there were no coherent words. Then suddenly he relaxed as unconsciousness swallowed him again. Marriner was whimpering like a puppy, the tears coursing down his cheeks. He felt horribly alone; and yet he was grateful for the broken man's quiescence.

And in the pause he thought of something to do. He took one of the clasp-knives from its pouch on Edrington's belt, opened it, and as carefully as he could cut away the clotted shirt from the wound. He slit it through from the neck to the arm, and laid it back. Already the flies, with the quiet industriousness of their kind, were investigating the sweet blood.

Marriner bethought himself of water. He went to the dead horse, but the canteen at the saddle was crushed and empty from the beast's rolling. His own horse, forgotten in the moment of discovery, had wandered away. There were blankets to get, a bed to make, a fire to set, tea to be brewed for a stimulant. Suddenly it was all too much for him.

Still whimpering, his face screwed up in what was, after all, as much an expression of self-pity as of concern for Edrington he thrust back through the scrub, prepared to find himself still more alone upon an even-remoter desert. But the horses, which had bolted for the horizons when that first agonized screaming arose, were already quieted; they were congregated by the water; and it was a welcome descent into routine to bring them to a campsite upon the bank. Hastily he dropped the packs, unsaddled his own mount, hobbled the herd, lit a fire and set water to boil. He plunged back and found Edringtion, unconscious still; but again with his body relaxed in new contortions.

With the axe he cut two heavy poles from the river gums. He brought Edrington's blankets and made a bed for him on the soft earth. Then gently he eased him over, straightening him out. The flies were massed about Edrington's face and exposed chest. Most of the blood had already dried into cracked and congealed blobs and runnels, and with warm water he tried to bathe these away. Then he covered the main wound with a shirt and, actuated from what forgotten source of knowledge he could not say, wrapped a blanket about the trunk as tightly as he could to prevent movement of the broken ribs. Gently he straightened him out, and, ripping the saddle blanket from the dead horse into lashings, secured him firmly to the poles at shoulders and legs.

"Bloody bean trees," Edrington said suddenly, and Marriner jumped. His patient was looking at him. "Never gallop—bean-tree country. Always holes . . ." Suddenly his face contorted again and he coughed, gently, slowly, with a terrifying repetition. A little blood dribbled from between his lips, and he subsided again into unconsciousness.

3

Throughout the night, Marriner sat with his friend. He managed several times to give him a few swallows of tea, warm and black and sweet; and in the morning, after the sun rose, Edrington seemed a little better. He even spoke rationally, a few words at a time. But those words horrified Marriner.

"I'm finished, you know. You'll bury me."

He seemed to speak with great difficulty, and tried to swallow several times.

"Watch the big desert. Take it easy. Watch your water."

And several times he gave directions: "South. Straight south and then west from the hills. Follow the hills."

He stayed quiet for nearly two hours and then when the horses of their own accord came in for water, late because of the unaccustomed freedom, shuffling along in their hobbles, he struggled to lift his head.

"The book. Bring me the book."

Marriner stared at him, wondering whether he were delirious, but Edrington insisted. The book was in the saddlebag under the dead horse. The saddle girth was cutting into the flesh and he had some trouble to get it undone. Eventually with axe and shovel he loosened the earth underneath and dragged all the gear away from the body. The book, doubly protected by rawhide cover and saddle pouch was unharmed, and he brought it the few steps back to Edrington, wondering whether, perhaps, it was some talisman. Utopia was far away.

"Write," said Edrington.

"I have no pen," Marriner said. Edrington stared a moment.

"A bullet," he said.

Marriner took a cartridge from Edrington's belt, now on the ground beside him. He sharpened the round end of its soft-nose lead to an approximate point, and tried it on the book. It tore the fine paper, but inside the end-covers there was a tougher sheet, and here it made a satisfactory mark.

"Write: I deed . . . to Davis Marriner . . . my horses, my gear, and my brand EGE. . . ."

"This isn't necessary," said Marriner.

"Write it," Edrington insisted. "My brand EGE . . . for services rendered. Now get my arm loose."

Marriner unwrapped the lashings and the blanket and held the book so that Edrington could reach it. He renewed the point he had put on the bullet, smoothing it out again on his boot. Edrington, without even a preliminary fumble, scrawled his name across the foot of the inscription. Then he sank back, exhausted.

"That'll see you right," he said.

Marriner looked at the inscription, looked again at the title page, and returned Sir Thomas More's *Utopia* to the saddle pouch.

"You can rub it out when you get better," he said.

Edrington looked at him without speaking, and closed his eyes.

In an hour or two, the dead horse had become a problem.

It was only an hour or two after that, with Edrington still unconscious, that Marriner realized that some of the stench came from the wounds of the man.

That night, Edrington was in a high fever. He spoke frequently when he was conscious, but it was the talk of delirium. Marriner recognized it only twice; once when for a long time Edrington asked for the book—" Blood is better,

41

write it in blood" he said once, clearly and distinctly—and again when he devoted some time to warning of the dangers ahead: "Due south. South across the desert; and reach the hills before you turn west. Pick up some black-fellows if you can. Take black-fellows—they will see you right."

Otherwise he was silent; or incoherent, with much babbling of an Evelyn of whom Marriner had never heard. In the morning, when Marriner woke, Edrington was dead.

Now the loneliness and the immensity of the plain seemed to be transmuted into a metaphysical force compressing Marriner's ego, restraining whatever endeavours suggested themselves to him, limiting his horizons inversely as his physical bounds were illimitable. For several hours he wandered between Edrington's body, the campsite where the gear still lay half out of the packs, the water hole and the fire, each time making an attempt to do some of the necessary work of the camp; each time discarding his preparations for some other just-remembered task.

He had food to prepare—he had eaten no solid food since they had left the hills. He had to bring in the horses, repack the gear. He had to bury Edrington, and it seemed right that he should make some permanent memorial in this lonely place.

At the death of his mother his problems had not seemed so complicated. And in actual fact, as he remembered now, his contributions then had been minimal—the parson had enlisted the services of the undertaker, kindly neighbours had shouldered his domestic problems, he had closed the little family store for the remainder of the week, and left the remaining details to his father's friends—the old family lawyer, the middle-aged doctor, the retired country bank manager. Now there was only himself and the universe.

His first accomplishment was the building of a cairn. There were rocks near the end of the water hole. He dragged these up to the top of the bank, above reach of the floods, and there erected a small stocky pile. At its top was a cross of light timbers, axed flat and fastened with horse-nails from the packs. It was an inadequate and impermanent memorial, he knew, but it satisfied some instinct in him. When it was done, he went to bring the body to this place.

The changes in that which was Edrington horrified him. He wrapped the body tightly in the soiled blanket on which it lay and tried to drag it through the scrub. Twice he stopped, retching, before he had moved it a yard. In the end he took a shovel and dug a shallow grave beside the body, working at a frenzied pitch, chopping with the axe at the many roots which obstructed him.

Throughout the task he was aware that Edrington, faced with a similar situation, would have been efficient, would have expended no useless energy, made no foreseeable mistakes. But for himself, when finally he rolled the stiffly awkward body into the trench, he had a moment approach-ing horror as he realized the excavation was not wide enough. Finally he covered the body as it lay, jammed in the trench not far beneath the level of the ground, and piled the surplus earth high above it.

He stayed a day longer at the water hole, conditioning himself for the journey ahead. He shot a kangaroo without much difficulty, and cooked it to his own satisfaction. The damper he baked was heavy and soggy, but it was edible. In the extra time at his disposal he went carefully through all Edrington's belongings, making a mental inventory. With the thirty-six horses, the four packsaddles, the three riding saddles, the water canisters shaped like twisted pear-drops to hug a horse's ribs, with all the innumerable tools and gadgets, the rawhide, the cured leather sheets of kan-garoo and cowhide, he was a whole man, equipped physic-ally to tackle and overcome the desert's problems. But he took little heart from his new possessions.

And somehow he delayed his departure from the water

hole until after the sun had been two hours above the horizon. The horses were nervous, playing up. They had the freshness of several days' rest, and they saw no reason to leave a place so well provided with food and water.

On that day, Marriner travelled perhaps eight miles only. At this distance he came to another water hole on the same river. Although he knew Edrington would have carried on, and although, in the distance, at about five miles, the signs pointed to yet another water hole, he camped. He shot a duck for his meal and ate it with the rest of the sodden damper. A great deal of the afternoon he spent in idleness, and when the dark came he slept soundly, exhausted mentally and physically by the aftermath of the tragedy.

Four days later, still pressing south, he had fallen into a new routine in which his day's travel had been reduced from between twenty and thirty miles to somewhere between ten and fifteen. He was still following the course of the river, or cutting its far-reaching convolutions at selected points; and he had recovered to a great extent the confidence with which Edrington had invested him.

On the fifth day, an hour before noon, he cut the river again. There was no water. He followed its course, twisting and turning with its banks for five miles; and in that stretch no water hole remained. When he came to a turning from which the river bed ran endlessly into the east he herded the horses into its bed, and they shuffled along, breaking into a quickly suppressed trot at times, sending the loose, water-washed sand flying in small fountains from their hoofs.

So they traversed bend after bend, hour after hour. More and more frequently Marriner loosened the canteen from the saddle and put it to his lips. At about three in the afternoon it was empty; and he forced himself to face the possibility of making a dry camp. He dreaded it; though with the big canisters filled on the pack horse there was not much danger in it. There would be a mouthful of water, a couple of quarts maybe, for each of the horses, and ample for himself.

Then, just as he had made up his mind to camp, as the evening came, he rounded a bend and saw the ground carpeted with rose and grey, a fluttering changing cover of galahs. The horses, whether from the sight of the birds, or from the evidence of other senses beyond Marriner's knowledge, broke into a run, and, screaming with all the exaggerated cadences of the parrot kind, the birds took flight. The horses replaced them, pawing and scratching at the sand with nervous hoofs; and as he rode up Marriner saw the minor miracle. For each bird had dug himself a little well on that expanse. The water lay immediately beneath the surface of the sand and already, before he himself arrived, the first horses were sipping noisily at their excavations.

In a flood of relief, Marriner made camp. He hobbled the herd, and by the time he shot his kangaroo the dark was closing down. Game was still plentiful; the soak at which he was camped drew the animals, apparently, from a wide expanse of country; and just as apparently, this in itself was a warning that water was going to be still more difficult to find in the miles ahead.

In the morning, when he awoke, the horses were still near the soak. He had heard them, indistinctly, at intervals throughout the night just as, with half his mind, he had listened to the howling of the dingoes, the occasional scurry of the disturbed game.

Three of the horses had lost their greenhide hobbles overnight, stretching the leather in the damp pools until it had fallen over their hoofs; but they had remained with the herd. Marriner looked for the hobbles, rather more than perfunctorily: the swivel chain which connected each pair of leather loops would not be replaceable, though he guessed he could follow Edrington's example in contriving some substitute of leather. He didn't search long, for he was anxious to get away. By all the evidence his river was running out. In a few miles its last traces would probably disappear among sand ridges in the desert; and it would have been foolish, as he realized, to imagine it could supply his herd any longer with drinking water. Also it had been running for a long distance in the wrong direction. He had, therefore, to gamble on crossing the plain, heading southward again, and finding water at his journey's end.

The herd itself was opposed to leaving the river country. They turned and doubled, so that he had some difficulty at first in heading them on their way; and this difficulty was at first increased because that way led over the sandy spinifex ridges where the needle-pointed grass irritated their fetlocks. But in a little while they settled down to the accustomed travelling and began their ceaseless jockeying for preferred positions in the line of march.

By the time the sun rose, they were far out on an apparently endless plain. Looking back, Marriner could see the line of trees that marked the river he had left stretching on towards the east, becoming broken, and continuing as a lesser demonstration upon the horizon. Ahead, and to the west was nothing, a little darker spot here and there that marked the presence of a bush, a desert orange, perhaps, a witchetty bush, or a group of the hardy persistent fuchsias.

Long before the sun reached its zenith Marriner was feeling its effects. Several times his hand wandered to the canteen strapped to his saddle; once he unbuckled it and held it up; but he replaced it without removing the cork. The sun was so hot that when he closed his eyelids it was as though a cool shade had been drawn; he took delight in the sensation and kept his eyes closed of deliberation for several paces of his horse.

Constantly he moistened the inner surfaces of his mouth with his tongue; when at last there was no more moisture there, when his tongue clung to his palate and had to be forced away he gave in at last and drank. Intending only to moisten his mouth, he drank deeply instead, and felt almost guilty as he replaced the felt-covered metal flask. The felt had long since dried, and cooling by evaporation was no longer effective; the water was hot in his mouth, but no less desirable.

At noon the horses slowed, and had to be driven. They had accomplished their usual stint; they sought the shade, the comfort of standing, bemused by heat, in the company of fellow sufferers. But there was no shade.

Once they passed a kangaroo family disposed about a hakea tree, five beasts trying so to accommodate themselves that the gaunt and twisted branches stood between them and the sun; but the hakea, like all the desert plants, had learned from ancestors ages before to reduce its foliage to a minimum, and so to dispose that minimum that it did not intercept the hot vertical rays of sunshine. The plants and the animals feared the sun; the snakes and the lizards and the lesser furred animals lived underground, the dingoes crouched in caves in the rocks or in the hollow trunks of trees, the emus were at some far water hole in this heat, and the night-loving kangaroos slept at isolated stations in the plains, wherever they could best avoid the brightness.

Only Marriner and his cavalcade moved on under the sun.

At this juncture he could see in the far distance a disturbance of the horizon, a low hill; and he determined to reach it. Somewhere among its impermeable rock there might be a reservoir that caught the rains; in his mind he could visualize it; and so he headed towards it. It lay nearly on his route; it became his target.

By midafternoon it was prominent in the line of his advance, an isolated rock, flat-topped, perhaps three hundred feet in height and twice as many yards wide. But by afternoon, too, his horses were showing exhaustion. Three of the younger half-broken beasts stopped frequently and had to be hunted forward. When they stopped, a muscle behind the forearm quivered and jerked; they were near to collapse. But Marriner, as he prodded them onwards, urging them from his own tired horse, took heart from the fact that the laden pack horses were still plodding on, even the heavy black (almost a prototype for the London cab horse) that carried the hundred and twenty pounds of water, the twenty pounds of packsaddle and gear that secured it.

And they were nearer the big rock than he had thought. By half-past four the procession had moved gratefully into the shade of its eastern shoulder, and there stopped.

Marriner, when he had dropped the saddles and the packs, left the horses standing and walked round the rock. Over his shoulder he carried a shovel. He circled the base and found no sign of water. There were two places, one to the north and one to the southeast, where clumps of trees pointed to underground nourishment, or at least to a site where the surplus water had run from the rock in the infrequent rains, and, first at the north (in the direction from which he had come) and later on the other side of the rock, Marriner dug deeply into the sand at these points. But he found no water, not even any dampness.

To each place he returned and deepened the hole he had made, but still without result. He would have to make a dry camp. On an afterthought he climbed the rock, circling it high up, hoping that somewhere he might discover a hole in the formation, a cleft that caught the rain water in season; but he was unsuccessful, and the sum of his endeavours was to bring him to darkness again with the work of the camp not done.

He went from horse to horse, taking the hobbles from the neck-straps and adjusting them about the fetlocks. They nickered at him, almost whimpering. Several of them began to paw at the big filled six-gallon canisters standing near the packs, and Marriner chased them off, halfheartedly, for he was as thirsty as they.

Then taking a leather bucket which he had not as yet used he measured a couple of pints into it, and offered it first to the big black pack horse. The rest of the herd clustered about him, excited, nickering and bowing their heads.

It was a measure of how much he had learned, how much he had identified himself with this world of horses, that he was able to give each individual a share—not enough for any of them. But none was watered twice. Each had two pints, a little more, perhaps of the life-giving water. When that was finished there was, perhaps, a half-gallon in each of the canisters.

It was a brooding camp. Some foresight had seen to it that Marriner still carried a supply of the previous night's meat, liberally covered with coarse salt and still edible. He made himself a fresh damper that, for once, was as good as Edrington's had been, and almost as inviting as bread.

The horses hardly moved from the camp all night. They fed a little on the leaves of the bushes, but they abandoned their usual systematic foraging. After midnight there were several small disputes among them, a little squealing and kicking of heels. They were mentally disturbed.

And perhaps it was on account of this that Marriner's start next morning was earlier than usual. His horses were at hand; there was no problem of unhobbling to water them before the saddling-up. He ate his meal, drank a surfeit of sweet black tea, filled his saddle canteen and put on the packs.

This time he put the heaviest load, the tools and the leather, on the big black, shifting the now almost empty canisters to his weakest pack horse. His best weight-carrying mare had carried him the day before, and now, like a majority of the others, she showed signs of exhaustion. He finally saddled a young bay mare for himself, a tired horse, but well enough muscled. He made the choice not without misgivings. None of the horses looked ready for the day's trek; but there was no alternative. They could not be spelled here, without water.

The rising of the sun, after they had been an hour on the road, lifted his spirits, for as its reflected rays crept along the horizon they disclosed a mountain range ahead. Directly in his path, due south, there was a gap in this range, a natural pass to which, even had he not been severely pressed, he would have directed his journey. But the climbing sun, a little later, brought the keen skin-lashing heat; and very early the horses began to show symptoms of exhaustion. The three younger horses that had been brought to near-collapse on the previous day were his first concern. One at a time they stood stubbornly, letting the herd pass them by; Marriner had to round on them, drive them like a dog with sheep.

In midmorning the first of them went down. He propped, stood stock-still, shaking violently, then slowly he went down on his knees. Hind quarters ridiculously in air he seemed to hesitate, then like a boulder falling went down on his off-shoulder. He grunted, stretched his legs, and lay still.

Marriner dismounted. The horse was not dead, but he could do nothing with it. He sat there for a while and then remounted. His own horse was trembling. And already the second of the young horses was down between himself and the herd, which now seemed to be moving purposefully enough towards the range. In spite of the condition of the horses they had made good time towards this point which to reach they had, perhaps, twelve miles to go. The third young horse lasted another hour. It collapsed suddenly and, simultaneously, one of the others, a fine-drawn skew-bald picked out a sandy space free of spinifex, circled twice, dropped gracefully to her knees and, as though at journey's end, began to roll.

Marriner, in a quandary, took Edrington's long stock-whip coiled at his saddle and swung it, endeavouring to reproduce the free rolling action of the expert cattleman, but the returning lash caught his own horse on the legs, and, tired as she was, she took fright and jumped away. Marriner dropped the whip, got her under control, dismounted, tied her to a bush and, retrieving the whip, advanced on the rolling skewbald.

He was angry now, and he cut her twice, heavily. She squealed, struggled to her feet and ran after the herd, which had now found a new access of speed from the sound of the whip. Marriner watched them go, walked back to the young horse lying in the sun, and found it already dead. He felt tired, dispirited; and he sat on the smooth bay shoulder for a moment, his head down.

It seemed a moment. But he had sat a good while before he decided to walk back to his saddled mare. He felt sick and lonely. He unbuckled the canteen and took four measured swallows of the warm water and then replaced it, noticing without really registering that the mare was trembling violently at flank and shoulder, that her head was held unnaturally low and her hoofs spread more than usual.

By the time he had remounted, the ambling herd was so far ahead as to seem like dots among the yellow grasses, an assemblage of moving dots, now walking, now ambling quietly, with a thin cloud of dust rising like an ethereal pillar to the cloudless sky above.

Marriner kicked the mare into a smart canter. She responded unwillingly, but she responded. Then, freshened by the water and touched, perhaps, by the madness that precedes an impending doom, he shifted his weight to the stirrups, leaned forward over her withers, and shook out the reins by her head.

Immediately she broke into a gallop. The spinifex here was only patchy; it was giving way to the lightly grassed

51

plains, and the footing was good. And Marriner settled down to an enjoyment of the gallop; urging the game little mare when she flagged, and shouting in a brief access of joy. They had covered, perhaps, two-thirds of the distance to the herd when the mare died in her stride.

She fell heavily and threw Marriner ten yards ahead of her. He was unhurt. He rolled along the plain and was scarcely bruised. He lay for a moment nevertheless and then got up, brushing away the sharp seeds that clung to his skin as he limped back. He grabbed the bridle and tugged.

"Get up," he said. "Come on, get up." Then he was caught with the horror of realization.

"You bastard," he yelled. "You soft-gutted bastard."

Savagely he kicked the unfeeling bay hide at the shoulder, screaming incoherently. As the words gathered meaning his vehemence subsided to a kind of sobbing.

"Just when you were needed most. How the hell am I going to catch up? How can I ever catch up? How can I ever get anywhere?"

When a returning sanity brought calmness he dropped to his haunches, surveying the damage, though the details mattered little, now that he was marooned here under the sun.

She had come down on her off-shoulder, and the canteen and the saddle pouch were unhurt. Beneath the saddle the rifle seemed undamaged in its holster. Though the saddle still lay under the mare, girth and surcingle were broken, and some straps of the martingale. All this was unimportant.

The mare was dead, with blood at her mouth, and the rest of the herd was far ahead.

Marriner squatted on his haunches until his mind was clear. Then he took the unbroken bridle from the mare's head and began to walk in the track of the herd. He now showed no discernible emotion. The truth must have been that he was so stunned at this sudden deterioration of his fortunes, from hazardous to infinitely worse, that his emotions had ceased to stir within him.

He walked a quarter-mile, trailing the bridle from the crook of his arm. Then he stopped, struck with a sudden fear.

Laboriously he walked back. He unbuckled the canteen from the saddle, strapped it to his belt, took up the bridle and set out again. This time he walked only a hundred yards before he stopped.

He came back to the mare, unbuckled all the harness, carried the saddle fifteen or twenty yards from the corpse, and there stacked it properly as though for an overnight camp, standing it on end with the loose gear, the broken girth and surcingle, the whip, the hobbles and neck-strap, the martingale, saddle pouch and rifle in its holster disposed tidily within the flaps, and the saddle blanket thrown over all, to be dried of its sweat. Then for the third time he took up the bridle and, equipped with water, set out on the trail of the herd. He sampled the water in the first quarter-mile. The canteen thereafter contained only a small cupful.

He could not see the horses. There was no trouble in following the freshly kicked earth of thirty-two tracks; and as though that were not sufficient the column of dust rose to the sky ahead; and beyond that lay the gap in the range, for the horses were still following the course that he had set them. He guessed that from instinct or from knowledge born of observation they knew that water waited them in the hills. Thinking of water he raised the canteen, took a measured four swallows again, and found to his consternation that they had emptied the vessel.

The sun was close to the zenith. The hills beckoned, but between him and the hills the air danced and shimmered. The heat blasted down from the sky; it struck up at him from the ground. Suddenly, about fifty yards on his right hand was born the sound of a steam engine gone mad, and looking over he saw a fine column of air rising, carrying soil with it, and small sticks and leaves. From its base the grasses and bushes strained in towards it, lashed into submissive obeisance by some fantastic force. The dust-devil weaved and twisted from the centre of this storm-lashed plot, and slowly it began to advance across his path, gathering speed, whirling and twisting, a force of destruction where there was nothing to destroy. The air was calm where he stood, calm and baking hot; and when he followed in the path of the dust-devil and crossed its tracks, it was calm again.

He plodded on, for there was nothing else he could do. He saw a snake, green and red, glide swiftly away among the grasses. He saw lizards, bright, sharp, with beady eyes. He saw a kingfisher in a tree, and thought aggrievedly that kingfishers should have belonged with water. But mostly he just gave himself to the automatism of walking. When he had walked another hour he sucked at the empty canteen, forgetting he had finished it. The hot metal neck burned his lips. His throat was dry, his eyeballs were heated and sore. His knees didn't properly straighten. He gave way to moments of panic.

On one of these, he started to run, heading for the hills. He ran a little way, and cursed himself for a fool.

Again, at another time, he stopped to stare at the dust-cloud now far ahead. Away off to the right was the more substantial column of a distant dust-devil—a whirlwind on the far horizon; and after adjudging the merits of these two columns he left the track of the horses to follow the track of the wind.

Yet again, in a moment of lucidity, he realized the folly of this and headed back at an angle, hoping to cut the tracks of the horses ahead. He succeeded, but didn't recognize them as tracks when he came to them. He was staggering now, and he went on, into nowhere, following nothing. There came a time when he lay down.

This was, perhaps, midafternoon; and it was a tribute to his stamina, to the strong lean body and the years of quiet living, that he had lasted so long. But the body had been betrayed by the foolish mind. No man could have walked in that heat without the constant refreshment of water, without renewing the supply of which the body, in its efforts to achieve coolness, was so prodigal. Now he was parched in all his parts; now the great heat of the desert had its will with him, no longer foiled by the refrigerating processes of evaporating sweat.

True, he lay only a little while; and then, with some illusion of refreshment, picked himself up to walk again. But when he walked he followed his own tracks. In a little while he was walking on his knees.

His consciousness now was limited only to a knowledge, or a fallacy that seemed like knowledge, of the need for movement. And while any fragment of consciousness remained to him, he moved.

But there was an end to stamina, an end to consciousness; and when it came he dropped into the sand. The slanting sun beat upon him, and a lizard looked at him unwinkingly. But even this he could not know. He was the shell of a man upon the sand.

4

Consciousness returned to Marriner as it must have come to him at life's beginning. Before there was anything on which the mind could fasten there was a confused haze of impressions; awareness of light and shade, of noises harsh and musical; tactual impressions at finger's end, at cheek and back; scents both welcome and unpleasant; a taste stale, sour and wholly objectionable. At what stage these impressions became reality would have been hard for him to determine; as hard as it would have been to determine just when, for the baby Marriner, consciousness was translated into the actuality of life.

But it was a matter of minutes and not of years before he was aware that the light and shade came from the sunshine probing the interstices of a bough shelter, striking in patches on his exposed skin and on the rough blanket which covered the earth on which he lay. The musical sounds were the songs of birds and the chattering of children; the harsh rhythm underlying—a regular repetition, a combination of whine and groan ending in a slap and a splash—he could not identify.

There was a heavenly fragrance wafted from some near-by boronia bushes, and from time to time a wafting of the musky scent of people, objectionable because grown stale. He sat up; and, seeing the movement, a native squatting near by got to his feet and walked over to him.

He was a middle-sized native, his wavy hair blowing loose about his face. He was dressed in torn trousers belted up about his waist. He was grinning in a friendly sort of way and he spoke in what, for a native, was excellent English.

"Where am I?" asked Marriner in the time-honoured cliché of the awakened, but the native ignored the question.

"You been close up long finish, I think, boss," he said.

Over his shoulder, among the trees, Marriner could see his horses standing, and black figures moving among them.

"You found me. You brought me in," he said. "Who are you? What is your tribe?"

The native squatted again, to be on his level, the better to talk to him.

"Name belonging me, Activity, boss," he said. "That my white-feller name. This my people, Eiliuwarra people. This place, white-feller name, is Bloodwood Plain."

Now Marriner, with the mists of sleep clearing from his brain, traced the whine and groan to the rhythmic swing of a whip-pole in the creek beyond the trees, a long shaft pegged between the forks of a beam set up on the bank, set up and stayed in such a way that a weight on the short end counter-balanced that of a bucket of water dependent from the end of its upper length; so that it could be lifted with ease from a shallow well dug into the river bed not far below the bank. There were two lubras operating the pole now, one a heavy woman dressed in a rag of a brown dress, the other smaller, slimmer and quite naked.

"Is there some white-fellow lives here then?" asked Marriner. The whip-pole was definitely of European—or more likely Afghan—origin. Afghan camel-drivers had been introduced to this Australian island with their changes half a century before, and controlled its heavy transport.

"No more, boss," Activity said. "Long time ago Charlie Bottom stopped here. He stopped two years, maybe three, long Bloodwood Plain. Plenty horses. Some cattle. Then he go. No more man stop. One, two man come through Bloodwood Plain and head south. All the same as yourself."

"And where'd you get this name Activity?"

"Charlie Bottom, boss. Old Charlie call me Activity. Little fellow then, working along cattle."

He looked at Marriner.

"What they call you?"

"Marriner. Davis Marriner." Activity rolled the words over on his tongue. "Mar'ner. Davy Mar'ner. That right?"

"That's right."

"You stop here, long Bloodwood Plain?"

"I'm going south."

Activity shook his head and made a sympathetic noise.

"Big, big desert down south. You perish, my word."

"Well, I have to go south." He eyed this new acquaintance. "You come with me?" he asked. "Suppose you come I give you plenty tobacco."

"You wait, Davy. You wait here. Maybe some fellow come through and take you with him. More better to wait, my word."

What circumstances were there, Marriner wondered, that could induce him to wait in this desert place? A day or two, perhaps. And then he thought of the desert behind and more ahead; and he thought of the little bay mare and the dead young horses.

"This desert ahead, this dry stretch—worse than the one behind?" he asked.

"Plenty worse, Davy. Oh yes. My word."

"I'll stop here a little while," decided Marriner.

Later, he got up and walked about the camp. His first thought was for his horses and gear. A good herd of the horses now grazed in groups here and there; most of them at any rate had come through. His packs and water canisters —all his gear—were unloaded in the shade of a clump of the riverbank trees; and he was really surprised when he saw that the collection included the saddle and the rifle; all the gear indeed from the dead mare; even to her hobbles and neck-strap; and seeing them, he remembered that he had not removed the hobbles from the young horses dead behind him; they represented irreplaceable property lost.

Beyond the stack of his goods, the blacks were camped in little shelters among the trees. There seemed to be about eighty people altogether, as near as he could judge; of whom one half, or rather more, were adult. The children all ran naked; a group of them sat as though in school, making cat's cradles of string. Marriner saw, from a little distance, a most complicated figure of string—"Lizard," said Activity, pointing and grinning; and as he watched Marriner saw the indicated lizard, in response to the child's finger movements, working his legs animatedly as though he climbed a tree. But when Marriner went a little closer to examine the clever intricacies of the string figure the group ran violently away, little bare bottoms waggling as the thin legs leaped to the speed of a childish desperation.

Perhaps half the adults wore clothes of some sort; a majority of these being men, and the women mainly elderly; those who were naked had raised keloid markings, the filled scars of initiation, branded transversely across their chests. As he wandered with Activity those who saw him coming in their direction melted into an obscurity, or found some task to take them elsewhere; but never obviously.

Water from the whip-pole had been poured into a small, cracked and leaking trough, apparently for the use of the horses. Marriner did not walk long or far; he felt himself getting light-headed in the sun, and his awakening had left him with a blinding headache. Whether in appreciation of this or for some other reason, Activity soon led him gently back to the shelter in which he had recovered consciousness.

By question and answer he elicited the information that the tribe had seen the approach of the horses from a good distance; they had sent men out to meet the new arrivals and the men, when the horses with packs and saddles appeared, set out on their tracks to find the men who must have been with them, as their condition testified, on that morning. They had cut the rambling, staggering tracks of Marriner, had catered to his needs to the best of their ability, and when it was night had taken horses back from the whip-pole well and brought him in. It was not, after all, an unduly strenuous effort; he had had but a few miles to go.

After the sun went down Activity, who seemed to have appointed himself to Marriner's service, brought him pieces of meat, baked to a delicate turn. He carried them in his hands, but Marriner only briefly registered a mental objection and one that was not ratified by his stomach; he stretched out his hand and took the meat, eating it and savouring it to the last fragments adhering to the bone. Afterwards he walked to the trough and drew himself water to wash it down. And then returned to the blanket and collapsed.

When he awoke the sun was high, and only a few natives remained in the camp. Towards noon, some of them came drifting back; the men with the results of their hunting, the women with their bark dishes filled with roots, seeds, small frogs and lizards, wood grubs, or those members of the honey-ant communities which had been converted by their fellows into living receptacles, their black-striped bodies rounded to a half-inch sphere filled with golden honey, their useless heads and legs projecting from the top like the necks of bottles; each head, indeed, the neck of the world's most ancient bottle, and a bottle filled with sweetness.

By evening the camp was full again, and twinkling with the glow of sixty small fires. Except for the friendly Activity, none of the natives offered much communication to Marriner; and Activity was at hand only when Marriner indicated a desire for his presence. But there was no hostility in their avoidance of him. It was founded rather, he decided, in a peculiar mixture of shyness and confidence. In the meantime they watered his horses, and twice a day they shared their food with him. It was good food, of considerably greater variety than he would have imagined, and it was cooked well, with the flavour retained.

He lazed through the days. On the fourth morning, when he arose, only six horses remained in the camp, and a collection of hobbles had been added to the gear stacked under the trees. Marriner was at once alarmed and called Activity.

"They orright, Davy," that consoler said. "Some fellows puttim long the Argadala water." He pointed east with his chin. "Plenty good feed, Davy. Plenty water. Good country."

"How far back?"

"Not far."

"We'll go and look at them."

"Yowai, Davy. Yow yow."

He walked over to the gear and selected a bridle, calling to the tribe as he did so. After a moment Marriner joined him, and somewhat to his surprise another native and two of the young girls, lubras about sixteen years old, also wandered up and caught horses. Marriner noted, without much surprise, that the horse left, while a likely kind of a beast, was the worst of the six. The lubras rode bareback.

Activity, as of right, rode in the lead, Marriner next, with the third man, Ngumbanalu, riding at Marriner's side, sometimes moving up or back; sometimes making little excursions off the track, the lubras rode quietly together further back, often a hundred yards or so to one side or the other. To one of them his eyes kept wandering again and again. She was slim; slimmer than her companion, and with too-thin legs and arms; but her body was well enough fleshed. Her hair, unkempt, still shone with rainbow lights where the sun struck it; it was almost fair. She had a merry face, all the merrier for its shy, sad eyes; and her lips, overfull like those of all her people, were yet curiously attractive.

Her companion was more heavily built, with coarser

61

features. Neither were beauties, Marriner decided, but the slimmer one had that indefinable attraction possessed by a very few in any community of women anywhere.

There was no talking as they rode along; but there seemed, nevertheless, a communication. Once or twice Activity turned to him to point out a herd of kangaroos, or an insect-searching bustard near the trail. On these occasions Marriner was struck by the arrangement of his fingers in the gesture. His hand and wrist adopted the neck-stretching, cautious movements of the bustard's gait; the lolloping action of the kangaroos. With the latter, the fingers were outflung; with the former they were bunched at the tips; and after the fourth or fifth time Marriner realized that the attitude of the hand itself supplied a communication.

His next discovery was that even when Activity did not turn directly to him with such information, his hand registered a variety of signs. At times, indeed, his fingers went through a long sequence of contortions, one following the other with such continuity as to seem to form some kind of deaf-and-dumb language.

At other times he would ride along, the same right hand listless at his side, for a considerable distance before he lifted it with some new communication.

At one such stage Marriner kicked his horse ahead and asked Activity directly what the sign stood for.

Activity repeated it—a bunching of the fingers, a turning of the wrist. "Dingo," he said.

Marriner recognized the resemblance to the dog's head, the way a dog when he halts in the wilds turns his head from side to side to pick up a scent, a sight, the sound of a possible quarry. But something else puzzled him.

"Where is the dog, the one you see?" he asked.

Activity looked at the ground, reining in his horse. In the soft earth Marriner could easily distinguish a dog's footprints.

"He walked along this morning, first thing."

Marriner also pointed to other prints alongside. When he looked closely the ground became a record of the passage of living things. Several dingoes, it seemed to him, had come this way in company; but Activity disagreed.

"No more, Davy," he said. "That other—one, two, three days old. Some more."

It was too much for Marriner. He realized that Activity's interpretation had reached a perfection he could not hope to attain, at least, not soon; for he could distinguish no difference in the sets of prints. He dropped back and continued to watch, with mounting amazement, as the graceful, swinging right hand recorded, in a never-ending continuity, the recent movements of game animals. In a little while he had identified several of the finger-symbols, for they were not obscure and they were frequently repeated. Often he could match them with the tracks, or with visible game.

Towards noon they approached the Argadala water over a wide, well-grassed plain where Marriner's other horses were feeding. They came running up to the party, nickering their joy at the recognition of friends.

The water itself followed the pattern of all the water holes; but it was the biggest he had seen, much more than a mile in length and several hundred yards wide. The banks were not so steep as at the average water hole, and there was a thick cover of trees to protect them. High in the trees, much higher than seemed reasonable, the debris of recent floods was jammed in the branches.

He rode round the water hole. When he returned the others had pitched camp, unsaddled, and hobbled the horses. The two lubras and Ngumbanalu had disappeared. Activity was hunkered near the saddles.

"Good camp," Marriner said appreciatively.

"I think tomorrow we go look some more," Activity suggested, pointing east with his chin. "Good country.

Plenty water." The idea appealed to Marriner. Suddenly, for the first time he felt the joy of this life's freedom. He could return or he could go on; no material things exercise their compulsion; the world was wide, and he fitted it anywhere.

"All right," he said. "We'll have a look out east."

That night they feasted upon goanna tails, rich and satisfying, like a superior and well-fattened chicken. They slept in their clothes or in their nakedness, just as they lay down, the natives each beside a small fire; the lubras at a little distance from the others. In the morning they rode on, and here again Marriner experienced a change of attitude, for he had mentally to condition his appreciation of his freedom by an acknowledgement of the sense of luxury he felt as he watched Activity and the others catch the horses and attend to the chores, admittedly minor, of camping.

They went east for three days, with the range of hills running parallel to their tracks all the way, a few miles to the south of them. At the end of the third day they camped in the hills, unsaddling at a site apparently devoid of water. Marriner commented, naturally enough; and Activity listened to him seriously.

"This place he's called Blowfly Creek," he said. "You come look."

The red-shouldered hill was easy enough of access, though there was not a trace of soil even in the interstices of the rock. The summit was a broad expanse, a quarter of a mile or more across, with a higher formation rising towards either end. Centred on this table of rock was an almost-circular chasm which, as they approached, disclosed walls that were perfectly parallel, but slanted at a steeply oblique angle to a considerable depth; so that on one side the rock walls overhung, and on the other formed a precipitous slide leading down to a placid pool perhaps thirty feet below the lip.

"Plenty water," Activity said.

"Plenty water," Marriner repeated. "But how can we get it?" Activity grinned, disclosing two rows of strong white teeth.

"You wait. You see."

There was no chink anywhere in the rocks, no cleft or chimney by which a climber might make his way down to the water. Nor had they, Marriner remembered, brought ropes. But soon Ngumbanalu came leading the horses up over the rocks, and behind him came the naked girls, laughing together over some secret joke. They approached the cleft as one approaches a familiar home, a seaside cottage or a remembered inn; and sat at the edge of the rock, near the horses; at the point where it formed a precipitous slide down to the quiet water.

As they sat Marriner discovered in his mental ramblings the reason for the name. Someone had christened this the Blowhole; unfamiliarity and the corruption of usage had brought it to Blowfly Creek. He knew it with certainty, and felt proud of his small discovery. It meant, though, that other white men had been here before; he had imagined himself the first who had ever penetrated this wild red landscape; and there was no trace anywhere of the passing of the others.

The girls sat by the brink, and the younger, prettier girl took some black and sticky material from the palm of one hand and gave a considerable part of it to her companion. They both spread the stuff liberally over their hands and the soles of their feet, working it particularly into the palms and fingers, spreading it over the lightly boned, graceful arches of their feet so that no fraction of the skin there was uncovered. Then, to Marriner's amazement, they went lightly over the lip of the crater-like flue.

The action had something of the quality of a dream as he watched them. They went down the slope—so steep that it was inconceivable that any matter could be supported

c   65

there—with the surety and the speed of lizards. Nor were they unburdened, for each carried a canvas bucket which belonged with the horses' gear.

Facing the rock, so that they walked backwards, but otherwise displaying no awkwardness whatever, they went lightly to the water's edge, filled their receptacles, and returned with them to the top, looped over the elbow and sliding against the rock. They poured out the water in a depression in the surface rock; to which Ngumbanalu led the first two horses to drink. In the meantime the girls, lithe and laughing, went down again, up and down the rock as though they climbed invisible ladders.

To Marriner, watching, the sight was unbelievable. He walked round the lip to the place where they emerged, and they hung back, smiling at him but too shy to approach, even after these three days in which they had camped together. But Activity, behind him, called them up, took the heavier girl by the wrist, and led her to Marriner.

He put his finger experimentally against her palm and invited Marriner to do the same. The skin was sticky; a peculiar form of stickiness not like a syrup or a treacle; but nevertheless, strongly adhesive. The girls giggled and laughed, the one behind holding the back of her hand against her mouth.

"Some stuff—you know this sugar-bag? They got some black stuff——" Activity was finding it hard to look for words with which to explain, and Marriner guessed. "Beeswax."

"Beeswax," Activity confirmed. "And some water from this bloodwood trees. Mix all up."

Beeswax and bloodwood sap; doubtless in a correct proportion; the materials at hand in nature; the beeswax carried from the last hive found; the bloodwood sap on hand wherever the trees grew; and the bloodwood's as common as any trees on the plain. But even with this aid, the operation needed a remarkable sense of balance, a clear head, a deft agility taken for granted, a confidence in one's powers stretched to the ultimate, an outstanding courage—it had taken more than beeswax to see the horses watered. The girls whom Marriner had so far noticed merely as willing and useful attendants thus acquired personality; became entities. He viewed them with a new respect.

"I'd like to try that," he told Activity. "Is it easy?"

"No more, Davy," Activity warned. "Suppose you're a little weeai—" he held his hand a couple of feet from the ground to indicate the size of a small boy—"then you learn him. Then it would be easy."

"Did you learn, Activity? Can you do it?" Marriner asked.

"Yowai, Davy. I learn him," Activity claimed; but apparently had no desire to display the accomplishment.

The next morning, before the sun rose, the girls repeated the performance, and Marriner climbed the hill to watch them. Muscles lightly rippling the naked skin, they seemed to gather a new kind of beauty in their exertions; a beauty not at all compromised by the incongruities of their attitudes upon the rock: the buttocks thrust sharply outwards; the limbs moving in a controlled rhythm one at a time; the long lean black thighs, skinny calves, flexing gently about a central equipoise; the feet spread wide; the toes splayed; the delicate fingers like tree roots veined to the rock, with the half-moons of the nails gleaming white. They never stopped an accompaniment of chatter and musical laughter; though the work itself was strenuous and demanding.

Marriner spoke to them when they had finished. The words were, he supposed, incomprehensible to them, but they understood well enough when he patted them admiringly between the shoulder blades; and from that moment neither of them, ever again, shrank away from him. He felt this at the time; he felt that he had established a communication as close as that which Activity had established with him in the first place.

"Have these two lubras got any names?" he asked Activity while they saddled their horses. Activity, setting the saddle with precision behind the withers, looked over at the girls and did not immediately reply.

"You give them white-feller name, Davy," he said at last. "They got no white-feller name."

"You want me to christen 'em?"

"You give them name."

"All right. This one Mary, that one Rosie." Mary was the pretty one, and she was smiling now. Activity repeated the names two or three times, savouring them. Then he called Ngumbanalu and spoke to him in the rapid-fire language of the tribe, quite a long speech in which the simple English names were repeated over and over. Ngumbanalu himself repeated them once or twice, and added a little speech of his own.

"He wants a name too, Davy," Activity said.

"All right. Call him George."

Activity imparted this new name to Ngumbanalu, who tried it out with apparent delight and then called the lubras over to the circle. They left their horses standing and came, and the newly christened George began a long series of introductions all round. Rosie giggled uncontrollably; Mary took her new name more quietly; but the introductions seemed to constitute a little ceremony of *brüderschaft*; and when they rode out they rode as a company, unified in their intent and their feelings.

In the three days, while they returned to the camp at Bloodwood Plains, Marriner was lulled into a hedonistic happiness; a kind of mental suspension during which all his emotions had their birth only in the manifestations of nature through which he rode: the strong and warming sunshine, the delight of horseflesh moving effortlessly to his intention, the red earth, blue sky, grey-foliaged trees, the songs of birds. The lollipop tree was in bloom, a straggling desert banksia with needle foliage and a few ragged spires glorious with old-gold flowers massed to their very tips. Riding past, Mary and Rosie would snatch a handful of the flowers and eat them. Marriner tried it, and found the blooms sweet and fragrant, overflowing with a honey which kept them besieged by a variety of the country's insects. Sometimes the girls would rein in at a bush of which the brittle branches were intersected by a vine; and from it pick a bush banana to add to the commissariat; an unexciting green vegetable more reminiscent of a pea than a banana. The little group never hurried; they made their short stages without any waste of energy; and their numbers made the task of finding and preparing food no more than a passing interest.

At the two overnight camps on the river between Blowfly Creek and Bloodwood Plains they all went swimming. The lubras and Marriner spent at least two hours in the water, washing and resting in the warmth near the edge. George and Activity also visited the pools, but their stay was brief; they washed the sweat of travel from their bodies and then went out on their hunts.

Marriner swam a great deal while the women watched him; he had not expected that they could swim, for they never ventured far from the edge, until Mary discovered a reason for crossing the water. When she plunged in, Marriner, somewhat to his mortification, found she was swimming more strongly and more rapidly than he had ever done. As with swimming, so with everything else; they made no slightest gesture without having a reason for it; they carried conservation of energy to an extreme.

He discovered also at this time that Mary and Rosie would conduct long conversations with finger gestures; and that neither George nor Activity were privy to what they were saying, although the gestures were not in any way concealed.

"Women's talk," Activity grunted shortly when Marriner once asked him what they were saying. And no translations were ever made, either to himself or the two other men.

The horses were still grazing at Argadala; the camp at Bloodwood Plains seemed unchanged. A good number of the people were no longer there; whole families, with children and babies had moved out, and only a few of the older people remained in the camp. According to Activity the absentees had gone hunting; they would return in a few days, a couple of weeks, perhaps. It was normal; conservation of food supplies demanded that some, if not all of the people kept on the move.

For himself Activity implied that he felt his own place to be near Marriner; there was an unexpressed hunger here, Marriner thought, for an indoctrination into the ways of the white man. Activity's manner remained independent; there seemed no plea, latent or expressed, for tuition; it was as though he had simply established an alliance that time would cement. And because, with this attitude, he seemed to shoulder responsibility for the chores connected with the horses still in camp; because he provided the meals which Marriner ate, and found or suggested some solution to every difficulty, some satisfaction to every manifestation or curiosity or desire, Marriner welcomed his presence.

One such solution was of more than passing moment. By the time they returned to camp, Marriner's eyes and his mind were so continuously engaged with the figure and the actions and even the insignificant movements of the girl Mary—the wild songs fashioned from her husky throat, the manipulations of her fingers in that voiceless communication —that he knew he wanted her for his bed. Perhaps, as much as anything else, it was a sign of his assimilation into the country. Perhaps the desire arose purely from the unsatisfied hungers of a body long condemned to isolation. But the girl grew more beautiful in every passing moment; or, more truly, the beauties which she possessed—the rhythms of free movement, the exquisite delicacies of fingers and wrists, the liquid depths of her untamed eyes, the soft and tiny orbs of her breasts that adjusted themselves to her attitudes—all these beauties implicit in the girl grew more important to him than the attributes of the ideals he had long possessed; more important even than that mental communication which is the basis of harmony in a sexual partnership.

Activity noticed his preoccupation.

"That feller Mary look pretty good, eh?" he asked.

"You think she'd come and sleep with me?" Marriner asked bluntly.

"You like him, eh?"

Marriner nodded.

"I fix something, Davy. Tonight, maybe."

Marriner, living on native food, was hungry for bread. He made his preparations, set his damper in the pot and was beginning to put the unused ingredients away again. Activity, near by, squatted on the sand, showing little interest. On an impulse Marriner heaped a little pile of flour on a sheet of loose bark and gave it to him. Activity looked up, pleased.

"Belong me?" he asked.

"Belong you. You send that fellow Mary along."

"Orright, Davy."

To his surprise Mary was there in a minute or two, holding out an empty coolamon. Behind her was Rosie. He grinned, said, "What the hell," filled both receptacles—and already there was an old wrinkled woman waiting for her share. Oh well, he thought, they've fed me. He parcelled out flour to every adult in the camp, exactly halving the store that was left to him. But he had no fear of hunger any more. The people of the desert would keep him satisfied.

He sat a long time by his bough shelter that night. There was a little sporadic singing in the camp—no full-scale corroboree, for that would demand the youth and exuberance

71

of the hunters, an abandon which the old men imitated, even led, but which was initiated by the young. Then the camp closed down quietly as usual, never completely asleep; given life always by some individual tending his little sleeping fire, or studying the stars, or listening to the night sounds of animals. Belatedly Marriner decided that Activity for once had failed in his ministrations; that Mary, perhaps, had refused to consider him; and, a little downhearted, he slipped in between the blankets and within moments was asleep.

He awoke, seconds later it seemed, to the touch of a skin amazingly soft and satiny; with a musky fragrance of flesh in his nostrils, with the sound of a girl's muted giggling and incomprehensible words. His arms opened to enclose her, happiness suffused his brain and warmed it, as a blush enlivens the cheek; his early upbringing with half its ancient shibboleths receded forever as he established this ultimate communication with the people of the desert.

5

Marriner awoke, as usual, before the sun, in the cold clear air that was close to freezing even here, well within the Tropic of Capricorn. The dim light of dawn was not yet adequate; between the boughs of his shelter he could see a man moving near by; a man in silhouette, big against the lit horizon.

It was dawn like any other dawn; it was a dawn outside his earlier experience; and he sensed that in it there waited something special. He lay wondering what it could be, and then he realized that his cheek was pillowed between wrist and biceps of a bent bare arm. Even so he was only puzzled until his searching hand touched the point of an elbow in front of his face, and memory flooded back.

"Mary," he said, and sat up. The girl at his side buried her face in the blankets. Her shoulders were shaking, whether from laughter or tears he could not be certain. Then he heard the sound of a giggle. He caught the sound of an English word and bent to listen.

"Rosie," she was saying, and the light dawned.

"By God," he swore, and pulled her over. It was Rosie all right. She lay on her back giggling, her hands over her face, one eye twinkling at him through the interstices of her spread fingers.

"I thought you were Mary," he said foolishly.

"Rosie," she said again, and laughed louder.

"Your name's not Rosie. Your name's trouble," he said.

But he couldn't help joining her laughter.

"Now get up, you little brat. Get up and get some work done."

"Trubby," she said.

"That's right: Trouble," he said. She could see that he was not angry, and she got to her feet, still giggling. She wandered off into the half-darkness. He picked up a pebble that lay near the blankets and for a time just squatted there, tossing it at an ant exploring the earth near by. After two or three minutes he threw the pebble aside, laughed again, and got ready to meet the new day.

It was introduced, as usual, by Activity. He had been up still earlier, and somewhere had tracked down an echidna, red-brown and golden, which, Marriner knew, they would share for breakfast, probably with yesterday's bread fried in the pan.

"This fellow Terrubbidy, she's good for you, eh?" Activity asked.

"Rosie?"

"No more Rosie. White-fellow name Terrubbidy, she says. She says you told her no more Rosie. Name is Terrubbidy."

Marriner thought.

"I told her she ought to be called Trouble."

"That's it, Davy. Terrubbidy. That other fellow Mary, she's not good. Wrong skin. Old men say she's wrong skin for you. Say she's not to come for you. This Terrubbidy, she's all right, eh?"

Whatever part Marriner had been allotted in the totemic structure of the tribe he could not guess; but he realized it was too strong an influence for him to contest. Anyway he was filled with content. Nor did he even make a token stand upon the change of name.

"She's a good girl, that Trubbidy," he said, and the conversation lapsed.

Later in the day he looked out an old shirt, though his store of clothes was scanty enough, and tossed it to the girl. She accepted it readily, and put it on with an apparent appreciation. It covered her from her neck almost to her knees; and while it added nothing to her appearance it seemed to please her, and it pandered to the bourgeois in Marriner's make-up.

For a more intelligent man, life in the camp at Bloodwood Plains might have proved impossible. Day followed day, bringing only those tasks which would enable a man to see it through. When these included such chores as hunting they were pleasant enough; though Marriner's part in this was usually to accompany and watch a few of the young men; for some innate caution prompted him to conserve his little store of cartridges. He kept nothing for himself, except a sufficiency of clothes and his tools, and handed out the tobacco, the flour, the tea and the sugar with a regal munificence. The thought of continuing his journey was always with him; and on several occasions he ventured southwards with Activity to try the land. But the menace of the desert grew as he proceeded; and he was always happy to turn back.

On the other hand, a man less intelligent, less sensitive, might have been unhappier than he. For Marriner learned to identify himself with the black people, to appreciate their feelings, to feel the lift of excitement when the desultory singing round the campfire strengthened, and was mated to the rhythmic clapping of sticks, and throbbed loud and compelling until it developed into the full-scale dancing of the corroboree; and the half-dressed natives threw off their clothes to be with their fellows in nakedness, and sang and chanted and acted out the incidents of their recent days. He learned to appreciate the woodcraft that could distinguish the difference in the tracks a dingo made when he was hunting, and when he was carrying dead game in his mouth. He learned to accept the philosophy of the unburdened man who, rather than accumulate wealth and possessions to the end that he might be happy, learned instead, painfully sometimes and sometimes easily, to be happy with the least that would suffice him.

He could not have told at what stage he began to find almost an enjoyment in the discomforts, just as later he could not have told at what stage Trubbidy began to speak to him in a few halting English words. She kept to him as close as any wife; she was his woman, and respected as such by the tribe; and unobtrusively she began to take upon herself even such wifery duties as were unknown to her people—the washing of clothes, for instance; and, while the supply lasted, the brewing of tea.

But even with his acceptance he longed to get away. He watched the northern horizons for signs of men travelling, but they never appeared. There was little else for him to do. Once or twice he tried to read Edrington's *Utopia*, but he didn't persevere very far. For one thing, the limited reading of his lifetime had all been done in the evenings; and here, in the evenings, the firelight was inadequate; the native fire was economical of fuel and seldom showed a flame. In the afternoons the lazy sun defeated him; in the morning he had a habit of pseudo-activity; tidying up his possessions, examining the traces left by the white man who had been here before him, or simply walking among the trees. His skin toughened in the sun, for he usually went shirtless; his physique developed, his mental energies were channelled into learning some elements of the tribal language and a skimming of the amazing fund of tribal nature lore.

After three or four weeks he could follow a track well enough; even to giving an estimate as to the manner in which its maker had travelled; slowly, or at a fear-induced high speed, or at a brisk run born of high spirits. But he could never, not in a lifetime, achieve the mental dexterity of the native, who transposed his reading of the tracks into a lively, authentic picture, as detailed as life itself.

Marriner came to this realization one morning when, with Activity, he had walked about four miles from the whip-pole. George—who had forsaken, forever it seemed, his given name of Ngumbanalu—was walking a hundred yards ahead, and stopped, searching the ground. He laughed quietly and went on.

Activity, on reaching the same spot with Marriner, also began to laugh. He was thoroughly delighted with what he saw. But Marriner, when he examined the ingredients of the joke, had no reaction whatever. He could see the prints of a 'roo, made apparently on the previous night, and there was a place where speed had been abruptly gathered, as evidenced by the distance between the sets of parallel claw marks. There was also a broken branch. And about ten yards away there were the prints of a dingo—all familiar things, not usually calculated to give birth to risibility. But Activity was thoroughly amused.

When Marriner complained, he explained.

In the previous night's twilight the kangaroo had been easing himself gently over the ground near the trees, not interested in anything very much, certainly not afraid or even nervous. He had seen nothing of the dingo that sat in plain sight, his head alert, watching. The 'roo was too big for the dingo to tackle by himself except under the compulsion of extreme hunger; and so the dingo evinced no more interest than any other dog would have done in this familiar intrusion. He sat where he was and waited.

But there came a moment when the 'roo, at close quarters, got a plain view of the dingo, and in a moment of panic, quite uncalled for, leaped high. He had cannoned into a dead branch of the tree, snapped it off, lost balance and rolled over, picked himself up and taken off into the distance as though all the devils in hell were after him. The dingo meanwhile, his senses assaulted by the unpredictable snapping of the branch, the confusion of the 'roo, the turmoil when branch and animal hit the ground, leaped into startled action himself, and ran into the distance.

The joke explained, like any joke explained, was not a very good one. Marriner could only account for the hilarity of the normally phlegmatic natives by realizing that the tracks on the ground were for them like writing in a book; that in this deserted place they visualized from the evidence not only the approximate positions and reactions of the animals involved in the little drama, but also the subsidiary details—the expressions on their faces, the discomfiture of their equipoise, the anticlimax of the dog's departure in panic.

Well, a less sensitive man might not have found in this the stuff to keep his mind occupied; might have dismissed these things as trivial; and a man more intelligent might not have found here material enough to compensate for the known world lost; but Marriner, with no ties of blood in the outside world, remained happy enough. The hope that another man might pass that way remained with him; he was determined to take the first opportunity to leave, but there was no desperation in his resolve, and no sense of urgency.

After he had been at Bloodwood Plains four months his opportunity came. With Trubbidy, Activity, George and a youth named Colin—there were white-fellow names now for nearly all the tribe—he had been on a four-day ride to the west. Long before they came in sight of the Bloodwood camp on their return, the natives were aware of the movement of horses, their senses alert, keen to read the meaning; and when they arrived, Marriner's herd was being watered. Activity rode forward to make enquiries, and when the others came up he had the whole story.

A small party of the young men had been camped at Argadala water hole—uncritically, Marriner suspected they had been trying their prowess with his horses—when they saw in the distance the dust of a new arrival. With commendable

foresight they had driven Marriner's horses back to Bloodwood Plains, leaving two of their number behind to find out
details of the new arrivals. They had ascertained that the
party consisted of a white man, four native drovers, about a
hundred horses and five times as many cattle. The cattle and
horses, they said, were very poor.

The news heartened Marriner considerably. He would
have taken horse straightway for the Argadala water, except
that he was tired, the horses were all tired; and upon reflection he could see no advantage in it.

In the morning, instead, he and Activity saddled up and set
out. They had covered about two-thirds of the distance when
they saw two riders coming in their own direction. They
pushed their horses into a canter, a gesture to which the new
arrivals did not respond. When the parties met, Activity
stopped his horse a few paces behind, as did one of the newcomers, a young native.

The other man was a heavy thick-set fellow with a heavy
black curling beard that looked like a swarm of bees dependent
from his ears and nose and covering his chest. He must
have weighed close to two hundred pounds, and he rode
a heavy-set, thick-legged bay, powerful enough to pull
a plough. Marriner rode forward, introducing himself and
holding out his hand. The other man took it in a mitt like
a gorilla's, a thick, heavy hand covered with coarse strong
hair.

"Bob Eichardt," he said. "You own these horses we've
been following the tracks of?"

Marriner admitted to it.

"You lit out yesterday in a mighty hurry then. What's the
matter? Scared of company? You'd think a fellow was going
to lift your horses. Or maybe take them back."

Marriner was affronted.

"To tell the truth I wasn't there," he apologized nevertheless. "Some of the lads brought them up to my other camp

last night and told me you were here. So I came out to look for you."

Eichardt grunted.

"What sort of a trip did you have?" Marriner asked.

"Well, we got here. What's it like, further south?"

Marriner pursed his lips.

"Never been over it. But pretty bad for the first stretch. Two long hauls and a dry camp between before you come to water; and then not much water; that's what they tell me. Worse than the bit you just came over."

"Could be a lot worse than that," Eichardt said, brushing into insignificance the trials and tribulations that dominated Marriner's memory. "Up ahead here—dry all the way?"

Marriner nodded.

"Then where did you take your horses?" Eichardt demanded.

"Oh, there's one camp—Bloodwood Plains, where I am now. It'll be a job watering cattle there, but we can manage. It's beyond that that the dry stretch starts."

"I'll have a look round," Eichardt said, and started his horse. He forged ahead, not caring, apparently, whether Marriner fell into line or not; and Marriner felt himself wishing he'd said "you" instead of "we"—"You can manage." It was a while before Eichardt spoke again, and then it was an attempt at affability.

"Good country here," he said. "Plenty feed," and Marriner agreed.

"We had a stiff pull further back. Water holes dried up. I've been losing cattle the last sixty miles. Got a few more to lose. I'm going to spell them there—how do you call that place where I am?"

"Argadala."

"All right. Argadala. I'm going to spell them there, build them up a bit. Can't give them more than a week. If that.

Can't afford the time. To hell with this route. Nevermore for Eichardt."

"It's tough going," Marriner said. He was relieved more than anything. He had been wondering how he could broach the proposition of accompanying Eichardt south. A week would give him plenty of time. In the meanwhile he would let it ride.

"Rough camp," Eichardt commented when he surveyed the Bloodwood Plains site. "You'd think you'd fix the old place up." He pointed to the standing walls of the old shack. "Square them off, build them up, put a roof on and it wouldn't be too bad," he said.

Marriner had never thought of it. He didn't think much of the suggestion now.

"Yes, well, it's only temporary," he said.

Eichardt looked him over.

"You'll want something when the rains come." He pointed with a coiled-up whip. "Let's have a look at your water."

The whip-pole with its bucket made him more morose. The old trough now had a most limited usefulness. It held only a gallon or two of water.

"You'll get along that way with horses but not with cattle. You'd think, though, since you've been here all this time, you'd have a bit of a yard and a trough that would hold something."

"I didn't count on staying."

"No? Well, even a week or two. You've got plenty of labour." He gestured towards the little bough humpies where the natives lived. "You've got quite a tribe here."

They dismounted, and Eichardt and his native companion tied their horses to bushes thereabouts. Eichardt asked for an axe, and Marriner sent Activity to bring his. When it came all four of them walked along inspecting the larger trees. There was a big river gum not far from the whip-pole.

"Here, Felix. Try this one," Eichardt said.

The native took the axe and tapped the butt of it lightly against the trunk of the tree. He eyed the trunk up and down its length and then nodded.

"All right, Felix. Bring her down."

There was a large, leaf-shaped scar on the trunk recalling the time some forgotten lubra had cut a coolamon from the bark to cradle her baby. The tree crashed down, and Eichardt went over to inspect it. The base was hollow and he nodded approval. He sliced casually with the axe to cut the smaller limbs away; the larger ones he parted at a little distance from the trunk. The largest of all carried the hollow of the tree for a considerable distance. The inside was filled with a variety of detritus; black flakes of dead wood mixed with the recent debris of a cockatoo's nest.

Eichardt worked swiftly and neatly, cutting away one side of the log in such a manner that the hollow was everywhere shielded by solid wood except at the butt. The whole thing made a large and adequate watering trough; and he asked Marriner to call natives and have it carried to the whip-pole site. Here he plugged the open end efficiently with a block of the spongy wood from a bean tree. He staked the whole trough very securely in position, sinking it a little in the earth.

When it was filled, it leaked only slightly, and even this small deficiency was made smaller with a plastering of mud. In two hours' work he had provided a convenience that would have saved Marriner hours of slow watering of horses. Marriner? It would have saved him nothing at all; it would have saved the tribe a little time they would not otherwise be using. On second thought, it saved exactly nothing; yet the display of enterprise impressed Marriner more than he would have cared to admit.

Eichardt was openly contemptuous of the meal with which Marriner provided him that night.

"Abo tucker, black-fellow tucker," he said. "All right for an emergency. A man has got to have flour; flour and tea and sugar."

"No chance to get supplies up here," Marriner defended himself.

"I daresay not. How long you stopping here?"

"I hadn't thought of it," Marriner lied.

"You taking up land?"

"I might at that."

The man repelled him. This was no Edrington, to share the long days with, to share the sunshine and the campfires, the joys and the hazards of travel. Quite suddenly he decided, and with a finality unusual in him, that he would not leave. Not yet. He had waited four months for a companion, and he could wait longer. Once he had made the decision he thought of nothing else but getting Eichardt out of his camp. He was not introspective enough to see that it was a decision of renunciation and not of resolve. And that to that extent it also was an expression of weakness.

However, he was not long saddled with the presence of the stranger. Eichardt rode back to Argadala on the following morning, and Marriner saw no more of him until, five days later, the herd of cattle, preceded by a lively band of horses under the control of one rider, came drifting up the plain.

The majority of the tribe people had already left for some other camping site far to the west. Of the remainder, Marriner, as he had previously arranged with Eichardt, sent some with the horses, to avoid a confusion at the overnight camp. There were left a couple of elderly women with the middle-aged husband they both shared, two old men each with young wives, and Marriner and Trubbidy and Activity.

Eichardt's horse-tailer, on his arrival, immediately made camp near the whip-pole, watered his horses, hobbled them, and had them feeding quietly under the trees long before the first cattle appeared. By the size of the packs, Eichardt's outfit was well supplied. The horse-tailer was taciturn. He spoke neither to Marriner nor to the handful of tribesmen remaining.

An hour or two later the slow and languid stream of cattle flowed in over the plain, seeming to possess the land their numbers swallowed. Their soft, pained bellowing dominated the senses, even though their numbers were small. There were, as Marriner had been told, about five hundred of them; none in good condition. They were mostly cows. There were perhaps fifty bullocks and a sprinkling of bulls, about a dozen. Most of them had the white Hereford face. They were a well-bred lot, but there was a strong admixture of Shorthorn blood among them.

Now that he was on the move, Eichardt proved a little more sociable than he had seemed at first meeting. Marriner's impulse to avoid him was obviously ill-thought, and he joined Eichardt by the trough after the last cows had been watered and, still protesting, been left to graze out on the plain. He found the drover genial enough.

"You'd better eat with me," Eichardt said. "I can do you a little better than that abo tucker. I bet you're hungering for a bit of white man's food, eh? How long you been out?"

"Five months. Yes, all that."

"Yes? Well, it's long enough. Now how much can you tell me about the route? Let's have it over again."

Marriner, as well as he could, retailed instructions for the next few days of travelling. He accepted the invitation to eat; and in truth he was glad he did, finding the plain meal strangely satisfying. Eichardt had cooked a bread fancied by the addition of beef-dripping and currants; his meat was beef, salted and carried over from the last camp.

"I'll leave you a bit of beef too," he said. "There's a couple more cows I have to draft out. They won't make a dry stage. I cut out about fifty at the last camp—Argadala you call it. They're a bit rocky on their legs and they hold us up too much. I had to nurse them in. I dropped another fifty here and there, in ones and twos, all over the last dry stage. The crows will have them. The crows and the goannas."

"How many did you start with?"

"I haven't lost many up to date. And with a bit of luck I'll get the rest through. But I'm undermanned. I'm short-handed. The boys I've got are good, none better, but a man can't do everything. And my plant is good. Good horses. I notice you've got a couple of good beasts yourself."

They discussed inconsequentials for a while. The stockmen were sitting at their own fire twenty yards away, talking also in lowered voices, at home wherever they stacked their saddles.

"Now stores," Eichardt said. "I can't let you have flour. I got plenty tea. Not enough sugar—you got sugar?"

Marriner shook his head.

"I'll drop off twenty pounds of salt—I've got too much. You got any money?"

"A couple of pounds." There had been about thirty in Edrington's belt.

"All right. Give them to me. You can have some tea and some cartridges. Your rifle a twenty-two?"

"Yes."

"All right then. Tobacco?"

Marriner, about to reply that he didn't use it, thought of Activity.

"If you can spare it," he said.

"Well, for Christ's sake, a couple of quid won't go far. See if you can dig up a spin and I'll see you right."

"Five pounds? That's getting down to bedrock," Marriner said wryly.

"You're pretty near there, looks like," Eichardt returned. It needled Marriner, but he took no notice.

"I can find a fiver," he agreed, and Eichardt nodded.

85

"Matter of fact, you can't lose, if you're staying here long," he confided. "There's a little fortune back there at Argadala. About forty of the cows I dropped will live, and the best part of them in calf. If you've got any brains you'll put a brand on the poodies. I won't be coming this way again, you can bet on that. It'll be a bit of beef for you if nothing else."

A rider had brought the wandering cattle together and bedded them down. They lay or stood now, chewing the cud, in the quiet familiarity of the night camp; the nearest of them only a hundred yards or so from the fires. There was a constant muted lowing from the cattle. Three horses, saddled and bridled, stood by the trees. The rider on a slowly trudging hack circled the herd, singing softly the words of some monotonous aboriginal chant; thus signalling his position at all times to the cattle, so that an unplanned noise from his movements, the clack or a hoof on a stone, perhaps, should not affright them.

The men at the fire did not talk long. An hour or two after dark Marriner stood up to go; and at the same time Eichardt threw his arms above his head, yawning and stretching in anticipation of sleep. His night, like that of the others, would be broken by a stint of circling the night herd; his sleep would be uneasy against the chance of having to throw himself, just as he slept, upon his saddled horse if the threat of a rush—a stampede—should develop. The remaining two stockmen, with the adaptability of the native, were long ago asleep. The horse-tailer, at the beginning of the night, had made his own fire and settled down apart; his day began three hours before the others.

When Marriner awoke in the early morning the cattle were being watered, ushered to the trough in small groups. Soon they were moving off; and only the horse-tailer was left, packing the camp gear, filling the water canisters, harnessing the pack horses, unhobbling the herd. A couple of hours after the cattle were on their way he, too, departed, his horses raising a sky-high column of dust as they trotted through the gap in the hills to the southern desert.

A couple of days later, Marriner left again for Argadala, curious to inspect the cattle Eichardt had left behind, though as yet he had no proprietary feelings towards them. They had grazed widely over the lush flood-plain that extended from the western end of the water hole; the young bushes of supplejack and bean had been nearly stripped of their leaves; and the cattle now were grouped in twos and threes over a patch of three or four thousand acres.

Without exception they were gaunt and scary. There were no bulls among them that Marriner could see; only one big-framed bullock. The rest were cows, good breeding stock; now worn but rapidly recovering even at this early stage from the worst effects of the journey—as they showed plainly enough by a spirited evasion of the approaching horses.

"Plenty good tucker," Activity suggested with his mind on beef, and Marriner agreed. There was now a storehouse of meat that would be difficult to exhaust.

There was something else, too. A thin and nervous Hereford, its ribs raked down from a jutty backbone, reacted out of character to their approach. Head down, she bellowed, tossed her horns, made the most effective threats at her command against the party.

At the base of a bush near by a little red and white calf raised an uncomprehending head, its skin still wet with placental fluid and the cleansing saliva of the cow, its hair newly and lovingly plastered into wavelets against its hide. Marriner reined in his horse and looked at it a long time.

"Don't kill any cattle for tucker yet," he told Activity. "I think we'll keep them. Maybe later on we'll eat them. You tell those other fellows they can live on kangaroo yet awhile."

87

"Yowai, Davy," Activity agreed. "He's a pretty little pickaninny, that one."

The cow had approached and was nuzzling the calf, which now made its first staggering attempts to get on its feet. In three months there were thirty-two calves at Argadala, and their mothers were smooth and glossy in the peace of the water-hole country.

6

When he returned to Bloodwood Plains Marriner almost immediately transferred his attention to the broken walls of the hut. With Activity and Trubbidy his main helpers, he levelled the walls off, raised them to an adequate height, and with saplings bored and pegged he made a framework for a roof. He worked slowly but methodically, taking his time to get what he wanted, and achieving, indeed, far more strength in his simple construction than its purposes would require.

In the end he had a habitable room, about ten feet by sixteen, with a smooth mud floor. There were two open windows and a door, all of which could be shuttered, if necessary, with heavy slab constructions he had split and pegged from the wood of the gum trees. He had the hut thatched with a rough, shaggy roof of spinifex grass, the carting and placing of which cost him a considerable irritation, for his hands and arms were spiked through and through with the needle-sharp points. When the shell was complete he began to provide himself with a few amenities—a bench and a table. He also built a fireplace, but Trubbidy continued to cook at fires outside, and he never interfered with that. Still, the fireplace added considerably to the comfort of the nights.

He never faced up to the proposition that the building of the hut betokened a relinquishment of his plans for continuing his journey; yet that was implicit in his proprietary interest in the seventy cattle which he frequently rode to inspect at Argadala and the further water holes to which they had wandered. It could have been, indeed, the sight of that first small calf that induced him to begin construction; or the suspicion that many more months, years perhaps, might elapse before a rider came that way again; a rider, at least, with whom he could establish an acceptable liaison.

But when the clouds began to build up in the north, and day after day became a little heavier, a little nearer; when the electric storms heralded the cold and driving rain, he was glad of his shelter.

It was a good year's rain. In three days the watercourses were filled, the flood-plains soaked. The day after that the tribe was swimming and laughing in water deep over the whip-pole site; within a week a green flush of grass had covered the plain. It withered in a few days, the grass and a sudden carpet of small flowers; but only to give place to plants a little more permanent. The growth on the desert was amazing. It made the game scarcer for a while; the animals had no need of the concentrated herbage near the water hole; and he killed the old bullock to share it with the tribe.

Activity, he found, was an excellent stockman, with capabilities for horsemanship far outranking his own. Trubbidy rapidly learned to become almost as good; as did the happy vivacious Mary, who took to riding with teen-age enthusiasm. There were one or two others among the tribe, particularly among the young lads of fourteen or fifteen who attempted any feat that Activity could show them. Marriner turned all the enthusiasm to good use when he set out to brand all the calves with Edrington's EGE irons; but he himself was amazed at the facility with which these untutored riders could throw a galloping calf, leap from the saddle and secure it, and wait for the fire and the branding iron.

Of necessity, when it was carried out in this manner, the job took a long while. About twenty of the thirty-two calves they branded in two lots, cutting the animals out from a herd they had rounded up. The remainder were caught one at a time in the open. They branded them on the left flank and cut a keyhole earmark in the left ear.

There was almost a sensual pleasure for Marriner in the operation; a pleasure far removed from the perversity of sadism, but inseparable just the same from the struggling flesh, the spurt of heavy blue smoke when the iron pressed the skin, the bellowing and the fear. The smoke in the nostrils, the sun in the face, the rough hide under the hand, the fellowship of shared exertion and accomplishment, the company of men and horses—of people and horses, rather; for half his stockmen were women; and more than once he marvelled at the delicacy of the hands that held and controlled the thick muscled hocks of the beasts.

Twenty of the calves were female. There were four bulls, born early in the season and well-shaped, that he left entire. Activity or one of the girls castrated the remainder with the deftness of a surgeon. He had the nucleus of a herd when it was all over.

At Bloodwood Plains again he began on the construction of cattle yards, placing them close to the convenience of the whip-pole, although the stream bed here still held plenty of water. He was engaged on this when, from the south, eight months after Eichardt had gone that way, a herd of cattle came north. This time the drover rode in ahead.

"You've had rain," he said, before he dismounted. "Thank God for that. It stopped just the other side of here. There's been none south. You're Marner, aren't you?"

"Marriner, Davis Marriner."

"Tom Copeland. Hang on a minute." He dismounted, trailed the reins over his elbow and walked forward. Behind him the horse-tailer urged a good-looking but weary band of horses towards the water hole. Copeland shook hands ceremoniously.

"They told me I'd find you here; but I've been half sick with worry whether there'd be water. I've got twelve hundred head of cattle on their last legs. They're dropping all along the track. They'll be here in a couple of hours."

"Pleased to meet you. As far as I know your worries are over. Plenty water from here north. At least there's plenty here and at Argadala, next stage. Then you've got a dry camp. Only one."

"One's plenty. Too much. Well, we'll see."

He was a pleasant young fellow, slightly built. As he talked he began to help his native horse-tailer, unsaddling. With the water hole filled there was no need to use the troughs; the herd scampered away, light with the promise of the night's rest and good herbage, to the water. The horse-tailer went with them. He had to watch and bring them back for hobbling.

The cattle when they arrived, seemed indeed to be about on their last legs. They broke into a stumbling run to the water, streaming down the banks like a flood and splashing into the water hole, adding their excrement and their urine to the water before they drank and stirring the mud up with their churning hoofs, after the manner of ruminants. Thirsty as these cattle were they did not drink until they had conducted these bovine rites; but then they filled themselves long and eagerly and waded out into the deeps to let the water soothe the worst hurts of their travel-tortured bodies.

Three of them died that night near the water, one of them lying at the edge, half-in, half-out of the pool. When Copeland left Argadala a couple of days later he abandoned twenty-five worn and broken beasts. All survived, adding their number to the nucleus of the Marriner herd.

Less than a week later, when the dust of Copeland's passing was hardly settled, and before the tracks of his animals had lost the clean-bitten edges that proclaimed them fresh, still another herd came north upon his trail. But this time it was a small herd of about eighty cattle, accompanied by an even smaller plant of twelve horses. Both cattle and horses were in good condition and Marriner guessed, correctly as he later found, that the drover had spelled and fattened them at every opportunity upon the track. Both cattle and horses bore a variety of brands; the collection of an owner operating on a limited budget; or perhaps the spoils of a horse thief and cattle duffer.

There were only two riders with the outfit. In the formula of greeting, one, a slim native, stayed behind. The other rode forward.

He introduced himself as Bluey Dallas, proud of the nickname that any Australian would inevitably give him at the sight of his red unruly hair. He was a thick-set man, his heavy cheeks so deeply creased in the line from nostril to corner of mouth that they seemed to be carrying scars. He had heavy-lidded eyes, a mouth in which cruelty was accentuated rather than diminished by fleshy loose lips. His jaw was set rock-hard; and his body, loosely built, heavily muscled and immense, matched his face. His oversized hands carried a thin coating of coarse red hairs to the edges of the fingernails. His dress: shirt, trousers, boots, hat wide-brimmed and set on the back of his head, was the dress of a bushman, a stockman of the Outback. His voice, though gruff, was affable enough as he chatted easily with Marriner, sitting relaxed in the saddle.

His black companion seemed little more than a lad, a youth dressed in faded blue shirt and blue denims, with bare feet in the stirrups. The face was almost obliterated in the shade of an enormous felt hat, wide-brimmed and with a peaked crown.

Dallas was, he announced, in no particular hurry to move on.

"You headed north?" Marriner asked him, though the question seemed redundant. To his surprise the big man shook his head.

"I don't know," he said. "I didn't aim to ride much

further. Going to homestead me a piece of land. You got a claim on this around here, I guess."

"As a matter of fact, I haven't," Marriner told him honestly.

"Well, doesn't matter. You've got this tribe of coons in your hand—it wouldn't pay a man to push you out. What I'm looking for is some good country, sure; but I want some coons to work it for me. Strike out somewhere new."

"There's nothing much to the north of here for a hundred miles or so," Marriner said.

"How does your country lie? You centred on it here?"

Marriner thought for a while. The tribal country lay to the east; very few of the hunting parties went off west; and those few not far. There were other desert people out there.

"I'd say I'm close up to the western edge of it," he decided. "I've got my cattle all out east. Never been more than a day the other way. Can't tell you about it."

"If it's okay with you, then, I'll leave the plant here a day or two and ride out to look the place over. If it suits me I'll take it up. If not, I'll head on north."

At long last he dismounted, and went to help his stockman.

"I'll have a pot of tea ready in about ten minutes," Marriner told him. "You'd better eat with me tonight."

"Be glad to."

A little later Marriner heard him bellowing: "Maudie, Maudie."

He looked out in some surprise, for the stockman was answering the call. With a shock Marriner recognized, from some nuance of movement, some response from the slim body, that the stockman was a woman. She was a girl; rather, a young girl whose face was full of pathos, as though it were relaxed in sadness, its expression fixed, recording what must have been her major reaction to life's treatment of her.

The shirt and trousers were not intended as disguise; not by Dallas anyway, as Marriner discovered when, later on that evening, they ate together in the hut; for Dallas spoke of her without any discoverable inhibitions.

"You got your gin pregnant," he said, nodding towards the open door which disclosed Trubbidy bending over the cooking fire. "You want to get rid of her. By God, it looks like I got to get rid of that one of mine too. It looks like she's got herself filled in as well."

Trubbidy was indeed pregnant. She had been carrying the child for some time, and her body was now taking new shape; a softly swelling shape that at this stage rather enhanced her attractions.

"I guess these things happen," Marriner said easily enough, but Dallas was of different timbre.

"The bitches breed like rabbits when they get mated up with a white man," he complained. "They can look after themselves in the tribe, you bet. Never see them with a family then. But come to bed with them yourself and they're in the family way before you can hang your trousers up. You mark my words: before long this country would be stiff with yeller-fellers, give them their way. And the yeller-feller will run the white man into the ground one day. Lying, sneaking, thieving rats the lot of them."

"What do you expect to do about it?"

"It won't happen to me. No yellow bastard of mine is going to roam this country, stealing a good man's horses, shooting his cattle—they'll take your job and your land some day. Look here, mate, these coons are right enough if you can take them. They know their place and they'll stay in it. Get a man half-black, half-white; the black part of him hates the white and the white part of him hates the black. And he understands both of them, both black and white. The blacks will stay on their tribal country; the yeller-fellers got no laws, they got no decency. They haven't got a good habit.

Get enough of them in this country and the white man's had his day.''

"I still don't see what you can do about it," Marriner observed mildly. Dallas was working himself up to something; pursued, maybe, by some fear that was stronger than his control.

"I told that Maudie bitch of mine," he said. "I warned her. 'Watch yourself,' I said. 'You get yourself filled in and that's the end of you. You can string along with me as long as you watch yourself.' Fair warning. Well, the bitch took no notice, I think. Good enough for a while. She's been along with me close on two years and looked after herself good as gold. Now we look like settling down somewhere she's gone and got herself pregnant. I'm not going to have it. I'm not sure yet, but when I'm sure, by God she'll be sorry. There's no second chances with Bluey Dallas. I'm straight with them that's straight with me, but I don't let no one cross me.''

There seemed no answer to this, and Marriner addressed himself to his meal. The choler to which Dallas's face bore testimony decreased, and the visible effects with it; and when Trubbidy came in again with fresh mugs of tea he watched her movements quietly. But as she went out the door he repeated his advice.

"Get rid of her. Straight away before you've got a litter of kids around the camp. Send her to hell and gone with some bastard going through with a mob. Get her off where you'll never see her again. Then you're not so likely to have the same trouble with the next.''

Marriner made no reply. Dallas gulped a few swallows of the hot tea, and with a rapid change of subject said:

"It's okay with you, I suppose, to leave these cows here a few days. Will you keep them tailed close to the water? Is there much feed further back?''

"There is. But I'll see they don't wander. A little

mob like that should hold all right. Don't worry about them."

Dallas and his Maudie rode out of camp before dawn. For the next five days Marriner, mostly by proxy, kept a careful watch upon the cattle and the remaining horses of the plant. Each afternoon a rider, Trubbidy or Activity, or sometimes a group of tribal adolescents, headed the cattle in to drink at the home water. Once or twice, when the vigorous cows, coddled and looked after for months back and not at all afraid of men or horses, wandered further afield, the riders followed the tracks until they located the animals and brought them flying home at a gallop.

All the natives loved this work. They seemed to have been born with a love of horses, a love much more intense than their love for the hunting dogs which, from time immemorial, they had tamed and kept around their camps. Yet for thousands of years of their history the dog had been the only animal to which they had extended friendship.

On the fifth day Dallas came back alone.

"I figure that's the country for me," he said. "Won't know for sure; but I'll give it a year or two. There's a crowd of coons out there that ought to make good stockman material. There's good water; and there's the promise of a lot more further back."

"I should be seeing something of you then," Marriner commented.

"Now and again," Dallas agreed laconically. "I figure on setting up camp a fair way back though. Don't want to perch on the edge of a holding. Not like you."

"I don't know how long I'm going to stay," Marriner said defensively.

"None of us do, I guess. Still, a man's better off on his own."

"What happened to Maudie?" Marriner asked suddenly. Her absence had been worrying him.

"Eh? Oh, her. Well, it was what I thought. She's in pup all right. So I got rid of her. I gave her marching orders."

Marriner considered this. Any native outside his tribal country had only a small chance of survival. Except at certain seasons, their incidence and duration established by long habit, when one tribe would visit another, perhaps to share an awaited vegetable crop, perhaps to trade, no native was safe in another's tribal country unless he was a messenger. It was the province, the duty of each tribe, to despatch the interloper, and this was sound tribal sense. For he might be outcast, he might be the herald of an invasion, he might be on the run from the justice of his own people. In any event, they would not be held accountable for his death.

So Marriner said slowly, "That's a bit tough. She's in strange country."

Dallas laughed without humour. He gave Marriner a queer sidelong look.

"She's in strange country all right. Well, I warned her. She knew what was going to happen. And that's that."

He stayed another couple of days at Bloodwood Plains. Then early one morning, when Marriner was just stirring, he came up to the hut.

"I'm on my way," he said. "Be seeing you in a few months."

Marriner came to the door.

"Good luck then," he said. "You need a hand to pick up the cattle?"

"No, we can manage." Dallas gestured to where the saddled horses were standing ready, and Marriner, to his surprise, saw another stockman, waiting patiently; standing as still as a tree in the dawn, holding the reins. For a moment he thought that Maudie had returned to the camp. It was the same slender figure, the same boyish stance, the same— actually the same—big hat with the peaked crown; the same blue denims and light blue shirt faded nearly white.

"She came back then?" he commented.

"What? Oh no. I picked up another gin from out of your mob. Seems to be made of good stuff. And she knows her way about a horse already. Man gets used to travelling with a gin. Gets lonesome by himself, someway."

The swelling of the breasts under the shirt was evident. Under the big hat the features took shape. It was with a sense of shock that Marriner recognized Mary. He had never seen her dressed before.

He walked down to where she stood.

"You going away, Mary?" he asked.

"Yowai, Davy." It was straining their mutual vocabulary. She looked neither excited nor downcast; and Marriner realized that for the last night or two she had probably shared the bed of the big fellow. A brief jealousy stabbed him. She was, to him, still the most desirable woman in the tribe. He could not understand his failure with her; though to be sure he had exerted only a half-hearted effort.

"Best of luck then, Mary," he said, though she wouldn't understand. "And goodbye."

"Yowai, Davy."

The affirmative indicated, he supposed, acceptance or reciprocation of whatever he had had to say. He stood and watched as Dallas and his companion mounted, and rode off together.

A couple of days after this, Marriner, Activity and Trubbidy, whose pregnancy in no way interfered with her pursuits, set off on the trail of Dallas's cattle and horses. There was no apparent purpose in this expedition; it was a change from the building of yards. Marriner suspected that Activity had promoted the idea (though if he had it was through the most subtle of suggestions) in order to know whether Dallas had camped within or beyond the bounds of the local tribal territory. It was easier to ride than to walk, and Activity had not yet progressed to the stage of using the horses purely for his own purposes.

On the way, as always, Activity continued to impart his knowledge of bushcraft to his companions. His finger-talk was routine; sometimes for Marriner's sake he amplified it with more detailed instruction. He did so on this journey, when they were returning late in the day. They had gone no more than fifteen miles, by which time they had been able to ascertain that the Dallas stock was not quartered at the last tribal water.

Activity now found a place where the tracks of Dallas's horse two days old ran briefly beside other tracks of the same horse a week old, and he demonstrated the altered appearance of the prints. It was a fine distinction, and Marriner was not certain that he could be sure of it, even when he knelt on the ground beside them. The older tracks were headed the way Marriner was going, back to Bloodwood Plains, but they veered sharply from the line of march, and as an exercise in observation he followed them. Activity seemed pleased, but he and Trubbidy remained on their original course, as they would in the normal order of march. Separation never worried the natives. No native, not even a child, could get lost; the traces of his passing were too distinct to the eyes of his fellows.

Marriner followed the tracks until half a mile or more separated him from his companions; a half-mile studded with the cover of bushes, so that he caught only occasional glimpses of them. He was about to ride back and join them when he saw the naked black body lying on the earth. He reined in, shocked. Then he dismounted and tied his horse to a bush, and approached on foot.

It was Maudie. She lay on her belly, hands clutched, arms above her head in the attitude of surrender. A bullet had smashed her spine. Another had penetrated the back of her head. Her legs lay limply together, feet folded to one side as though she had dragged herself a little.

Looking again he saw it was true: she had dragged herself

a yard or two before the bullet had smashed into her brain.
Her arms had threshed the earth; there were riven troughs
where her bent and straining fingers had dug the soil.

The booted tracks of a man had approached the body and
walked away. Marriner followed them. The ground was
rich with the evidence of what had happened; even to his
unpractised eye the story was written as clearly there as in a
book.

There was the bush where the horses had been tied, a few
yards only from where his own mount now stood quietly,
unconcerned. And here the bare feet had made a little pattern
that confused him for a while until he remembered that the
naked body was that of Maudie. Here, under orders, she
must have stripped, and thrown her clothes in a little pile
on the ground; a little blue pile. And from here she had begun
to run; only a little way until the bullet hit her back.

Then, conscious and paralysed, she had struggled, digging
at the sand while Dallas dismounted and walked quietly close
to give her oblivion with a bullet in the head. Then, leaving
her here, possibly without a backward glance for his movements were definite, he had gathered up the clothes: the hat,
the belted trousers, the faded blue shirt; a bribe for her
replacement. And ridden to Bloodwood Plains. And to
Mary. Mary had probably shared his bed that night.

Marriner found himself sweating, his breath harsh, his
heart jumping crazily behind his ribs, the pit of his stomach
heavy almost to aching. Here was evidence of violence
premeditated. He was shocked, incapable of thinking.

He remembered Dallas: "No yellow bastard of mine is
going to roam this country." . . . "The bitch got herself
filled in." . . . "I gave her fair warning." . . . "By God, she'll
be sorry." . . . "No yellow bastard . . ."

And he remembered Dallas a few brief hours after the
murder: "She's in pup, all right. So I got rid of her. I gave
her marching orders."

And that queer, sidelong look: "She's in strange country all right."

Carefully stepping in his own tracks he went over the scene again unable to believe what he saw. But the tracks could not be misread; the body with its bullets would not alter. Not in any seat of judgment. The hot sun had done its work, and the carrion-eating lizards. But they could not alter or even faintly disguise the evidence of the body. Not even when these remains were only bleached and scattered bones would the evidence of the crime be hushed. The broken skull, the shattered backbone would shout to the skies.

But Marriner knew too, somewhere inside himself, that they would shout in vain. He was first in the country and Dallas was second. The law had not caught up. It would take a little time.

Did Maudie know, then, what she prepared for as she stripped herself in the empty desert? Was she in fear? And if she was, did she fear the bullet, or the death of an exile in the desert? Did she just fear a brief loneliness, perhaps?—a search for a shelter in which she could wait for her baby? Was she sobbing as she pulled the shirt over her head? Was she defiant? Did she curse her lover as she stepped out of the trousers? Did she know the clothes would cover another skin and so soon?

As Marriner envisaged that moment the sad repose of her face was unchanged; the emotions were locked behind the features. She did not plead, nor did she argue. And the evidence was there—she had taken four or five quiet steps before she began to run, and then gave way to panic, matching her speed against the speed of the bullet, and losing; clawing at the sand then; raking those deep furrows with her fingers.

Marriner stood a long time before he mounted his horse; and when he did he rode round the body, round the short line of tracks; circling the whole scene three or four times. Then he headed his horse in the direction in which he could expect to find the others.

They had waited for him; and suddenly he had a conviction that Activity at least had some knowledge of what he had found. Perhaps the tribe had known and delegated Activity to lead him there. Had Activity prompted him to follow the tracks at that juncture? He could not remember; there was only the little lesson in tracking, a direction to the mind. Did Activity possess a power beyond explanation? He shivered a little in the hot sun.

Trubbidy sat leaning a little forward in the saddle, her hands on the pommel with the reins, her body relaxed, so that the swelling lines of her pregnancy were obvious.

"No yellow bastard of mine will roam this country. . . . Get rid of her."

Marriner shuddered and reined in his horse. Then he turned in behind a bush, dismounted, and was violently sick.

He staggered to a new shade and sat down. He rested perhaps ten minutes or more, holding lightly to the reins. Only when the horse became a little restive did he remount.

The two natives still sat their horses in the same place, quietly, waiting for him. When he joined them they said nothing. He looked sharply into Activity's eyes, wondering whether in fact he knew; but he could neither read them nor bring himself to mention what he had seen.

"More better we hurry, Davy," Activity said. "Plenty dark tonight, early."

They would talk some other time of what he had seen. Not now. Once or twice he imagined himself confronting the monster that was Dallas; braving the heavy-lidded eyes, the loose sensual mouth, the gorilla shape of him; but he knew he would not. Dallas lived by his own law, Marriner by his. Neither would interfere.

He had come to a hard country.

7

Marriner slept badly that night and looked to Trubbidy's presence, not in vain, for his comfort. For a week the scene on the desert haunted him vividly; then it grew dim, and there were days together in which he did not think of it. In some searching for relief he stepped up the work on the station, and he found that the work began to claim him. When, nearly seven months later, Dallas rode over one day, Marriner talked with him as they had talked together when they first met, and neither of them made any mention of Maudie.

Mary accompanied him, in the same shirt and denims; but they were now so tattered that they performed little service for her. Dallas had a purpose in coming; he needed stores. He had an order written out and twenty pounds in notes. The order was addressed to Masterman's, a firm of stock and station agents, at their branch in the little South Australian town of Quorn.

"Anyone going down, send this with them," he said. "They can send it back whenever any drovers are coming through. Doesn't matter when I get it; it'll be nice to know it's coming sometime. Send a coon over with a message if it should arrive."

When he was riding away he had an afterthought: "I've got a shirt and trousers for the stud down on that list. Write on it a dress for her as well, and they can leave off some of the flour. I'm getting tired of watching a girl in trousers."

He waved, and was on his way.

Marriner made out a list of his own. He ordered some clothes for himself, and three women's dresses, and made out a good list of items like tea, sugar, flour and salt. Then he thought of the children and added sweets, and tobacco for the men. He had to wait a month, and then entrusted the lists, and all of Edrington's remaining money to a drover headed south with horses.

It had been a year of development. Cattle were moving in the Territory, and the route that passed through Bloodwood Plains had become a recognized one. Five large mobs had gone north, two smaller ones, and several droving plants without cattle had headed down to the South and the markets. Most had staged at Bloodwood and rested a day or so at Argadala; and Marriner had shifted his own cattle, more or less permanently, to the good water further east and off the route.

Even without the natural increase his herds had grown surprisingly from the culls of the travelling mobs. Nine of his mares had thrown foals, and the horse herd had otherwise been augmented in a couple of deals he had made with drovers, trading one fresh fit horse for two. He had also made an outright sale at terms that were advantageous enough.

Trubbidy had borne her child, a boy baby whom Marriner christened Henry. At its birth it was pink and wrinkled, differing not at all from any of the white babies Marriner had ever seen; and for a little while he deluded himself it was going to be as white as himself; but within a few days the skin had darkened; not into the rich brown colouring of tribal children, but into a dusky medium hue, unlike either white or black, and unpleasantly reminding him of Dallas and his references to "yeller-fellers."

The child was a happy baby, and its presence never inconvenienced him. He grew to like the sight of Trubbidy, her tattered shirt pulled up round her neck, squatting to suckle the child at her now capacious breasts. Within a couple of months of the birth she was pregnant again.

He finished the building of an extensive holding yards, and though there were now seldom cattle of his own at the Blood-wood water hole, the yards greatly simplified the handling of the travelling herds as well as that of the small band of horses he always kept with him. The life of the water hole, from the time the rains filled it until no surface water remained, proved to be only three months; at the end of this time the whine, screech-and-grunt of the primitive whip-pole mech-anism again dominated his mornings and his evenings.

He loved the sound; and he loved it more particularly when, to water a large herd as well as to cater for the needs of the natives, it carried on, as it often did, for hour after hour. He never analysed the feeling, the sound existed, perhaps, as the clarion of his steading; it was the recognizable sound of his own place, and peculiar to that alone.

In this short time the character of the native encampment had also changed. It was now never entirely deserted. Activity, George and a youngster named Jacob, with their wives, were constantly there; they could always be depended upon to work cattle, to escort the travelling mobs safely through Marriner's country and Marriner's herds; they were good hunters, and they could butcher a cow or a steer on the infrequent occasions when Marriner decided to sacrifice some comparatively useless animal to his appetite—and theirs.

A few old men and women also haunted the camp; but most of the tribe clung to their nomadic habits; and if they had not, their feeding would have presented a considerable problem. They came back frequently to Bloodwood, but they seldom stayed long; and while they were there their hunters ranged far abroad.

About four months after Marriner had sent the orders south, a drover came up with the goods on a pack horse.

"You were lucky to get them," he said. "Prices have gone up. You didn't send enough money. But Masterman's bloke sent the lot. He said he'd send them if I'd carry them; but to tell you to send a few cattle down and work up a credit there, and then you'll be able to get what you like any time."

"I owe you for transport, then?"

"Not a thing. If I can use your yards. I'll probably be back. If no one comes through before I do I'll take cattle down for you—you can give me an order on Masterman's to take care of droving fees."

A letter enclosed with the order embodied similar suggestions. It was a long letter, with several enclosures intended to establish a business relationship between Masterman's and Marriner; and an assumption that his business was worth soliciting made Marriner laugh. He put the papers all aside and erased them from his mind, except for a resolve to send cattle if and when he had the opportunity and the right cattle to spare.

The stores had a short life. He gave out the tobacco, the sweets, most of the tea and flour. He had new clothes for himself and passed his old ones to Activity who, in turn, gave his rags to the lad Jacob. But it was a pleasant change to see Trubbidy attired in a dress. It increased the atmosphere or the illusion of domesticity in the hut, simple and even ugly though the dress was. Apart from clothes, at the end of four days all he had left was an adequate supply of tea, some flour and salt.

There remained the stores for Dallas. He loaded a pack horse and took Activity and Jacob over the desert to the west, for as yet he had only a little hearsay knowledge as to where the big fellow had pitched his permanent camp.

Dallas had set himself up comfortably on good water. He had a hut built with slabbed logs placed upright in the ground and roofed with spinifex thatch. And, like Marriner, he was surrounded by an encampment of natives. Most of his stock was grazing in the vicinity; at least, within ten miles of his camp.

Marriner's cortège made no attempt to establish relations with the other natives. There were a few distant greetings from one side or the other, but that was all. However, they were quietly joyous in their reunion with Mary, thin now, and angular; and with the lines of sadness more than ever pronounced; but healthy enough. Marriner understood, without anything being said, that even after this passage of time she had little to do with the tribal natives on Dallas's holdings, and he was sorry for her in her loneliness. He was also afraid for her.

Dallas himself was unchanged. He also had some communication from Masterman's. He read it, grunted, and tucked it away in a saddle pouch that depended from the flaps of a saddle pegged inside the hut.

"The bastards want cattle," he said. "They'll get them when I'm good and ready. I'm not making any trip back there this year."

"I'm going to send a small mob, next time a drover goes through," Marriner suggested. "You could leave a mob with me to add to them."

Dallas weighed the suggestion and grudgingly acceded to it.

"That'll do for once," he said. "But if a man wants to get down there and see them sold. If it was a big mob, that is. Otherwise they'll steal the pants off a man."

"Can't go down there every time."

"No. But in a year or two it won't be necessary any more. The buyers will be travelling up this way. That's the shot, if there's enough of them. A man will get a price per head, on the property."

"Well, there's no buyers yet."

"No. Well, in about six months I'll bring a little mob over. But it will be three years before I've got anything really fit for travel. My cows are too young to sell and I'm eating the bullocks."

A little later in the evening he brought up a subject that Marriner would have avoided.

"How's that stud of yours?" he asked. "She have that nipper?"

"Yes. A boy. He's no trouble."

Dallas grunted.

"Should have given her marching orders. They're no good, them half-castes. You want to see what it's like up top, up in the North. They'll be running this country in fifty years."

The company of Dallas meant less than nothing to Marriner. When he and his people saddled up in the morning he was glad to leave. They did not return on their tracks, but struck through the mountains to the south to emerge on a plain heavily grassed with spinifex. Re-entering the tribal territory which Marriner now identified with his own holdings, they crossed the mountains again; and it was at this point that Marriner made a discovery that seemed, at the time, of little moment.

He was dismounted when he made it, standing alongside the horse, looking across an elevated mile-wide plain that sprawled across the top of the hills. There was a crow near by, cawing, cawing with a persistence that annoyed him. It was sitting on the branch of a bleached and long-dead tree; and with a gesture of annoyance Marriner stooped quickly to pick up a stone to throw at it. To his surprise his fingers slipped off the stone at first try; and the crow rose, cawing still more energetically, and flapped away.

Marriner tried the stone again. It was embedded slightly in the ground, but came away easily. The weight of it was what had tricked him. It was surprisingly heavy, of an even, dark colour. He showed it to Activity, and might as well have shown him a pebble from the water hole.

"Plenty stone like that here, all round about," Activity said, jutting his chin out and pointing with it. And Marriner saw that the surface of the ground here was, indeed, covered with the stones. But at the time he thought it sufficient of a curiosity that he slipped it into his saddle pouch instead of throwing it away. When they reached Bloodwood Plains he tossed it up on a shelf in the hut; a long shelf running the length of the hut just below eye-level that had become the repository for all kinds of small items of gear.

He felt glad to be back. The sight of Trubbidy and the baby was a comforting one; he had already begun to recognize this small rough hut as home. The sound of the whip-pole, a lonely intrusion like the cry of a curlew, welcomed him; the tribe had arrived back in force, and the laughter of children supplemented the thin screeching of wood against wood.

The yards at Bloodwood Plains became a recognized stage on the north–south stock route. A zigzag route from water to water became refined, replacing the uncertain judgment of each individual drover, and the travelling herds in certain seasons became a feature of the life. Between the herds came others: a few prospectors, some wandering adventurers, men bound for the crocodile rivers or the buffalo plains of the North; disappointed men heading back to the security of the settled areas. And the Afghans: swarthy silent men with their swaying camels, the transporters, the hucksters of the region.

Sometimes there was a groaning line loaded to capacity with galvanized roofing iron, the sheets cut short to fit the camel saddles, to offer a lesser resistance to the wind, and to facilitate unloading. They were quiet, hard-working men who accompanied the camels, mysterious men allied to the desert soil, yet alien as their beasts of burden. They mixed well with the Australians, though they drank no liquor, and were proud in their nightly prayers, kneeling to face Mecca in the far northwest.

Under the constant pressures of contact the dark people of the country themselves changed, subtly, a little at a time. The whole tribe became clothed; at first women who were rewarded for temporary favours by a dress-length of calico or a cast-off shirt; or their menfolk, to whom such rewards belonged. Afterwards the others benefited—from the games of chance they were so quick to learn, or in the ordinary commerce of the people, or as the beneficiaries of the natural generosity of their fellows.

From learning the uses of tobacco they developed a hunger for it; for tobacco and white flour, and sugar to replace the wild honey from the hollow trees. They learned a broken talk; the youngsters became stockmen and disappeared for long periods, sometimes forever, with outgoing drovers. Cooking utensils, rawhide ropes, and battered, broken riding boots were wedded to the natural furniture of the hunter.

And by insidious degrees their health deteriorated. They accepted clothes, but not the responsibility of keeping them clean. The new foods which supplemented their diet were not such as would maintain a balance in that phosphate-poor country. Only a nation of meat-eaters could have survived here, drawing on the concentrations of phosphate in the flesh of beasts, and in the ripened fruits of grasses and trees. Neither Marriner nor any of his fellow adventurers was capable of the realization, but this was a country for the exploiter; the farmer, the conservationist, unaided, must have perished here.

The changes, then, were not good. But they were implemented by such slight degrees as to be inconspicuous. For a time they did not alter the life of the tribe; the cattle and the game flourished together; the juxtaposition of white man and black created little discord.

These early years were happy ones for Marriner. Trubbidy's second child was a girl. Two years later there was another boy; of which the birth nearly coincided with the

birth of a half-caste boy to the wife of Jacob. This was also
Marriner's, conceived almost in carelessness at a camp far
out near what Marriner accepted as his eastern boundary.
None of the tribe, not even Jacob, registered any criticism,
nor even surprise, in regard to this event. Marriner, however, was ashamed of it; and probably for this reason never
experienced any joy in the company of either of these, his
youngest children.

The eldest boy, Henry, was an engaging youngster; inseparable from his sister, Casey; and at times when he lazed
about the camp and there were no white men in the vicinity,
Marriner played a good deal with these children, taking an
interest in their growing accomplishments: the games they
played with string, the dingo puppy some hunter gave to
Henry, the lizards and small birds he caught, the tracks they
imitated in the mud of the water hole with sticks and finger-
tips.

The cattle demanded an increasing share of his time. By
the end of the fourth year it was taking three months and
more to carry out the branding muster, so widely were his
herds spread over the country. To facilitate the work he had
built a couple of roping ramps, each enclosed in a holding
yard, and situated at points about thirty miles from Bloodwood Plains and from each other. Some of his horses, one
small band, were running wild beyond his control; and occasionally he would make an attempt to go out, shoot the
stallion who guarded them, and run the others in for handling.
He was never successful; but about this he was never really
sorry; the buck, racing behind his mares, slashing at their
flanks with his teeth, guiding them to an escape route, was
much too beautiful for destruction.

And he had no need for extra horses. He had a plant of
nearly a hundred. Edrington's basic stock had been good,
and there was a small and steady demand for replacements
from the miners and drovers. Some careful streak in him

led him to keep his mares; those he was willing to sell, the worst of his plant, were not acceptable to the buyers; but the better geldings commanded a good price.

By the end of the fourth year, too, he had settled into a regular habit of sending cattle south to the markets. They were of no particular quality; he had brought neither bull nor stallion; but they made a price, and in return now, the Afghans were coming twice a year with stores for himself.

He had far more than he needed; he was well supplied with saddles and riding gear; with clothes and blankets and boots; with flour and salt, sugar and tea. As each consignment arrived the tribe, forewarned in some manner known only to themselves, was there to greet it in full force; there was a celebration with singing and dancing, and great stores of sweets, of bottled cordials on rare occasions, of flour and tobacco disappeared by magic. At first Marriner was back to eating native foods after these occasions; but his way of living gradually changed until he was at all times supplied with sufficient of these comforts for himself.

When this stage was reached, he found that the travellers, the drovers and the Afghans, the loud-talking adventurers, the introspective miners were beginning to depend on him for replenishment of supplies. He built himself a new four-room house a little further from the yards and the whipple-pole, but still within range of its protesting music. The old hut was devoted to the purposes of a storeroom; and it was only barely adequate.

There seemed no shortage of money. He hardly glanced at the letters and statements which Masterman's sent him at regular intervals—he had never yet finished the reading of *Utopia*, his only book; and when he came to write his lists of requirements the operation was tedious, requiring his full concentration for the manipulation of the worn pencil to make a proper record of his needs. He had a comfortable feeling that the herds he sent down were probably adequate to pay for the stores he received; if they were not, he supposed that Masterman's would cut down on their consignments.

As he had done with the horses, so he dealt with the cattle, keeping the breeding potential as high as he could. He frequently slaughtered cattle for his natives; indeed it had become necessary for several reasons. In the first place, a considerable team was now engaged on his work for six months of the year, and they and their dependents had to be fed. In practice they could have been sustained by the remaining hunters. These, however, if too big a burden were placed upon them, would walk off to some other section of their hunting grounds; and it was simpler on occasions to feed the whole tribe.

His men had also come to make certain demands upon him. They were not overt demands, but had he not met them he would have lost their services; for good stockmen were acquiring a value. Therefore he supplied them all with blankets, with clothing and with tobacco. Sometimes he gave them a few shillings to spend on sweets and canned goods when the Afghans came; and sometimes this nucleus of money was gambled for by the tribe.

They had other sources of money and supply. One or two of the more aggressive openly offered their women to the travellers and received payment in advance. Sometimes they sold a well-carved boomerang. Sometimes Trubbidy, for instance, in her affluence, was generous to her friends and relations; and these small acts always had Marriner's acquiescence.

"You're too damned easy with that bitch," Dallas told him once. They were sitting on a barked log near the yards, Dallas and Marriner and a bird of passage, a prospector who went by the name of Mission Mo.

"The only way to handle them is to get on their hammer and stay there. Keep them down. Let them get away with nothing."

"You've got it all wrong, Blue." Mo so seldom disagreed with anyone that Marriner was surprised by the statement. Mo was a little man, with a cocky, quizzical, small-boy look that belied his wizened features and his greying hair. He was small in stature too; small and thin and tough; an old bird well-cooked by the desert sun, though his years were not so many more than Marriner's. He came by his moniker through a legend that he had once been a layworker for a mission in the North; and the legend also supplied several bawdy variations of a story that explained his severance from that institution. Which one was true he would never admit; he seldom talked about himself, and the probability was that none of them had much foundation in fact. He had called at Bloodwood Plains twice before, a tiny figure perched on top of one of his two horses. The other carried pick and shovel, dolly-pot and prospecting pan; for Mo was one of that vast army that sees the pursuit of gold as the aim and end of existence. He had found gold before. He would never be happy with what he found; the pursuit and not the discovery was his fierce joy.

Mo as a philosopher was something new.

"A man has got to depend on his woman in a country like this. He has to treat them right," he said then.

"It'll never be a country till white women come. You can't count these gins women," Dallas said contemptuously.

"You're wrong again," Mo said. "No matter what brings the white man here, it's the black woman that keeps him here. Not me. Women are not for me. But the rest of you. A white woman would be on your backs. 'Let's get out. Let's give it away,' she'd say. She'd have known better things and she wouldn't want to go downhill. But the lubra cooks and works and musters the stock and chops the wood and carries the water, and you fellows sit back and take it. You wouldn't stop five minutes otherwise. She's happy with what she's got; she knows no better, and she won't worry you."

"You're right," Marriner admitted.

"Bloody rot," exclaimed Dallas.

"I won't argue," Mo said. "Just have a look at yourself, that's all. You're sitting settled like an egg in a nest. Take away your woman and you'd be over the horizon tomorrow. And if she was white you wouldn't be here in the first place."

Dallas spat, and said nothing.

There were women at the whip-pole, pulling at the line that held the bucket, and tipping it, when it appeared, into the trough. The pole, in its socket in the fork screeched slowly, a long-drawn-out sound as the weight swung downwards. Then there was a groan as the upper end of the pole, just above the fulcrum, came in contact with the fork; then the splash of out-pouring water, then the swift sound as the bucket was sent down, the muted message of its arrival at the water level in the well. After a while Dallas got up and walked away. He didn't excuse himself or explain his departure, but he was not being rude; it was his normal procedure. Mo had been waiting for this.

"Tell you what, Davy," he said, "I'd like a yarn with you. I want you to stake me for a while. I won't tell you I'm on to gold. I'm not. But there's gold in this country, that I'm sure of. There never was a country without gold. And sooner or later someone's going to find it. Well, I'm looking. But I'm flat to the boards. I got my gear and my horses, and that's the lot. You stake me and I'll cut you in on a share of what I find."

"What do you need, Mo?"

"Tucker. The usual. That's all. Except boots. And a couple of bits of camp gear, a bucket and a butcher knife."

"I'll lend them to you. You can pay me back."

Mo shook his head.

"Not good enough, Davy. I'd owe them to you. And that would be on my mind. Then I'd have to find something. I'd be racing round trying at this and trying at that, and giving nothing a fair go. No, give me the gear and we'll be partners. Half-shares."

"Too much. Give me a third."

"Half's the usual, Davy. It's okay with me."

"It's too much, Mo. You're welcome to the tucker, what I've got. You don't have to cut me in on anything."

"It's this way, Davy. When I'm running short I'd like to think there's more where that came from. That's a big thing. I might strike colour next week; it might be six months. It might be a year. Or more, even. Should find something, though, up there in the North."

Marriner nodded.

"All right, Mo. I'll take a third."

"Make it half, Davy. I don't want to be beholden to you. When I find it there'll be plenty for me in a half. We'll be as rich as El Dorado, Davy."

"All right, Mo. If that's the way you want it. You'd better take fresh horses, too, and leave those hatracks of yours behind. They could do with a spell."

"Got something quiet?"

"Plenty. You can take your pick. When do you want to go?"

"I'll pull out in the morning, Davy."

"Well, you better come see what I've got and fill your packs."

The storeroom had not long been replenished. It was piled with burlap sacks of flour and sugar and tea. There was a case of nails, a case of canned goods, a couple of caddies of the sweet, black, sticky trade tobacco, some cans of cane syrup. They worked over them for a while, sorting out the stores into handy packs.

"Next trip it might pay me to take a third horse, if you can spring a new packsaddle," Mo suggested, and Marriner nodded.

"I'll see what I can do."

117

Mo picked up the *Utopia* off the shelf.

"A bit of reading too. I'll take this along, if it's all right with you."

"Right. Look after it though. That's my title to my brand." He showed the inscription on the flyleaf and Mo read it.

"Geoff Edrington, eh? I thought I knew that EGE brand. Whatever happened to him?"

"Thrown by a horse. Got ripped on a stump and died."

"Well." Mo was silent for a moment. "Nice bloke he was, too. And a good rider. It can happen to any of us. You better hang on to it." He replaced it on the shelf and took up a black stone sitting alongside, turning it over in his hands.

"Where did you get this?"

"South and west of here. There's plenty of it. I've had a dozen blokes look at that. Nobody knows what it is."

"I know what it is, all right. It's wolfram."

"Is it any good?"

"Don't waste your time on it. There's a few bob in it. By the time you've paid the 'ghans to cart it, you'd have no profit. No, gold's the only thing. And by God we'll find it. If it takes a year."

He put the black lump back on the shelf.

8

It was two years more before Marriner went south with his own herd, his own drovers. The journey was no more arduous than the succession of conjoined little journeys which added up to the normal muster. It was, in fact, much more pleasant, once the cattle were accustomed to the routine of travel; for they became drilled to the order of march, like soldiers, and anticipated with the desired reaction the marshalling movements of the riders.

The great desert, the fear of which had first chained Marriner to Bloodwood Plains, now presented no insuperable difficulties. In the meantime the probing calculations of the drovers had established the best watering places; and the route was now as closely defined as a constructed roadway, zigzagging purposefully across the countryside, directly enough from one night's halt to the next, but sometimes appearing to be almost opposite to the imaginary line of the total journey.

At the southern edge of the desert the settlers had sunk bores, and great windmills turned at the insistence of the south-easterly which dominated the plains weather, filling great earth tanks and long lines of metal troughs. Marriner, too, had chosen his season well. From his privileged position between the deserts it was almost impossible for him to make a mistake with his droves; his subsequent ones were as successful as his first; so that his cattle arrived fit and market-able, commanding superior prices; and their condition became connected with his name.

He had left the young stockman Jacob in charge of the work

at Bloodwood Plains. For the journey he took no women, though some were among his best riders. He wanted no strangers hanging about his camps, creating animosities for his men. Jacob could have the women's services; and Jacob was as efficient as himself in the tasks about the station.

Even on the drove Marriner was in the hands of his men. Twice they objected to the night-camps he would have chosen, moving on perhaps half a mile in each instance. The first time Activity shook his head.

"This frog-dreaming, Davy. No good for camp." It had been a short day; Marriner, rather than irritate the superstitions of the tribe moved on. Each tiny area of country was sacred to one totem or another; and the Eiliuwarra never camped on the country of the frog. Frog-dreamings were evil places.

The second time he was disposed to argue, believing some such factor, unimportant to himself or the cattle, was at work.

"This is frog-dreaming again, I suppose," he said with some impatience, almost with a sneer.

"No, Davy. This drummy ground. Frighten the cattle. Tonight they'll rush, if we stop here."

It was true, and a very timely warning. The ground was hollow. The sounds made on the surface seemed to reverberate through some underground caverns. The thudding of the night-horse's hoofs, thus magnified and dispersed in unaccountable directions, could be sufficient to start a stampede in which the sleeping men would be at the mercy of the unheeding hoofs.

The thought of a stampede was always in the minds of the riders: their blankets were so arranged they could jump in a second from their light sleep to a running start; their bridles lay to their hands in the night; the shovel stood always by the fire so that a man, hard pressed, could throw live embers into the faces of the running cattle, split their onrush, if he were in luck, and so create an island of tenuous safety; the night-rider was always keenly aware of each cow's movement, and its significance.

Marriner said nothing more. He left the establishment of the camp to Activity.

As always, it took no more than a few moments to convert the unsettled plain into a home. The horse-tailer had already attended to his charges; he built a fire now and brought up a load of wood. Activity, who was cook, cut a few slices of beef and threw them to the edges of the camp to divert the meat ants—a horde of hungry insects inevitably present which would otherwise have conducted unceasing investigations for food. The other two brought water, slashed down a few whitewood trees to make bough breakwinds, dragged the packs or the canisters into position to serve as stools, and then, usually, brought out a battered pack of playing cards. One solitary rider attended the watered cattle while they foraged over the plain—this man would have no night-duty.

No orders were ever given. None were needed. Sometimes the resting stockmen would hunt; as a rule they preferred the beef that was now a staple—fresh beef if the beast had been slaughtered that day, salt for the succeeding week. Bad beef after the fourth day, often enough; but they ate it just the same.

So they came, eventually, to Quorn. The journey took them nine weeks, and was without unpleasant incident except in a flat stretch of mulga country where some of the cattle snatched mouthfuls of the smooth, moon-shaped leaves of the desert poplar; and seven of them dropped dead almost in a line. The remainder of the herd got through safely, and Brannigan, Masterman's man, when he had introduced himself at the yards, commented on their condition.

"You're Marriner himself, eh?" he said. "I hope you've got a couple of weeks to spare. I've been on the point of coming north to see you myself a few times."

"You wanted to see me?"

"Yes. But now you've come this far, I think you ought to go on down to Adelaide. You don't have to do it if you don't want to—we're only your agents after all—but I think it would be a good idea. What's that country of yours like, up there?"

"Fair enough. Suits me," said Marriner, and Brannigan nodded.

"We've had good reports of it. These cattle are a good enough advertisement. I'll go through them later, but as it is they look about the best mob to come through. You must have had a good season. Plenty water, eh?"

"And plenty grass."

Over a bottle of whisky they laid the foundations for a good friendship, that night. Brannigan arranged agistment for the cattle until the sale—there was one listed for a date ten days later—and in two days Marriner was a passenger on the weekly train that linked Quorn with the city of Adelaide.

Masterman's here maintained an enormous stone building in which the offices occupied one ground-floor corner; the rest consisted of stores for wool, hides, tallow and grain, and a capacious repository for farm and station equipment. There was a little excitement when Marriner announced his name; a little flurry of the male clerks who sat on high stools at sloping desks, or stood at their work the better to move from one place to another.

Marriner waited only a few minutes, and then a hurrying, beardless boy ushered him into the presence of the manager, whose name was Watkins. He was a portly man of considerable presence. He had a drooping, straw-coloured moustache that almost concealed his upper lip and the expression of his mouth; but expressive and twinkling blue eyes made this concealment unimportant.

"Marriner, eh?" he said, almost repeating Brannigan. "Well, Mr. Marriner, we've been beginning to wonder whether we'd ever see you at all. You're not a very good correspondent—you probably don't even read our letters."

Marriner flushed. "I lead a pretty busy life," he lied. "Don't get much time to write."

"In any case, it's better to talk at firsthand. I think we have a fair bit of talking to do. Scotch?"

He reached in a cupboard, pushed a bottle and a glass across the table, followed that with a water carafe, and indicated a chair. When they had each taken the first swallow of a drink he turned to business. At his tongue's end he had more of Marriner's affairs than Marriner knew himself; and while some of his facts were fairly obviously gleaned from a letter which Brannigan must have dispatched on the train Marriner travelled in, to be delivered with that morning's mail, a great many of them related to matters that Marriner had never thought of.

"You've been doing pretty well with us," he said. "You've got a very pleasant kind of a surplus in our books—I wish all our clients were in the same position. I'll have a good talk about that later. First of all, you don't mind if I assume the mantle of an adviser? We are agents, as you know; but our position is, you might say, wedded to that of our clients; and there are some disturbing factors at the moment dominating your current situation. Oh, nothing that can't be rectified, Mr. Marriner, I assure you. But you're a practical man; you don't bother your head about paper details—that's very apparent. Now don't you think for instance that it's about time it would be wise for you to get some title to your holdings?"

"I never thought of it," confessed Marriner, though the question was obviously rhetorical. He had the nervousness of a countryman in unaccustomed surroundings, though he was flattered by the delicately deferential air of this man of business. In answer to a push-button on Watkins's desk an elderly, bespectacled clerk now brought a file of papers.

Watkins explained them at length. They were applications for lease of the properties.

"Take your time. Read them. You'll find they are not complete. We have no idea of the boundaries you will require. As a matter of fact, we have the very vaguest idea of where you are. We can spot Bloodwood Plains itself fairly accurately—luckily enough. Most of the country is very inadequately mapped, but there is some indication of where your river meets the stock route."

His pencil hovered over a spot on a large map which seemed to consist mostly of white spaces. The hills running east and west of Bloodwood Plains were, however, hachured in as a mountain range, and the river was marked fractionally, unmapped beyond an irregular series of loops which Marriner recognised as existing far east of Argadala water hole.

"Now, you've got no neighbours, I take it?" Watkins asked.

"Dallas. He's over to the west of me."

"Another man we'd like to see. He's quite close to you then? And he's the only one?"

"That's right."

"Well, have you an accepted boundary?"

Marriner leaned back and smiled uneasily. "I guess we have. At least the natives have. The tribe with me is Eiliuwarra; Dallas has the Wailbri. They don't mix. The tribal boundary would be ours. There'd be no argument about that."

"Well, can you indicate where that would be?"

They worked over the map for a while. Then at the older man's suggestion Marriner sketched in lightly the area he thought he would like to take up. Watkins went over it with ruler and protractors and made a few calculations.

"You're very modest, you know." He smiled. "It's the sign of an honest man. But we mustn't put modesty before more practical considerations, must we?"

He could be almost arch at times. He went on:

"You've marked out a piece of country about nine hundred square miles, give or take a little. Now that's all very well. But believe me, you'd get nine thousand just about as easy. The Government is trying to encourage some settlement there—have you any trouble with the blacks, by the way?"

"None at all."

"Good. But they're not so lucky further north, from all accounts. Anyway, back to business. You've marked in here the country you know; the country you think will be good. If you'll take my advice you'll extend your boundaries into desert country—for one thing, if settlement takes on, you'll have to think of fencing someday. That's in the future. A good stretch of desert will save you a fence. It will also save you from neighbours perching close; and that's another factor worth money, believe me. So extend those boundaries well past where you know there is water. And take in all the good land you've ever heard of. Get it under your name now while the going's good, that's my advice."

From the boundary that presumably marked the holdings Dallas would claim, Marriner obediently sketched in new lines, and again Watkins measured them.

"Three thousand two hundred—that's a better size. You've no objection to a big place, I take it? Right? Well I'm going to mark in another couple of thousand miles and get your signature. We'll apply for the lot. How many cattle have you got running there now?"

"Eighteen hundred, near as I can make it. Practically all breeders."

"Right. You'll be talking in thousands, eight or ten thousand, six years from now. You've got to think ahead. And you'll need fresh bulls. Fresh blood. Something else we'll discuss later. Now water. This is all well watered?"

"About half of it."

"There's underground. Never forget the underground water. Boring plant. Windmills. Never forget it. Look for it before you need it for expansion. God knows what that country will carry someday. Someday I'm coming up to have a look at it. Must be strange country, on the reports. But the cattle are good—yes, they're good. Branningan tells me this lot's the best yet."

The interviews with Watkins lasted for four days. He was six hours in the office that first day; the second day only an hour, but he and Watkins sweated over a table, drinking whisky and marking papers, for seven hours that night. Marriner was amazed. He had not thought his business so important. He was also amazed by his credit balance and the fact that he had money in his pocket to spend on whatever his fancy asked.

He signed orders for blood stock and for galvanized roofing, as well as for the items he had planned to buy—saddle and bridle mountings, hobble-chains, buckets, pots, axes and implements. That some of these were blank orders temporarily disconcerted him; but he had developed a good deal of faith in Masterman's Mr. Watkins.

"Don't worry, old fellow," that worthy said. "We don't want to break you. We can see the makings of a substantial citizen in you, a substantial citizen, yes; and that suits our book, you know. It will suit us very well, very well indeed."

"Don't stint the station. Don't go without," he said on another occasion. "Whenever there's something you think you need just let us know. We'll do what we can even if, temporarily of course, there isn't any money. Just build up those herds and don't worry. And the water. Develop the water. Don't forget the underground."

At the end of the sessions Marriner was the owner of some five thousand four hundred square miles of country; and even though his ownership still had to have the final stamp of Government ratification, there seemed no hurdle there. He had also registered the change of ownership of the brand EGE; and had promised to send, for Watkins's safekeeping, the copy of *Utopia* in which Edrington had written the testament.

"It's more of a memento, you might say—very romantic story that. It must have been very distressing for you at the time. Truly one half never knows how the other half lives," Watkins added somewhat inconsequentially. "But yes, it will be just as well to have the evidence, just as well. It'll do no harm to keep it with the rest of your papers."

Towards the end of these sessions Watkins introduced him to a banker who not only accepted his account, but undertook to advise him on investment possibilities. The city men took a good deal of pleasure in his company; he was receptive and had a good brain, so that he easily grasped the drift of their remarks; and he had no preconceived ideas of his own, so that he disputed none. When they questioned him on his life they found his surroundings exotic enough so that he became something of a figure of romance. By this time, too, he had a little fund of anecdotes, these mostly connected with the drovers, the adventurers, the prospectors and the "hatters"— the "Mad Hatters," men so identified with loneliness as to seem queer to their fellows.

His background had been urban, so that he was never uncouth in the stiff and formal company of their womenfolk, to which they once or twice subjected him; and he looked for so little that they were never ill at ease at leaving him out of their plans. Stevenson, the banker, who seldom came in contact with such men, was particularly pleased with his acquaintance.

"They're arming for war in Europe," he said. "Maybe it'll be this year." It was March of 1914.

"D'you think it will touch us?" Marriner asked, and Stevenson smiled tolerantly.

"Hardly likely, except in a special way. It will stimulate

the export beef market. Oh, and tallows, hides, what have you. Everything we supply. Minerals too. Are there minerals in that country of yours?"

"Some say there's gold. A few fellows are looking for it."

"Gold is where you find it," Stevenson quoted sententiously. "But gold is not the only pebble on the beach." He laughed. "That's a good one. There's not enough such pebbles."

"What others?"

"Nickel, for example. It may bring high prices—double, perhaps, the current market. There's already been some movement. And metal for the cannons. Wolfram. Almost anything. If there is metal you want to keep a lookout for it."

Marriner remembered the black stone.

"Wolfram, eh? There's wolfram. Is it valuable?"

"It's going to be worth having, mark my words. You know where you can lay your hands on it?"

"There's a little outcrop."

"Send it down. Get title to it."

"Will it pay the cartage?—there's the thing. These Afghans don't work for nothing. It's a long way to the railhead."

"You've got your head screwed on the right way, Davy. I can see that. But if the market jumps it almost certainly will pay. Play it safe anyway. Get title to it. Register a claim before you go back."

Watkins echoed the advice enthusiastically when Marriner broached the subject.

"That's the ticket. Get it down on paper. Then no matter what happens you're covered. The mining warden's a friend of mine as it happens. We'll go along and see him. Advice costs nothing. Maybe a second string to your bow—but don't neglect the cattle, Davy. Never neglect the cattle.

Look after the cattle and the water. Develop the underground water, that's where the wealth is."

Marriner registered the claim, or made the preliminary
steps, as just another in the series of non-significant actions
he had been taking all along. He still hardly regarded himself as a cattleman; that he was a landowner, a potential
cattle king was beyond his comprehension. He was amused
by, rather than involved in, all this activity; he chuckled
frequently as he rode the train on the first step of his journey
back.

Within a couple of months of his return the Afghans with
their camel trains arrived on the first of a long series of
regular transport lifts. They brought tools, building supplies, and heavy galvanized roofing sheets, cut into four-foot
lengths. And Marriner lost to them the services of Activity.

More outward-looking than the rest of his tribe, more intrigued by any novelty, he was fascinated by the great proud
camels, and spent much time in their company, working so
willingly and so intelligently that the camel-train leader
offered him wages. Activity accepted at once. He had no
diffidence in telling Marriner. After all, the obligation was,
in fact, on the other side; although it was true that Marriner
was annoyed.

Nevertheless, Activity was no longer essential to him.
The cattle station now practically ran itself. There was ever
more and more work to be done upon it; more cattle to be
branded, more distant pastures to ride, more yards to be
mended; but there were ever more and more workers
capable of accomplishing these tasks.

And now Marriner, following the advice of Watkins, began
to pay small wages to his men: ten shillings a month to them
all except Jacob, who, as head stockman, received double.
The money never left Marriner's hands for long. The men
paid it back for tobacco and flour, sometimes for a blanket
or a pair of trousers; so that in no time at all they were all in

his debt; and they were costing him no more than when he had made gifts of these things to them. But the trading added to the work and the responsibility at his headquarters; and his first building of sawn timber was a new store.

The timber was the local carbeen, the great white ghost gum of the area; a tree so magnificently lovely that Marriner felt a pang each time one crashed to the ground. The timber was a dark brown in colour, so hard that it had to be fastened, nailed, planed or sawn before it had had time to season; and so heavy that it doubled the work. After it was put into place it dried and twisted into strange shapes. Its only recommendation was that it was strong, and that no other timber was available. The river gums were useless, hollow and rotten. The bean trees were so soft and pithy that the cattle ate even the trunks—but for making benches beans were good. Sawn exceptionally thick they made furniture that gave an impression of solidity, but was lighter to lift than if it were made of balsa wood.

Marriner staked out his wolfram claim, completing all the requirements of the law. Towards the end of the year a party of prospectors came up from the south. There were three of them, Harris, Hanrahan and Edwards; and they brought news that the world was at war. Armed with Stevenson's forecast, Marriner took the news with an assumption of foreknowledge, a grasp of contributing details that obviously impressed the newcomers; and he put a proposition to them.

"Work the wolfram?" Harris said. He was almost elderly. "Wait till you get a railway up here. What's transport going to cost?"

"Not as much as you think," Marriner told him. "Camels going down with empty packs pretty near every month now; oftener sometimes. And besides, the war will push the price up. The stuff's there. You will only have to throw it in a bag."

"Where do you come in? What's your cut?"

"Twenty per cent of the net."

Harris considered this for a while, then turned to his fellows. Marriner walked off and left them. "Think it over," he said.

They didn't take long.

"We'll have a look at it. See how it goes," said Harris. The return from the first consignment made them enthusiastic. They stayed on the ground, built themselves huts, ordered stores.

Mission Mo, riding in from one of his prospecting forays, was openly contemptuous of them. Marriner told him of their presence half-heartedly; wondering whether, perhaps, he had let Mo down in not assigning him the wolfram field, but the little prospector rapidly reassured him.

"Working for wages. That's what it is. Making yourself into a glorified labourer. They'll have good wages for a year and then go broke staying on the spot trying to keep it up. It's temporary. The price depends on the war. They'll be working like horses. No, gold's the only thing. It may take time. Once you're on to it, that's the finish. You're made. Champagne and silk sheets the rest of your life. And there's gold in this country too, don't forget. And I'll be the one to find it."

He had come, humbly enough to ask for a new grub-stake. Marriner let him help himself, as he always did.

The store now almost constantly claimed his attention, so that he could no longer ride out to the ends of his domain as he loved to do. He had an additional purpose for wanting to go out; for the ends of his domain now lay at a greater distance, in some directions, than he had ever ridden; he had no knowledge of some of the holding accredited to him; and for his own benefit he wanted to establish this country in his mind, and record its details on a map which Watkins had asked for.

It seemed to Marriner that he was under a pressure of work; and that the store was the hindrance. There was seldom more than a day or two when it was not in use. The miners drew on it for supplies for their natives as well as for themselves; of recent months Marriner had had a fair supply of overproof rum packed in and now frequently in the evenings the miners rode over for a convivial hour. About once in two months Dallas rode over, accompanied by his lubra. While he drank in the store she would sit quietly on the sand outside, and once in a while he would walk out to her with a rum-filled enamel cup. She would drink, sipping the strong liquor so delicately that she would take an hour to empty the mug—swaying backwards and forwards, and, as the liquor overcame her, singing wild snatches of native songs.

She was not Mary. Mary had long before disappeared; and when the newcomer had taken her place, Marriner asked about the substitution.

"What happened to Mary? Where did she go?"

"Didn't she come back?" Dallas countered. Marriner shook his head.

"She didn't ever come here."

"Well, God knows where she is then. She could be dead. That Wailbri crowd of mine have never liked her there."

"She left you?"

"I tossed her out. She was getting hard to take. You give them too much rope and they'll run you. If she didn't come back that's her fault. She knew the way."

Marriner eyed him in some disbelief. Those had not been the questions he had wanted to ask. "Was she pregnant?" he would have said. "Did you shoot her? Did you strip her and shoot her in the back?" He remembered, very vividly, the other lubra, outstretched on the sand. The latest girl was wearing clothes like Mary's, blue shirt and narrow blue denims.

If the natives knew anything they did not reveal it, either by word or sign. They disliked Dallas and avoided him; but they always had.

Bloodwood Plains, however, was seeing a great deal more of Dallas now that he had the miners as well as the occasional drovers to drink with. The latter now limited their movements to one season of the year; but in that season appeared in greater numbers than ever before. March, April, May and June saw most of them; there was another little current of moving cattle in October, November and early December. The adventurers and the prospectors were liable to appear at any time.

Creswell Cummings appeared, a gull among the crows, in a wild, unruly party of the adventurers. He was a tall, fresh-faced youth, tidy, neat, clean, and obviously uncomfortable in his company. Whatever had possessed him to throw in his lot with that of the men with him, he now regretted his decision. The others taunted him considerably; and though he stayed amiable he was apparently tired of their repetitive sallies.

In the inevitable drinking session he sat with a glass in his hand, sampling it briefly. Marriner himself, as of habit, was only a token drinker; the man and the youth stayed sober and talked. In a retreat from loneliness Cummings confided that he was a refugee, not from the war, but from the war-makers, from the fanatic women with their white-feather presents, from the drums and the brasses and the marching feet, from an excessively patriotic father who had seen the last two months of the Boer campaign in South Africa; and from the gap in his family left by two brothers already campaigning in the Middle East. He had no taste for adventure; he had been forced into this one through a dislike, and perhaps a fear, of the larger adventure in the Northern Hemisphere.

The upshot of their conversation was that, although he did

not actually apply for it, Marriner offered him a job. He
could look after the store, Marriner said; the store and the
work round the homestead. It was not arduous; but his
presence would free Marriner. It need only be on a temporary basis; if he did not like the work he could ride on when
he liked, or when the opportunity presented itself

9

Cummings dropped into a ready-made niche at Bloodwood Plains. He was a handyman, forever pottering about, constructing shelves, shifting stock in the store, making odds and ends. One of his first achievements was a baker's oven, the building of which he undertook, as at first he undertook everything, with apologies for what he imagined might be construed as interference. Like most of his other ideas it was successful.

In the store, he achieved a kind of drinking-cubby, a verandah with a separate entrance to the rum store—this, a half-door with a tabletop over which drinks could be served. His motive here was not so much to cater to the comfort of the drinkers, though this was certainly an effect, and one which increased his popularity, but to keep inviolate and undisturbed the rest of the stock. He conducted a stock-taking, made lists of the articles in demand and the articles soon to need replacement and took notes of the complaints of the buyers.

In the meantime, Marriner was off again on the kind of living in which he really delighted: sleeping with the horses at the stock camp, overseeing the branding, moving from one distant water hole to another. He also enjoyed a completely new interest—the company of his eldest boy Henry. It seemed only a few years since Henry was a baby crawling about the first old hut; now he was a slim lad of ten, already headed for man's estate, a capable horseman and an avid student of the wild. Now, to a degree, Henry took Activity's place; not altogether, for he was the student where Activity

had been mentor; but he supplied the company which Marriner had missed since Activity's departure.

Once or twice, sitting on the sand in the evenings, Marriner
tried to teach the lad to read and write, drawing the letters
with a twig; and Henry would listen and imitate with a
serious face.

And then at the other fire there would be a clapping together of the song-sticks, a chanting of wild words, and one
after another of the men would join in the song, and the song
would gather tempo, and they would fling their clothes to
the night and dance in the ancient rhythms; playing out the
long-established dramas, running into the night from the
mock vengeance, or stamping out the enactment of the
kangaroo-dreamings. Young Henry would look pleadingly
at them, his attention would wander, and finally Marriner
would give him the sign that he awaited and he would join
the men, a little mimic, loud in his clearly remembered
responses; and by the next night his European lessons were
to learn all over again.

Marriner was not a very good teacher, and his son no
pupil. Henry could see no use in the ink-tracks cluttered so
meanly in the pages of a book, though he proved sharp
enough with figures.

But with the other lessons of his life his application was
excellent; he was expert in the hunting lessons he had from
the tribe, and the newer lessons that developed the herdsman.
There is a moment in the mustering of cattle which calls for a
precision of judgment and understanding. The cattle are at
ease, grazing on the wide plain where they have remained
undisturbed for months, perhaps for years. The rider appears,
the cattle take fright, galloping with speed and determination
to some known place of safety.

The rider joins in the pursuit. After a while his course
parallels the course of the cattle, and there is a bovine
mental process which, if the rider plays his part well, will

induce the beasts before long to believe that they and the
mounted man are all fleeing a common danger. At this
point—neither before nor after—the man may ride to the
lead; and the cattle will follow him. When he turns they
will swing in behind him so that he brings them sweetly to
his own destination; and by the time they realize that they
are, in fact, under duress, the run is taken out of them.
Exertion is saved for both man and horse.

There is, of course, always an old cow who, for the protection of her calf, will turn away from her fellows to strike
out for herself. The rider must catch this movement in time
and change his plans accordingly. His whole judgment is
based upon the external signs—a fractional mitigation of the
desperation of speed, a turning of the head that indicates
awareness.

Intelligence marks the good stockman. And some other
intangibles. A rider who is attuned to the beasts he works
can save much effort; and Henry could handle these situations
like a veteran. He had no need to be told. The sound of his
whip never intruded upon a delicate manœuvring to cause
confusion; it was ready enough when its use was justified.
And he was friendly with his horses, and with the young,
half-broken horses of the plant. He would commune with
them by the hour, after the manner and the delight of all
young animals. Marriner had a great deal of pleasure in his
company.

When he came back from the first trip after two months'
riding, he found that Cummings had already reordered stores
from Quorn. He found that affairs at the homestead, indeed,
had progressed; they were in better order than he had ever
kept them. He had no hesitation in leaving the place again
and again. Only in the hot months from December to March
did he stay permanently at the house.

A new problem, of minor proportions, arose. At the end
of a year of Cummings's management, the supply of cash

and notes at Bloodwood Plains had reached surprising proportions. There was also a number of cheques, drawn by Dallas and the miners. For all this money there was no outward channel. The goods for which the money changed hands were charged against Marriner's cattle account. He sent in the cheques yearly with his drovers, but he did not care to trust them with his money. Consequently, there was this pressing reason for him to return to the South. He set out with a thousand cattle, with seven stockmen and a plant of ninety horses, sixty of which he planned to sell. It was one of the biggest movements in that season. He also carried nearly seven hundred pounds in money.

He arrived in Quorn to find himself something more of a legend. Brannigan, who was still at this branch of Masterman's, found himself busy coping with a little press of people anxious to attain and claim friendship with Marriner; and these in later years bragged of their brief acquaintance.

"A shrewd bastard that," they said. "To talk with him you'd think he had nothing. All the time he had a finger in every pie in the Territory."

At the time it was not true. However, the wolfram fields had developed to a surprising extent; the armaments industry of the world did not look at prices. Marriner's trading concern, though small, was the only one in five hundred miles of stock route; his cattle holdings had to be reckoned large. The legend was growing, however, in advance of the man. It was known that he lived as simply as a black-fellow; yet on acquaintance he was far from parsimonious; he seemed to look for chances to put his hand into his pocket.

The state of his balances, indeed, amazed Marriner; and though it had not been firmly in his intention, when the sale had been concluded—and cattle were bringing, at that stage of the war, unheard-of prices—he went on down to the city of Adelaide.

Stevenson, the banker, hailed him with delight, and some

relief. The arrangements Marriner had made with him for investment included the purchase of a variety of shares; some, though not all, were flourishing; and Stevenson, who felt that he had far exceeded his functions as they were understood in that day, was anxious to test Marriner's reactions. So far as he was concerned, they were entirely satisfactory. Marriner had no use for more money than he could hold in his pocket; he did not admit as much, but his equanimity in reviewing financial adventures that Stevenson was inclined to view as close to hair-raising gave him the appearance of a cool and collected investor.

He disposed of large sums between his more than substantial credit at Masterman's and a good current account at the bank. His affairs kept him busy for nearly three weeks; and in this time he made a number of social contacts. Watkins and Stevenson both saw to that.

It was Watkins, indeed, who was responsible for his meeting Peggy Delaney, though not of intent. Watkins had at last persuaded him to invest in a boring plant—he had a fixation about the development of underground water—and took him out to a distant suburb where, on a cluttered piece of ground, a corrugated-iron building proclaimed itself the headquarters of the Whitmore Engineering Company. A small office was tucked into a corner of the building, its windows guarded from accident by a fabrication of iron bars and wire netting which had effectively prevented cleaning. Through open doors, Marriner could see a handful of men working at lathes and drilling machines in the building.

The door marked "Office" was shut, but Watkins opened it and Marriner followed him into a narrow passage with two doorways opening on equal-sized cubbyholes. From the first of these a girl emerged, a small, dark-haired girl with a bright enquiring face. She was rather severely dressed—white shirt-front, ample skirt—in the office-girl's uniform of the day; but her small heart-shaped face carried a roguish

grin, the curls that clustered about her face seemed to adver-
tise a spirit free and untamed; and her voice, when she
spoke, was musical and gay. She came forward, holding out
both hands.

"Mr. Watkins!" she exclaimed, as though their arrival
had brightened her day. "Whitmore's favourite client."

"Delighted to hear you say it, my dear. I'd like you to
meet a favourite client of Masterman's—Mr. Davis Marriner.
Mr. Marriner, Miss Peggy Delaney. Mr. Marriner is
from . . ."

"From Bloodwood Plains," she supplied. "Do come in,
both of you. I've heard of you, of course, Mr. Marriner."

She led them into an office much more comfortable than the
exterior of the building would have led Marriner to expect.
It was cheaply furnished, but efficiently; and there were
touches—in the curtains, the two comfortable chairs, the
kettle already singing on a small spirit stove in a corner—
which obviously had been introduced by the girl. She was
the first career woman Marriner had seen. Few offices in
that day and age boasted a woman secretary. Miss Delaney
was something more.

"Mr. Whitmore has left us to fend for ourselves again,"
she said. "A business trip. To the East. He will be sorry
not to have met you—unless you'll still be here in about
four weeks' time, Mr. Marriner? In the meantime—I'm
at your service."

She showed a grip of business that Marriner found amazing. She explained the capabilities of the boring plants they
could supply, and their disabilities; and leaped to the point
at which Marriner would have arrived more slowly—the
necessity for him to keep his equipment as mobile as possible.
She questioned him on the amount of plant repair available
at Bloodwood; and obviously considered it inadequate.

"I'm going to recommend that we supply an engineer with
the plant for three months until you can get your men

trained," she said. "It would really be best. If that fits in with your ideas I'll go ahead with the arrangements. Come back the day after tomorrow, meet the man I have in mind, and talk with him about the tool situation. But what I'm recommending might involve more money than you are prepared to lay out."

"Mr. Marriner realizes that water's his best investment— don't you, Davy?" Watkins asked. "And I'm sure Whitmore's will give him a good deal—even if I have to stand over you, young lady."

They sipped tea and nibbled biscuits in the little office before they left.

"What an amazing young woman!" Marriner commented, and Watkins nodded, rather grimly.

"You don't know the half of it," he said. "Whitmore's trips 'to the East' have been pretty frequent of late." He lifted his hand to his mouth, went through the motions of tossing down a nobbler of liquor. "The brother's serving in the Middle East. That young woman is keeping the business together. Not only that, she's doubled it. And her workers are more loyal than any in the business. Amazing? She's phenomenal."

Marriner was alone when he went back to discuss his plant investment, and the vivacious Miss Delaney greeted him like an old friend. She took him through the dusty shop to meet a young, stooped, bespectacled engineer named Carson; and left them to talk.

"I'll come and give you a start if that's what you want, Mr. Marriner," Carson said. "As I see it, there's two things you can do. You can have your own plant and your own team; and you should be able, in that country, to keep them busy. Five thousand square miles? You'd keep them busy forever. But without an engineer on the job there's liable to be long idle spells. Breakdowns. Waiting for plant. And sometimes you'll have to have advice; unless your man is mechanically

minded to an unusual degree. Or yourself—what about
you?"

Marriner shook his head.

"Well, then, the other thing is to start a boring plant as a
separate business; and it might pay you to think of that.
Working under contract for yourself and for your neighbours
with a qualified man in charge of the plant. What about
neighbours?"

"None—one," Marriner qualified. "I don't know whether
he'd be interested."

"Perhaps it would be best to see how things go. I'll come
up and start you all right—Whitmore's will bill you for it.
After three months you can make a decision. It's just
possible I might be available more permanently. I want to
see how I like the Outback. Now, the plant . . ."

Marriner's commitments, before he left, were astronomi-
cally larger than he had envisaged. They amounted to the
purchase of two stationary engines and a small engineering
shop as well as the boring plant and the services of Carson.
Strangely, he had no very great faith that the acquisitions
would advance him. His attitude was simply that money was
available, or would be within a season. His decisions had
been made for him; he had an uncanny conviction that he
was a spectator of his own development. It was an important
deal, however. Peggy Delaney made no attempt to conceal
her delight. She pirouetted through the office with the signed
papers to file them in a drawer.

"I'd like to see Daddy's face," she said. "Back home he'd
never trust me to sell a dozen eggs."

"Back home?"

"In Wollongong, New South Wales. Oh, I'm a bird of
passage. Footloose, that's me."

"No ties?"

"Only Whitmore's. And that's only because I'm lucky
in my choice of financial friends. They like me for my sales

ability. And my typing." She caught one of the knobs of the old-fashioned press that stood by the wall and sent the lever whirling.

"We should celebrate this together," Marriner said, surprising himself with his own daring. "Would you have dinner with me?"

She looked in his eyes for a few seconds before she replied. "Yes, I think I'd like that."

They dined. They danced. He delivered her to the grim-looking boarding-house in a suburban street. At the week-end he hired a rig, and they drove into the flowered hills above the city. They attended the cinema. They dined again. On this fourth occasion he talked about his life. It was the first time he had ever seriously discussed it with anybody. He told her about Edrington and about Activity. He even told her about Trubbidy and Henry; though he made no mention of the other children, and felt the old guilt again about the one in Jacob's family.

"Is it lonely? Do you find it lonely?" she asked him, and he considered his answer for a while. He answered honestly.

"Not really," he said. "That is . . . I never have. But after this . . . after meeting you . . . You've changed things for me, Peggy."

She stretched out a hand and clasped the back of his where it rested on his knee under the tablecloth.

"Don't," she said.

"Don't what?"

"Don't say what you were going to say."

He looked steadily at her; very conscious of the pressure of her fingers, his hand motionless beneath it.

"I was going to ask you to marry me."

"I know. And now you have. And now I have to say 'no.' "

"I could give you riches—a new house. It needn't be a rough life. . . ."

"It's not that. I'd almost sooner have the hardships and the horse camp."

"Is it Trubbidy?"

"No. No, it isn't her. Would you think me immoral if I told you I almost liked you for Trubbidy? And certainly for telling me about her. I must be very forward, I think. Young ladies aren't supposed to know these things."

"If you knew me better, if you got to know me better first . . ."

She turned her dancing eyes on him, and they were kind.

"I don't love you, Davis. I'm still old-fashioned enough to believe in love. At first sight, perhaps. You've been good to me."

He protested, but she remained quite calm. Nevertheless, he did not give up. Next time they met it was at her boarding-house; in a sitting-room apparently made available to her by her landlady. She had several of her friends, and it was an evening of music, of staid selections played on a cottage piano, and vocal offerings by a tremulous tenor, a lusty baritone and a sweet soprano. Marriner found it very boring.

Towards the early end of the evening his hostess went to the piano herself to play and sing some of the catchy, lilting lyrics the war had made popular. Her voice was husky as a native's, quite untrained; her fingers were only a little more disciplined, but the music sprang to life.

The girl she had replaced at the piano took the vacant chair next to Marriner.

"Trust our Peggy to be first with the latest," she said. "I can't think where she could have got the music. I haunt the music-shops and I've never even seen a copy."

"She's marvellous." Marriner beamed. "I think she'd get anything she set her mind upon. Don't you?"

The girl looked at him. She had an oval face, beautiful in structure; perhaps a trifle full in the cheeks. Her nose was long, her mouth firm, nicely shaped. Her hair was pretty, though severely dressed. Her eyes were green, set in long ovals; and above the right eye the brow was now lifting slightly.

"Yes," she said. "I think she could, Mr. Marriner." Then with a little rush of enthusiasm she pursued the subject. "I've always thought she was a most remarkable girl. She works, you know. She's in business; and she practically conducts the business she's in herself."

Marriner, thus presented with the subject closest his heart, looked more closely at the speaker. She was beautifully gowned. Her height was above average; the beauty of her face was almost classical, and enhanced by a studied dignity and poise.

She was, as it appeared when the guests were departing, the landlady's daughter. Marriner, the last to leave, spent an additional half-hour with the two girls. He invited them both to the theatre on the following night.

He put off setting a date for his return to Bloodwood Plains. Although he knew in his heart that Peggy's refusal was final and definite, some stubbornness in him was blind to this truth; he pursued her avidly. When he could arrange a meeting with her he was happy; after their partings he was sad. Three or four times he shared her company with that of the statuesque Monica; several times she stepped into the breach left by an unavailable Peggy. He didn't ever resent this. He liked her company; and through the day when Peggy was at her office, it was always possible to pass the time with Monica. She was a good horsewoman, and he could always be sure of her company by hiring good horses, the best of the local livery stable's string.

And anyway it was practically impossible for him to see Peggy without at least encountering Monica, except when he called for Peggy at the engineering yard; and he soon found that that was not the best way to her good graces. Unless he had business to conclude, his welcome there was perfunctory.

But Monica was a ready listener.

"It's much too generous of you," she said when she found herself in his company for the third night in succession. "How on earth will you face life at Bloodwood Plains again? Won't you find it lonely?"

He nodded. "Yes, I'm afraid I will," he said. "I've had my eyes opened. I'm afraid I'll never be the same again."

He paused to examine his own words and was convinced they were the truth. "I've never guessed what a difference company can make—the company of charming women, like Peggy, and like yourself."

"Do you have to go without it?" she asked, and leaned forward significantly.

"No women in that country. It's not a country for women. You couldn't imagine it. It's hard country," he said.

"A woman in love, a brave woman, would belong with her man."

He laughed shortly. "You can say that, because you haven't seen it."

"I'm told it's beautiful."

"Oh, as to that, it's true. But if you were to go there with only the company of rough men, of natives, with none of the refinements of life that you're used to, then you might change your mind."

She shook her head.

"One makes one's own company. One can introduce the refinements of life. Far from being a miserable existence it could be made a task after any woman's heart. If she were with her man."

"Look at it in another way," he said. "I'm not fit to take a good woman to wife; not the kind of woman I could love. Nor is anyone in that country. It's too late for us. We've been too long in our rough society." That was a pause. He

146

would not have maintained that argument with Peggy. But he was thinking of Trubbidy.

Monica looked astonished. "You!" she said. "You've taken the attention of every girl in Adelaide. Not many would pass by the chance."

"You don't know all the story."

"There are so many stories." She looked mischievous. "A story about a dark mistress—is that the one that bothers you?"

He looked questioningly at her, and said nothing.

"Some women tell their secrets," she said. "Don't blame Peggy—we are the closest friends. But what shocks her is nothing to me. How could you be blamed, I asked her. How can she expect a strong and red-blooded man to live like a monk, without a monk's consolations? It's a new world. Those things don't matter any more."

He was red-faced, incoherent.

"Could you forgive those things?" he asked, forgetting that Peggy had never condemned them; and, in his embarrassment, far too ready to believe that she had discussed them. Such conversations on such subjects conducted between a man and a woman had been impossible in his youth; now that he was in his middle thirties they invested Monica with a kind of sophistication that enhanced her stature. He plunged headlong into the discussion.

"Would you really marry a man like me, with my background?" he asked her later in the evening; and again she raised that right eyebrow. It was a characteristic that delighted him.

"Do you really expect me to answer?" she asked, not at all coquettishly.

Three or four days later he asked her more directly and to his surprise she released herself to his too-ready arms. In the meantime he had cooled towards Peggy; the thought of the girlish discussions of his Trubbidy offended him; he tried to imagine how far they must have gone; and in any case resented that she had been mentioned at all. Before he left again for the North, he and Monica were married. Their immediate honeymoon was brief.

More disastrously, it was an anticlimax after the excitements of preparation for marriage; for this had been extensive. He found it unnecessary to disturb the investments he had already made; both Masterman's and the bank were willing to carry him to an extent that he would once have thought frightening; and so he and Monica laid out large sums not only on the furnishings of a house, but also on such items as glass for windows, a bath, porcelain wash-basins and sinks, and a laundry copper. It all added up to several caravan loads for the camels on the wolfram transport.

The idea was that the real honeymoon should consist of the five or six weeks on horseback; and Monica's expressed imaginings sometimes waxed poetical about their riding the wide plains together and sleeping under the canopy of heaven; and for the first two or three days on horseback she valiantly did keep up an illusion of being oblivious to everything that made no contribution to this romantic conception.

But the realities of travel could not be overlooked. The meals could not consist in their entirety of the delicacies which Marriner had thoughtfully provided; the mattress of earth was unyielding to unaccustomed limbs. George and the other stockmen, who had waited unquestioningly at Quorn for Marriner's return, were shy and silent with their white mistress; they accepted her orders only after Marriner had confirmed them. The unrelieved presence of her husband became too quickly tedious. Moreover, although she was a good horsewoman, an over-considerate Marriner saw to it that she was provided only with the quieter beasts; in the pursuit of their normal avocation the better horses were flighty and not to be trusted with an unpractised rider. A good camp horse, at the sway of a rein, might misunderstand its rider's intention and wheel in a flash; when they were stepping along in the scrub a sound mustering hack was responsive to its own instincts as well as its rider's commands —when these considerations were taken into account it usually happened that Monica was provided with a mount unworthy of her capabilities.

At her request, Marriner made the most elaborate arrangements for her privacy while sleeping and bathing. He delighted in this for a time; asking nothing better than to be her guardian in these isolations; but sometimes it seemed that she carried these precautions to an absurdity. He had for comparison the previous carefree company of the tribal women; and he was aware, he could not help but be aware, that his stockmen found amusement in these alien practices.

By the time they reached Bloodwood Plains he was truly thankful to be home again; and he was not prepared for the flood of tears she released after looking over her new residence. It was by no means elaborate; it had none of the niceties that a woman could supply; but Creswell Cummings, forewarned by letter, had seen to it that it was clean and tidy; considerably better furnished than it had been on Marriner's departure. It was also cleared of any traces of Trubbidy's occupation; and the girl herself had been shifted, with her family, to the aboriginal encampment, though that was only a couple of hundred yards away.

Monica was not hard to comfort. He had never deceived her about the amenities of the place; and she had steeled herself, long before, to the thought of pioneer hardships; her tears were little more than an acknowledgement of the enormity of what she considered her task; and he soon dried them. Sitting beside him, on the edge of the blanket-covered, rough-hewn bed, she relaxed in his arms, and leaned there quietly for a moment while he bent his head over her, his nostrils savouring the fragrance of her hair. Suddenly she stiffened.

"What's that?" she asked, her voice muffled. He listened. The old familiar screech and grunt, grunt and splash came from the river bank.

"It's only the whip-pole," he said soothingly. He smiled at her as she lifted her head.

"It sounds like home," he added, pleased with the thought.

"It sounds like a devil in hell," she told him viciously. He was amazed at the strident tones in her voice.

10

If the outcry was a portent of things to come, its message was not repeated for the next few weeks; a period in which Marriner was busier than he had ever been in all his life. The boring plant and the engineering gear arrived within a week of his return, and the homestead was loud with the sounds of construction. Carson, slow in his own movements, proved to have a talent for organization; his lean, stooped figure, moving dreamily from one place to another, seemed to arrive by calculation at the exact moment his presence had become essential. He would make an adjustment with an output of energy so economical as to seem inadequate; and leave instructions with his helpers for their next move.

Creswell Cummings, fresh-faced and bustling, seemed by comparison to be performing wonders. He was in charge of construction; yet at every stage it was Carson who waited for Cummings's share to be finished. To give him credit, Cummings was also much occupied with the store; the arrival of new goods had relieved a dearth of some standing, and the customers, appearing in late afternoon, chained Cummings—or sometimes Marriner—to the building while their buying developed into long drinking sessions that lasted through the night. There were four parties of miners permanently camped on the hills now; Harris and Edwards had split, and each was working a half of Marriner's claims, paying royalties; Hanrahan had staked a claim of his own elsewhere and acquired three working partners; and a newcomer, Johnny Loyal, was also in the field.

Almost constantly the camel teams were camped at Bloodwood, coming or going to the fields. Wagons were appearing on the road now—the engines and heavy gear had been brought by wagons—and there was some trans-shipment to the mines; so that at least one camel-team was regularly employed in the vicinity.

Marriner himself took a part in all this activity. Additionally he tried, as much as he could, to check the cattle work; but he had all the reluctance of a new husband to leave the homestead; and Monica was not backward in her suggestions for improving the homestead site.

Those which concerned material things he hastened to implement wherever he could. Bloodwood Plains had become a sprawling huddle of unattractive huts, with gear stowed at haphazard; and it was not difficult to see the advantages that would lie in reorganization. But when she set out to alter those features of his life which concerned his relationship with others he was made ill at ease.

She was shocked, for example, that the natives called him "Davy"; men, women and children used this name as naturally as they used their own. She at once insisted that they refer to "Mr. Marriner," and used this form herself when she spoke to a third party, even to Carson and Cummings. She gave such short shrift to any natives who appeared in the vicinity of the house that stockmen, who had been in the habit of calling on Marriner for their orders, now sat patiently on the top rails of the stockyard until he should appear.

But she, too, was occupied in these first weeks with the details of furnishing. Marriner had found her three young sturdy girls to work in the house. She drove them from morning until night. To her own credit she drove herself as thoroughly, though her occupations were, naturally enough, with the lighter tasks. She was a good housekeeper and seamstress; and no matter how she was employed she had a faculty of keeping a close eye on her servants.

She was impatient of their beliefs. By tribal custom each of them had relatives at whom they were not allowed to look, much less speak to; and consequently when they made their way from their overnight shelters to the house they would walk in a wide half-circle to avoid some little gathering by the stockyards; sometimes going as much as a mile out of their way. Marriner had always accepted and ignored such procedures; they seemed to drive his wife to distraction. She would send a girl to the yard with a message for him— another would carry the message; or sometimes, if it were a simple one, a woman near the yard, having watched the finger gestures relayed from the house, would suddenly volunteer it. The careless transfer of responsibility infuriated Monica; and she did her best to stamp it out, with no success.

In other things, she had her way. It was part of her routine that the women, when they arrived in the morning, should tub from head to foot in the laundry and change into clean clothes which they were on no account to wear, other than in the house. This bathing normally occurred before she was up and about; for she liked her morning bed. When she discovered that the chattering girls took no account of the casual presence of Marriner or any other man while they changed, she lost her temper. She ran out and hit them with a riding-whip. The girls made no attempt to run away; they covered their faces and bent their backs to take the blows; and when her anger was spent they were badly marked. They did not offend in this way again, but the lesson was a superficial one.

When Marriner questioned his wife about the split cheek of one of the girls she burst into tears.

"Those women. Those dreadful women," she said. "And that Carson. He should have known better. He shouldn't have been near the laundry in the morning."

"Was he in there with them?"

"They were standing outside, the black sluts," she said. "Right out in the open. They have no shame."

It was a strange thing, Marriner thought, to say of these

153

people of the desert, whom he thought of naturally as unhampered by either clothes, or inhibitions about their bodies. But looking round the encampment he could see now that the first impression the Eiliuwarra left was not that which they had left with him some fifteen years before.

They had acquired both clothes and dependence. The erect posture of the hunter, the calm encompassment of the daily round, the alert quietude and independence of a people who at a moment's notice were prepared to walk into the distance and there support themselves and their families indefinitely— these had all disappeared.

Instead there was an encampment of people waiting for gifts, waiting for the beef to be killed, waiting for instructions, their nakedness covered with materials they were not capable of making, their bellies filled with meat they had not hunted, their limited capabilities on offer to whatever miner, cattleman or camelier cared to give them support. The ground about their shelters was long worn bare; the old, impermanent cover of fresh leaves and branches had been replaced by scraps of building materials—canvas and board and some rusty iron—and the scents of eucalyptus had given way to the mustiness of incipient decay.

Some of the women at the encampment were fat; two middle-aged women and one man grossly so. Marriner remembered that he had never seen any corpulence in a native who lived on native foods. The balance of nutrition, developed over the ages, had been overthrown.

Marriner was uneasy when faced with such changes. He blamed them, unreasonably, on the people themselves; feeling that he had given them opportunity, a chance to work, the comfort of clothing against the cold, the solid sustenance of beef in place of the dainty flesh of lizards. He was apprehensive lest somewhere he had failed these people; they were not as they had been when he first came, but he could not put the blame on anything he had done.

He felt with his wife that, such changes having been brought about, more were necessary.

One aspect of the matter was brought to a head one afternoon by a young, bearded horseman named Monroe, who had ridden down to Bloodwood Plains to see the wolfram fields. He had said nothing about his mission; Marriner and the others interested took it for granted that he might have come across signs of metal elsewhere in the country and was trying to ascertain whether his find was worth developing.

Monroe was accompanied by a tall, extremely tall and statuesque black woman, a native dressed in a long, grey and dirty frock which failed to cover the lines of a startlingly beautiful figure. It was a figure such as was unknown in the desert country. Her face was well featured too, a face sad in repose; and seldom wearing any other expression.

Secretive though he was about the affairs on which he was engaged, Monroe was a braggart, a pleasant enough example of the kind. His lubra, sitting with three or four others on a log rolled out on the sand in front of the store, about twenty yards from the door, came in for a good deal of masculine attention.

"What is she? Where does she come from?" Dallas asked. His own lubra—fat and jolly, the fifth he had had since Marriner first met him—was sitting there also; her hands, between her outspread knees, drooped in the lap of her dress.

"She's a Mullik-Mullik, down from the Daly River country," Monroe told him. "There's a lot of them like that, tall, good-looking, the best-looking coons in the Territory. Hard to handle, but——"

"She wouldn't give you any trouble down here," Dallas commented. It was true. A thousand miles from her tribal country, the girl was condemned to sudden death if she fled the protection of her white man. None of the tribes was yet so civilized that their men would have let her encroach upon

155

their own tribal land without the most extreme of punishment, and there were many tribes between Bloodwood Plains and the Daly River in the far north. She looked unrelated to these desert people.

"She won't give trouble," Monroe repeated. He had a glass of rum in his hand; and he and Dallas with about six others were seated round the table on the verandah.

"She's a beauty. How did you come by her?" Dallas asked.

"I was over on the Daly. I was having a look at an old copper show there on the hills, and I came across this bunch in a lily lagoon, two gins and a buck, just the three of them. They made a pretty picture too—you know those red lilies?"

Dallas nodded.

"Well, I wanted her. So I got her. They went for it when they saw me. I shot the buck and rode her down. Never saw hide nor hair of the other one again. Too busy taming this one. She took taming."

Two of the miners turned to look at Monroe and raised their eyebrows. The others took no notice. Dallas was still admiring the girl.

"She's a beauty," he said, and Monroe called to her.

"Judy. Come over here. Jump to it, now."

The girl approached.

"Now strip. Reef that dress over your head, and show them what you've got."

Without a change of expression the girl did what she was told. She was wearing underclothes, a pair of coarse unlovely bloomers; but above her waist her skin shone naked and black, her upper body perfectly balanced with her long legs, shining black flanks; and her neck rose from her shoulders like a column. Her mouth was slightly open, contemptuous, her eyes emotionless.

"Turn round, slowly now," Monroe called to her; and himself turned to the others.

"Best-looking nigger ever you saw."

The girl turned half around, turned back, just as Marriner came up.

"Get that bloody woman covered up and out of here," he said. He seldom lost his temper, but he was heated now. "You fellows are going to have to take a pull. I'm not having this sort of thing round here."

Monroe looked at him, saying nothing; but the girl picked the dress up off the sand and put it on. Dallas banged his glass on the table and laughed shortly.

"It's no laughing matter," Marriner said, and Dallas picked him up.

"Have a good look at yourself, Davy," he advised. "You had naked women all over Bloodwood when every other camp in the country had its women dressed. You had your own stud here wandering round in a shirt that didn't cover her hips. What's the matter with you?"

"It's different now," Marriner protested, and Dallas interrupted him.

"Yeah, it's different. You've got yourself spliced now; you're respectable. But your old stud's still sitting down at the camp, isn't she? She's still looking after a bunch of yeller-fellers that's rightly yours. A wife doesn't change that, Marriner."

"You're wrong," said one of the miners. It was Harris. "I'm with Marriner. There's a white woman in the country now. Them old times are gone. Strip your women if you want to, Monroe. But not in the settlement any more, not right out in the open."

"There'll be a bloody policeman here next," Dallas sneered, and Harris nodded.

"True enough," he said. "And then Monroe will have to buy his women, same as everyone else. And that'll cost him more than bullets."

Marriner had calmed.

"Leave out the argument, lads. There's no need for it anyway. You came in for a quiet drink without that."

In his heart he was perturbed, not so much by the braggart Monroe, but by his own reactions. For the first time in years the image of the dead girl on the desert, her clutching fingers, her outstretched broken body, rose in his mind. For that he had made no slightest protest to Dallas. He had made no smallest enquiry when Mary disappeared. There were, he knew, a thousand crimes of greater import than this display of a woman who had no objections; yet it was now that he had spoken.

It was his motivation which bothered him. Certainly in the civilization that was coming, no man at his evening drinking could do what Monroe had done. But no man, either, could talk of the innocent men he had shot for his pleasure. No man could talk with approval, as men here often talked, of whole tribes of natives wiped out to give protection to cattle, of the Derriss family, moving their herds across the top of the continent, and not so many years before, poisoning the wells they left behind so that there would not be so many natives to spear their cattle, dealing with these people as they dealt with wild dogs, eliminating them as they would have eliminated (if they could, or if they had cared) the very ticks that lived upon the beasts, giving poisoned flour with a smile and a greeting to innocents who would shortly die, they knew, in the agonies born of phosphorus.

These things didn't belong with civilization either; yet they were not the subject of Marriner's protest. This was still hard country, wild country. It had been wilder, and black had killed black; yet not for profit, and not from safety.

Out of the confusion of his thoughts he arrived at no definite conclusions; except only that the simple fact of his marriage had made some indefinable alteration to his standpoints.

He aligned himself on her side when she demanded that
the tribe be moved. They could not be moved to any great
distance; the necessity of drawing on the people for his stockmen, her house-girls, his key men in the jobs of construction,
demanded that a majority of the tribe be kept within easy
walk of the homestead; but he sent them to a level, shaded
site, well provided with trees, about three-quarters of a mile
along the creek-bank. Here, after the rains, there would be
water for them. In the meantime they could carry their
supplies from the whip-pole.

To do this, they passed the house, so that there was a chain
of them in the early morning with buckets and cans, slipping
through the yard; stopping briefly, while they were unde-
tected, to relay gossip, either by word or gesture, to the
house-girls. Monica hated the procession, the ragged uncouth travesties of femininity trailing by the house, the
giggles and shouts which she always suspected had some
lascivious meaning, though she was usually wrong. By
normal transfer, she continued to hate the whine of the whip-
pole. Sometimes she put down her sewing and held her head
in her hands while it went on.

Two months after her arrival she was carrying her first
child; and because of this, because of the unaccustomed heat,
because of the impossibility of investing her house-girls
with any due sense of responsibility she had, by evening,
sometimes worked herself up into a state approaching nervous
prostration.

"You should bring in Trubbidy. She's good in the house,"
Marriner once incautiously advised her, and she rounded on
him.

"She's been talking to you, has she?" she asked. "I've
been watching her. She comes out with those yellow kids of
hers to waylay you; and you fall for it. I've watched you
stop and play with them. Well, she can stay down at the
camp and keep her kids with her. And that Henry. You're

with him all the time. Next thing you'll be bringing him
into the house."

"He's my son, after all," Marriner protested.

"He's a black like all the rest. He's been brought up
like a black. He's not fit to be in a house. He's not
going to learn in mine. And you spend too much time with
him."

"He's the best stockman on the place. He'll be my foreman
some day," Marriner said. It was a compromise. He had
been thinking that his son belonged in his house. But he
knew that his wife was jealous for the baby she was carrying.
He said nothing. But a few days later he rode out on a three-
week tour of the property, accompanied by Henry, by Jacob,
and another of the camp youngsters.

He had a twofold purpose in the journey. First of all, he
wanted to check the condition of the cattle and the waters
after his long absence. In the second place, he wanted to
select a site for the first bore, a site where its water would
do the most good. Such a site would be in country where feed
grew luxuriantly, preferably top-feed, the foliage of shrubs,
too far from natural water to be grazed by any cattle. For
each bore he sunk, he could number his extra carrying
capacity by the thousand; he wanted to make the best possible
use of the machinery.

Young Henry had shown a great deal of development in
his absence. He was all but a man now; a cheerful worker, a
capable enough foreman, able to transmit orders and earn
respect without diminishing friendship. He was reliable and
he was independent. He was disappointing to Marriner only
in his inability to read. He had a smattering of letters in his
head, but he showed no desire to advance his knowledge
in this direction. In other ways he was clever.

Once, when they were standing together unsaddling their
horses, Marriner, remembering his own inability to cope with
the desert at a time when he was more than twice as old as

160

Henry, and curious as to the lad's reaction, tried him with a question.

"Suppose some day you're pretty near perishing out there, no food, no water, no place to go, what would you do?" he asked.

Henry grinned up at him. He stroked his horse's forearm. "Mighty big veins he's got there. If I opened that up, maybe it would keep me awhile, eh?"

The reply was instant, and astonished Marriner. He hadn't thought of tapping such a life-source.

"Maybe I could have a mare with milk, too," Henry continued.

"That blood would be pretty thick in your mouth," Marriner said, though he knew the answer had been the right one.

"Mouth would be pretty sticky anyway," Henry defended. "You see this fellow here?" He wandered off among the spinifex tufts, looking from one to another, and then stopped, pointing.

Marriner walked up. There was a circle of disturbed earth, not three inches across, in the middle of a bare patch between the spinifex clumps. Henry squatted down beside it and started to dig with his fingers. Eighteen inches down, with his arm sunk into the loose earth to the shoulder, his fingers closed on something, and he withdrew it. It was a fat sleepy frog, its skin a superfine transparent tissue that seemed filled almost to shapelessness with liquid. Its sleepy eyes blinked once or twice as it lay on the boy's hand; otherwise it made no attempt at movement, let alone flight.

"You just find this fellow and squinch him into your mouth, see," Henry said. His hand enclosing the frog lifted above his mouth, and he thrust his head back as though to jet a stream of water down his throat. But his fingers did not close. Very tenderly he set the frog down again at the bottom of its hole, and filled the loose earth down on its back. When the hole was level with the rest of the ground he tossed the remaining earth among the spinifex. He had all the native instincts for conservation.

"You'd take a lot of killing," Marriner said, and his son grinned happily.

On this trip they penetrated country that Marriner had never seen before, though it was his own land; country unvisited because of its distance from permanent water. There were a few surprises—a line of corpses where cattle had been poisoned by grazing a grove of gastrolobium bushes; some scattered bones far from any water, where a few strays had gone beyond safe range, picking at the lush parakeelia or the munyeroo while these succulents flourished, and thus wandering so many days from a drinking source that a return was impossible after the plants had disappeared. Factors such as these would influence Marriner's choices of sites for his bores.

But while a great deal of country offered excellent opportunity for development, provided only that it be supplied with water from underground, the first site he chose was within a quarter of a mile of Blowfly Creek. There was water here in abundance on the rock, but it was unavailable to stock; and Blowfly Creek was a keypoint in his mustering routes.

He had two possibilities in mind. One was a simple windmill sited at the edge of the almost perpendicular shaft. This could lift the supply from the rock reservoir and pass it to a tank from which the troughs could be kept filled with a simple ball-float to control the stopcock. The other was a bore at a likely site a quarter of a mile away on the plain. The first had the disadvantage that it was drawing on the more readily exhaustible supply in the rock; and it would also require a good deal more piping. So he chose the other; deciding at the same time to build a yard near the bore. It seemed a

wasted investment from one point of view since he had so
much new land to develop; but it proved a good decision.

He was also pleased that, of the company with him, only
Henry showed any enthusiasm or understanding of the pro-
ject. For the others, water was water; and where cattle
could not exist, game could. The development of the land
with its promise of greater prosperity and more work for
their community was of no interest to them whatsoever.
Under instruction they would lend their energies to the
accomplishment of the change, but their minds would remain
apathetic. They did not believe in the new world to come,
and that to which they belonged was disappearing. They
would neither halt nor hasten the change.

He was realizing the strength of the ties that bound him to
Henry; for the moment he failed to realize that they were the
ties of his life with the tribe, and almost the only ones remaining. Trubbidy had taken her dismissal with complete
equanimity; as yet she had contracted no marital alliances
with her own people, but he would not be surprised if at any
moment she did. She did not even enjoy a specially privileged
position, although when the rations were given out, as they
now were weekly, he saw to it that she did not lack for anything. He had no particular attachment to the remaining
children; not even the girl Casey, with whom he had been
fond of playing. Sometimes he felt a little guilty about
this and tried to remedy it. When he had been back from his
trip a few days he suggested to Monica that she might take
Casey, at least, into the house, and perhaps impart a little
conventional erudition along with a knowledge of domestic
duties.

Monica stared at him.

"Are you crazy?" she said. "If I had my way they'd live
somewhere else altogether. Anyway, what claim do they
have? You don't even know that they're yours. They're
just little wild things."

"Maybe we could make them into something different," he demurred. "I feel I should try, at least."

"You want to forget you ever had anything to do with them. You'll teach them nothing. And think of me. What am I going to tell my own children, when they grow— 'That's your sister; that gin with the yellow skin, with a slash of red flesh for a mouth, and a big flat nose'? Bring them into the house, and I'll go out. That goes for your precious Henry too. Talk to him as much as you like down at the stockyard, but don't bring him here. That's another thing. We'll have to start soon on a new house."

Marriner nodded.

"I've thought of that. It's going to be hard to get the men. I thought we should get a start on it when you go south."

"What do you mean, when I go south?"

He was surprised.

"You'll go south to have the baby, won't you? There's nothing here, no doctor, no nurse."

"Go south, and let you go back to your Trubbidy. And fill the house with her kids, her yellow kids. Not likely. No, I'm staying. And sending for Mother. She's had her time nursing and she'll be glad to come. So you'll have no worries. But I'd like to have a room ready for her when she arrives."

"You'd better hurry up and get her here. It's a long trip," Marriner reminded her.

"I wrote. Long ago. She'll be here in August. You've got three months."

Marriner thought, ruefully and uncomfortably, that the matter was out of his hands. He was sorry. He would have suggested the arrangement himself if he had thought of it, for he was a kindly man, and disposed to give Monica whatever she desired.

"I'll see what I can do," he promised.

11

In the end, the only thing he did was to give up his place in the house to his mother-in-law; and the child, a boy they christened James, was born long before the foundations of the new house were even laid. In the meantime, Marriner simply shifted his bed out into the open air, on the occasions when he slept at the homestead. For the greater part of this period he was on horseback.

Partly, this was because the work of the station was now considerably increased. His earlier survey had shown him that his land was supporting too many mobs of brumbies, small bands of wild horses that ranged the country near the hills. They ate the feed, but more importantly, they constantly augmented their numbers from the station herd, and he had to start a programme of eliminating them. The simplest way was to shoot the stallions, and to trap the mares and the young stock. A good number of the wild horses were useless; he brought them into the Bloodwood yard and shot them for meat for the natives. But he got a useful percentage of stock horses too.

Activity returned during this period; on the surface a scarcely altered Activity. Jacob had shown a considerable talent as an engineer's helper; and Activity stepped back into his old position as head stockman. He and Henry rode constantly with Marriner—the black man, the white man and the lad who was in between. To Marriner's rather disconcerted surprise, Activity had much more to teach Henry at this stage than Marriner himself could. And to a certain extent, Activity produced the balls for Henry to fire.

Thus one evening the lad, sitting with the other two round the fire, suggested that, in future, they neck-brand the cattle.

"Suppose you're riding near a quiet mob. They've all got their heads out. You'd see a neck-brand. Now that we've got them flank-branded we've got to ride in and turn them," he said.

"That's not so much," Marriner disagreed. "We've always flank-branded. How about when half the mob is flank-branded, half neck-branded. How about that? Lot of trouble, eh?"

"With the neck-brand, you save the hide, Activity says," Henry continued. "Flank-brand there's a big patch of hide no good."

Marriner looked over at Activity.

"Peggotty Hill—they neck-brand," the black man said. "Good hides, my word. This shoulder-brand, flank-brand, they knock the hide around."

"It's worth looking at," Marriner said. The usual brand—"EGE" with a digit, a five, a six, or a seven to mark the last figure of the year in which branding was done, and thus give an approximate age to the beast—certainly spoiled a large area of the hide, particularly when the fire-brand was applied to a small calf. The ruined patch grew with the beast. In the following season the Marriner cattle were all branded on the neck. It made no immediate difference to prices, but as the years went by it made the Marriner herd distinctive among the Territory cattle.

Marriner, riding with Henry, cut new hoofmarks. He made the horse-sign to Henry, who reined in and looked more closely than Marriner felt was necessary.

"Something," Henry said; which meant he disagreed, though the horse-signature seemed obvious. But he was already calling Activity, who rode over. He inspected the tracks briefly and made his comment.

"Them horses got long ears," he said. Marriner looked at him and he explained.

"Donkey."

The wild donkeys, bred from escaped draft animals and thriving on the desert, had at last moved down from the North. They, too, had to be shot down, and ruthlessly. They, too, were rounded up to feed the native community at Bloodwood.

In addition, the boring plant, now getting rapidly ahead with its task near Blowfly Creek, had to be supplied. And the routine work of the station—the mustering of cattle, the branding of strays, the doctoring, training and breaking of horses, the killing of meat for Bloodwood, for the wolfram fields at Raggedy Peak, for the mustering team itself, all had to be maintained. They were days of constant, hard saddle-work; and Marriner, at the edge of his forties, worked as he had never done before.

It set an obstruction between his life and Monica's. But Monica, with the help of her mother, had raised her own obstruction anyway. Hers was the world of domesticity, a world which barely touched him. When he was at home they enjoyed good relations; but these periods were sometimes a month apart and of short duration. Between them, Monica became as set in her routines as he in his. She found much of her fulfilment in the circle completed by her child and her mother; even the frictions and resentments of her life were worked out on the household staff.

Marriner's relationship with his mother-in-law was as friendly, and even more remote. She was a smaller woman than her daughter; small and plump; a self-sufficient widow with a cheerful bustling manner, a great pride in her daughter and her daughter's son, and very few sensibilities whatever.

Once she commented on the appearance of Trubbidy's daughter Casey.

"You'd almost think her father had been white," she said. Before Marriner could say anything, Monica cut in.

"He was," she said. "Probably one of these drifters going through, or one of the miners. There are one or two other half-castes in the camp."

She didn't even look at her husband, and there was nothing more said on that subject. Again Marriner felt a twinge of conscience; he would have liked his children set apart from the rest of the dark people, but he supposed, after all, it would not be fair to his wife. He had never been unfaithful to her; he was more considerate of her than she knew. It was in deference to her that he recruited no more stockmen from among the girls of the tribe, though they were as good as the lads and gave less trouble.

Marriner sent down two thousand head of cattle in the year that young James was two; and as a kind of bonus there was nearly three hundred head of horses. The horses sold at Quorn for a flat five pounds a head; the cattle averaged four pounds ten. The agent's reports were so ecstatic that Marriner went ahead immediately with the long-promised new homestead, and placed orders for the materials. Really, it was no more to him than a decision to put his bridle on this horse or that.

Creswell Cummings, in almost hourly consultation with Monica and her mother, worked out the details, filled in the orders, made himself responsible for the whole thing. He was working now on a combination of wages and a share in the store-profits which, together, added up to a far more comfortable figure than some of the smaller station-owners could show for their efforts. He was wholly committed to Bloodwood Plains, or so it seemed. He had no taste for an independent life; his job kept him busy; and, with its combination of an out-door life and a sedentary occupation, was more attractive than any other he could envisage.

As a result of correspondence with Masterman's, Marriner

also acquired a "jackeroo," a cadet cattleman, a farmer's boy from the tamed hinterland of New South Wales. He was not a jackeroo in the accepted sense of the word—that would have been an English lad with some pretensions, both as to family and property, who was learning the cattle business with an eye to establishing a branch of his family in Australia. Young Roberts, instead, was of farmer stock. He had been born to hard work. He was quick and intelligent, and he had spent a good deal of his youth in the saddle so that most of what he had to acquire was an indifference to unimportant detail, a breadth of vision in management. His assistance, and his ability to lead a team of musterers, was of enormous importance to Marriner. Activity could have done the work; but Marriner felt the need of the companionship of his first black friend.

The new homestead was planned for the other side of the river, half a mile from the huddle of buildings which now constituted the homestead. The river trees saved it from the dust-clouds which sometimes rose from the vicinity of the yard, and there was an opportunity to make a good garden. It was to be quite a pretentious house, with six large rooms and two wide verandahs. Someday Monica wanted to add a columned porch in a Colonial style, and they made provision for this.

The boring plant was put to the task of providing yet another water supply. It was to go in before the house, so that the water would be readily available for the necessities of construction. The plant had already made a water supply for the homestead and the store. The whip-pole in the creek, however, still protested for hours each morning as the lubras drew their supplies from it. They were too lazy, Monica complained, to walk another quarter-mile to the tap.

"Why can't you fill that thing in?" she asked Marriner. "It wouldn't hurt them to walk that little distance. That's a terrible noise—creak, creak—every morning."

But Marriner liked the noise. The whip-pole was almost the only thing on which he didn't defer to her wishes.

"Let them be," he'd say. "In any case, it's theirs. It was here before I came. So let it alone."

Whenever the creaking protest started he could envisage the small encampment to which he had first opened his eyes, and the memory-picture was one which yearly became more attractive.

In the middle of the excitements of housebuilding, Mission Mo made his gold-strike. He rode in one afternoon, late, just before the sun went down. He came in from the south, though he had ridden into the west when he had last left; and he surveyed the new layout of the station for a little while, sitting quietly in the saddle. Marriner was also riding in at that hour, and came up beside him. Mo, who had been out for four months, greeted him as though he had seen him last that morning.

"You're giving yourself plenty to go on with," he said. "That's going to cost you something."

"I guess it will."

"Well, I've got a surprise for you," Mo said. "I've brought you the money to pay for it. I've made my strike."

He dismounted, and went to his pack horse. He moved quietly, as a man about a daily routine, but his hands began to tremble with excitement, so that he could hardly open the buckles. He brought out two large samples, one in each hand. They were of a greenish quartz, crusted with gold. Marriner had seen gold samples before, but nothing like these. The colour of the quartz itself was unusual in that country; the gold was undoubtedly rich.

"A big strike, eh Mo?"

"The biggest ever. The richest."

Mo was holding the samples tight, twisting his wrists slowly, to look at all sides of each of the specimens. He was fascinated, as though the metal had hypnotized him.

"The richest, at least," he said again. He looked up, suddenly a little troubled.

"I don't know the biggest," he said. "If I can follow the lode. It's faulted all to hell. But we're on to it. There's a fortune right there in my packs. And there's a good deal more to come. And the half of it's yours, Davy my boy. And by God you earned it. How many years has it been?"

Marriner could not remember.

Mission Mo was only one of half-a-dozen prospectors who now combed the hills at Marriner's expense. He never really anticipated any return from this. Nor was it a charitable undertaking on his part. He had the stores they needed, and that was that. He wished them success, not for his own benefit—he did not need it—but for their own. And above all he liked to see them returning, making his place the centre of their operations.

Mo made no secret of his success. And that night he had a considerable audience at the store. He talked quite freely about the claim, reserving information only as to its where-abouts.

"You can be on my tracks in the morning, the lot of you," he said. "Only thing is, it's a long way round by my tracks. And I'll tell you. I'll give you a week and still beat you to it, going straight. So you might just as well wait. And any-way I've got it sewed up. The claims staked and laid out and registered—yes, registered. I been south and registered it. And what I've got claimed takes in just about every colour I see there.

"Well, I'm not stopping you from coming. Them there's the best samples I could find—there's others I left at Quorn. And far as I can see it's a small outcrop, and no pickings left for anyone else. But the more the merrier, come along."

"How big a range is it?" Dallas asked. "Are they real big mountains?"

Mo pursed his lips.

"Not so big. Not so small. Give it a couple of days and come along with me. It's big enough for Davy and me. Far as I can see it's no bigger. But come along. Plenty of chances for looking."

Dallas grunted. He was a cattleman, and interested in gold only if he fell over it.

There were five of the wolfram miners, however, who went out with Mo three days later. Marriner and Activity went along. They had an arduous four days' ride before they reached the range, a small line of hills six or seven hundred feet in height and perhaps fifteen miles in extent. The hills were flat topped, as though they had formed part of an earlier plain that had eroded. The gold was in an outcrop in the bend of a water-worn gully near the top of a hill—a ragged, broken formation in which the rock veins seemed tossed and tumbled in all directions.

Here lay the evidence of weeks of pottering; a few narrow costeaned trenches, a shaft which led down beyond where the costean had uncovered a sampling of the greenish quartz. The gold samples had been taken from the surface, and the quartz reef that remained was rich with the metal. The claim was so located that there seemed little possibility of re-locating the reef beyond its boundaries.

Three of the miners returned immediately to the wolfram fields. The other two remained, deciding to spend some time in prospecting the hill. There was none of the real excitement of a strike, except for Mission Mo. For him it was the end of a journey, the exciting, anticipated end; and the shaking of his hands developed every time he came to a decision, every time he reapproached the workings, every time they talked over the problems or, as they sometimes did, lightly discussed the rewards.

From a man with a quest, Mission Mo had become a man with an accomplishment. The imaginary gold of his dreams had become reality; now it was for him to translate it into the rewards—the wine and women, the racehorses and the mansion. Strangely enough, these had little place in his thought; or the place, if it existed, was not much revealed by his conversation.

Marriner left two natives with stores and horses at the claim for the use of Mission Mo. There was good pasture near the foot of the range, and small water holes in several places. The claim would be no problem to work; though transport would present a difficulty.

When they returned to the homestead, Marriner was immediately involved in the racing, galloping, three-month rhythm of the delayed branding muster. He was at home here; cattle had become a way of life; and it was a way of life that absorbed his full attention and left him happy. The excitement started in the cold morning of the first day, before the dawn, when the horse-tailers—there were two now, for it was a big camp—brought the working horses up and the sleeping men arose. The fires were shaken up, and the men ate their meat and damper standing, or squatting in the shelter of the bush where they had spent the night. Then as each finished he caught and saddled the horse he would use that day and rode off, sometimes by himself, sometimes one of a little group; sometimes stating his intention, the country he would cover and for what distance; though of this there was little need.

Young Roberts, whose first season this was, found it an enthralling business. In the first few days of confusion it seemed to him that orders must have been transmitted by telepathy. It seemed also that the riders had left great stretches of country uncombed, until he realized that these men were much more in tune with the country he could imagine.

He would ride along with one of the younger men, Muggins or Clarence or Harold, and in the centre of the plain they would change direction.

"Cattle over there," they would tell him if he asked.

It was a while before he realized that on these occasions they had cut the fresh tracks of cattle travelling from water. If they had not cut them they would know of a certainty that the hill grazing was untenanted.

Then again they would leave such a trail after following it for half a mile or so; and the reason would be that another rider had cut the same trail, was now hunting the same cattle, and they had discovered the evidence of this activity in the tracks. From time to time a rider would push a small bunch of cattle down out of the hills, sometimes leading them, sometimes chasing them at full gallop; and having seen these cattle taken into control by the riders in the centre of the sweep, he would canter away again on a new pursuit. Sometimes the cattle they drove would pick up others. Almost imperceptibly the central mob grew from hour to hour. By night there would be two or three hundred head.

Sometime during the day a cloud of dust would rise on the horizon behind, and a little later the nucleus of the horse herd would come past at the run, the two horse-tailers riding behind, their mouths masked against the dust, as often as not, with the neckerchiefs they wore for display. By the time the cattle arrived at the night-camp the horses would be all watered and hobbled and feeding out, the cooking fires would be lit, the wood collected, a little hunting done, perhaps, some mending of harness; and the horse-tailers would be resting or asleep.

The first night they held three hundred head of cattle. The night-riders sang softly through the dark; the cattle camped quietly. Next morning they drove this mob across the range to Argadala, and there, with the acquisitions they made on the way, yarded four hundred and fifty by noon. On the third day they fed these cattle out on the plain, three riders easing their horses along with the herd, letting them roam a mile or two before turning them, holding them near the water, while other riders combed the remainder of the Argadala country. These brought back an additional hundred and fifty cattle.

The six hundred cattle stayed in the big yard overnight. In the morning they were drafted into the small yard where the branding ramp stood. This was a small fence, curving up from the ground to a V-shaped gap, the other side of which was bounded, only a foot away, by a tall post with a continuation of the fence running five or six yards to nowhere. At the back of this fence the fire was laid and the branding irons set to heat. There was an art in making the fire so that the branding irons were heated evenly.

Henry saddled the broncho horse—one of several heavy draft animals used for no other purpose. It had its own special saddle, long in the girth and buckled to heavy breast harness to which the greenhide rope was clipped. On this ponderous animal Henry moved among the yarded cattle, and dropped a rope over the head of any calf or cleanskin cow he could see.

Immediately, the broncho horse started at a fast clip round the ramp. The calf, encouraged to run elsewhere and needing little encouragement in any case, naturally put the ramp between itself and the horse; the rope mounted the ramp and dropped in the Vee, and soon the calf was imprisoned, choking, blatting, protesting, against the fence. Here, or on its progress hither, two cowhands on foot would have roped a leg before and behind on the near side, and made the ropes fast to either end of the fence. Whereupon, the broncho's rope being suddenly let go, the calf fell heavily or was thrown.

The team immediately went into action. One man held the animal's head down; another seized the hind legs, holding them steady with an iron hand on the fetlock straining against a foot pressure higher on the leg, or with the tail looped round the groin. A third man cut the earmark in the exposed ear. A fourth, if the animal was male, castrated it; and as the man straightened up at the completion of the job, the red-hot brand was pressed into the calf's neck and it rose, marvellously freed of ropes, and made its jerky, halting run back to the herd; thereafter nervous of ropes and men on horseback.

That, at any rate, was the ideal. When it came to grown bulls, and the cunning, vicious range cows, the programme got complicated. Sometimes the roped animal would take off after the broncho horse, scattering men on foot in all directions. Sometimes she would run the rope through the fire, and send embers and red-hot irons flying. Sometimes the cowhands would clear the high fence from a standing, scrambling jump even before the cow was brought near the ramp.

A big bull might have the tips of his horns sawed, to make them permanently tender, and thus cure him of the habit of using them for offence. The strength of such an animal would be more evenly matched with that of his holders; the straining of antagonistic muscles sometimes ended in a brief victory for the bull. The last man to let him up might spring from his head to the safe height of the ramp fence; if he neglected this precaution a bull or an old cow might chase him and the other tormentors about the yard.

The stockmen, happy, laughing, competitive, also varied the programme. Sometimes, if Henry on the broncho horse seemed to make one or two bad throws, or failed to come close to a particularly obstreperous target, they would walk into the herd themselves, foot-ropes twirling, fully alive to the dangers they invited from the bulls. They would rope a beast and drag him out, or be dragged about themselves, shouting happily for help while the rest of the natives laughed at their discomfiture. If their capture was small they would manhandle him out in the open without using the ramp; they

called this "scrubbing" a beast, for it was what they were
expected to do with a cleanskin in the scrub; and there was a
constant challenge: "Scrub him; scrub him" when the size
of the animal was on the borderline of what a man on foot
could reasonably be expected to handle.

Or, when a biggish beast was let loose at the ramp, one
of the lads would stand astride him as he rose, and rough-
ride him back into the milling herd. If he was thrown the
taunts rose all around as from a school playground. But if he
rode sweetly and lowered himself to the ground without
incident at the exact moment when the achievement could
reasonably be considered closed, there was an equally hearty
burst of applause.

For these riders were like children. They had nicknames
for most of the outstanding characters among the cattle.
They taunted them, flung insults at them, cheered them on in
their battle against the human whenever they chanced to be
winning, gave them serious advice, and were, in the main,
kindly. But they could be ruthless.

In the transfer from one yard to the other, a young bull
found freedom. Unlike most of his kind he had no thought
for the rest of his herd but, driven by panic, set out for the far
horizon. Two of the stockmen, Nugget and Muggins, set
out after him to turn him. He would not be turned, however.
Again and again, as they rode up on him, he changed his
direction momentarily, but again set out as directly as possible away from the yards. The horses performed magnificently, but the bull was not to be persuaded.

When he had done this several times, the two riders took
turns to throw him. They did this from the tail, not from the
head, after the American fashion. They would gallop close
alongside and as the bull swung out, off-balance because of
the change of direction, they would lay firm hold on the tail
and throw in the direction, or nearly in the direction, that
horse and bull were following. The bull fell heavily and at

speed. Sometimes he slithered along the ground or crashed into a small tree, but he was always up like a cat, and immediately away.

First Nugget, then Muggins, then Nugget again, and Muggins again threw him. Each time he got up bellowing, a little more slowly than the last. He had taken dreadful punishment from the impact of his own weight. He was gasping as well as bellowing. For the fifth time he was menaced.

Nugget rode in fast, reached out his left hand to grip the bull's tail and throw it, stopped his horse and in the same moment left the saddle, so that as the bull's head struck the ground Nugget struck its head. It was a slick action. The bull lay quiet for a second. Then he kicked and plunged, throwing the lightweight Nugget about a little; but he could not rise, the weight at his head was too secure.

In the meantime Nugget was slipping his castrating knife from its pouch on his belt, and opening it.

"Throw me your whip," he called to Muggins.

The knife flashed, and sank into the septum between the bull's nostrils. The bull bellowed with fright and pain, but Nugget's fingers followed the knife, and the whiplash in them. He tied the heavy leather securely in the open wound, so that the whip passed in one nostril and out the other. That done, he got serenely to his feet.

The bull was too cowed to follow. It lay there, where it had been thrown. Nugget called to it.

"You come, little bull. You come long. I got you by the nose, by Christ. By Christ now, you come."

Muggins laughed delightedly. Nugget gave the whip a twitch, and the bull slowly got to his feet. He lowered his head, but Nugget pulled it up again with his whip; and the exquisite pain brought the bull to subjection. Nugget walked a few steps, leading the bull this way and that, and the bull came quietly. Then Nugget mounted his horse.

"No more you run away, little bull," he said. He led it quietly back to the yard, dismounted, led it into position, pulled its head up against the ramp, and they went ahead with the branding.

It was one of the scrub bulls, not one of the studs, or they could safely have let it go in the first place; but it must have weighed close to six hundred pounds and it was well grown. The utter fearlessness which Nugget had displayed amazed young Roberts.

The natives understood the animals, and as far as it was practical for the cattle to have what they wanted, they got it. But as soon as there was a conflict of ideas, the man's had to be victorious at whatever cost. Thus, a consistently unruly bull might be thrown and have a few tendons cut in a leg. He would be in pain the rest of his life; he would limp throughout its length; but otherwise he would be a better and more easily handled bull.

Thus at moments that were not infrequent in the crowded bustle of the branding yard, the stockmen seemed utterly callous; at other times they were unnecessarily kind. The same Henry who would replace a desert frog tenderly in the sheltering earth would grin and make jokes as the horn-saw bit into the bleeding nerves of a bullock's armament. He and his people were unpredictable.

Over the branding yard there was a constant haze of dust, the acrid scent of burned and living hide, the sweeter and more subtle smell of blood. It was a place where the emotions were readily uncovered; a place to show some of what went to make a man. It was an elemental, raw, cruel kind of place.

Every third or fourth day they branded. Usually on these days they killed a beast for the camp. There was little hunting now. A rider would sometimes bring in a lizard or a snake swinging at his saddle; if it were a short day he might be minded to go hunting for a duck or a porcupine. Otherwise they lived on the cattle.

And there was something else happened on branding days —the corroboree. Branding days were short. The cattle were turned loose after the branding, and the men rested. Following the evening meal the natives would cluster round one of the fires. By and by a low song would start. Then one or other of the men would go to their packs, and produce a pair of rhythm-sticks to tap together in time with the words; or a screaming, whining bull-roarer, to pick up the chant as it rose to excitement.

The fire would die down. The voices would bring in a stronger and stronger response. Then, one after another, the men would shuck their clothes to stand up and dance, their disciplined bodies moving weirdly; so that a man, for instance, if the choreography called for it, might appear to dance flat on his back, his body jerking itself rhythmically clear of the ground, controlled by the muscles of his buttocks and his shoulder blades; or standing, with hands on knees and body bent, leap backwards with celerity on stiff legs, with such control as to complete a desired figure with absolute exactitude.

It was dancing wholly stylized, yet raw and elemental. They danced the hunting of the kangaroos; they danced the taking of women; they danced murder and fire; they danced the beginnings of things; they danced the stars—the secret of the Emu's Nest that darkens the Milky Way and the shooting stars that come from nowhere. Yet everything they danced was sheer joy and entertainment.

Just as when he was a boy, Henry joined them, always. He would sit at the fire with Marriner and Roberts and the black Activity for a little while until the call became irresistible. Activity, strangely, was rarely moved. He stayed at the white man's fire; sometimes calling an expected response, but not joining in the dance. But long before the other natives were all on their feet, Henry was with them, dancing with the others.

Marriner did not like it. But never once did he voice his disapproval. He just sat and watched; and sometimes he felt the surge of emotion and violence; and sometimes, when that was proper, he laughed with the dancing men.

12

When the branding season was over, Activity went away again. Marriner tried to persuade him to stay, and Activity was apologetic about going, but he remained firm.

"I kind of miss them camels," he said. "A man gets to like them. I want to go with the camels again."

"Plenty of camels here," Marriner said.

"Yes, Davy. But no jobs. They got all the men they want. I'll go south again. They know me."

"The day of the camel is coming to an end," Marriner said, for that was true; but the argument didn't appeal to Activity.

"I kind of like them camels," he said. "There's still a few about. Still a little work there."

Marriner's suspicion was that now the men were back at the homestead and camp life was over for a month or two, Activity resented the new house and "the Missus." But if this were so the black man didn't betray his feelings. He saddled up a horse, took a spare, and went.

There were a lot of travellers on the road at this time. A smaller percentage than ever before were cattlemen or miners; the majority had few prospects in the country and quite obviously didn't care. Most of them were soldiers back from the war; soldiers desert-hardened to the sands of Egypt or Palestine; soldiers antipathetic to the flag-waving populations which had greeted their return to the cities of the East Coast. Some of them had well-developed neuroses. A few seemed to have achieved a balance; but one that would have distressed the social reformers.

Nearly all were heading up to the sun, up to the deep tropics, up to the lotus lands far away from people. They had little money or none; they asked for meat or flour or salt as though it were a right.

"That plug of mine's dragging her feet. She could do with a rest. You got one you could swap for her? Something decent. I got a long way to go," one bearded giant said to Marriner. He was wearing his old army hat, and there was a grin under the mass of hair that camouflaged his face.

"Well, if I don't you'll run one off on me," Marriner said. He cast an eye over the mare. She would make a stock horse, with a bit of condition on her. He had a look at her mouth. She had all her teeth, with the crown hollows filled in. She was eight years old at least, then; but the teeth were still upright, not too slanted. She could not be much older than eight. She had a few years of breeding ahead of her.

"All right," he said. "You can have your pick of any gelding in the yard, bar two." His treasured camp horse, an educated beast that was worth half-a-dozen men in drafting cattle, was a gelding; and so was Henry's. The drifter picked a fine stocky beast, threw a saddle on it, and tried it out. It went quietly.

"You got a good one," Marriner said.

"You didn't do so bad, cully," the other rejoined. "You got yourself a brood mare." Marriner's stipulation of a gelding had not gone unnoticed.

"If she ever puts on enough condition to carry a foal."

"She'll live," the other returned carelessly.

"All right then. We'll have a drink to seal the bargain. Go up to the store, see the fellow there—Cres Cummings his name is—tell him I said you could cut out a quid."

"I'd like to take some of that out in tea. I got a couple mates with me. We're right out of tea."

"He'll fill your tucker-bags. You can still cut out the quid.

If you're still here tonight I'll see you there. I never drink before dark."

"Well, thanks, cully. We'll be seeing you."

There was no trace of gratitude. Marriner, who in his dealings with the black people was accustomed to getting no thanks, had no fault to find with this.

He found the bearded man with two apparently ill-assorted companions sitting on the edge of the store verandah that night, taking the pound out in rum. One was a small, sturdy, happy-looking fellow, the other lean, lantern-jawed, with a three-day stubble. Nobody else was at the store; not even Roberts who, when he was at the homestead, usually came for an evening drink. Only Cummings was leaning over the half-door, yawning.

"Give us the keys if you like," Marriner told him. "If you've got anything else you want to do."

"Well, thanks. I've got a book to read."

Cummings departed with alacrity, and Lantern-jaw watched him go.

"That's the kind of job I'm going to get me," he said.

"Not for mine." The little man disagreed. "Kind of job I'm looking for there'll be no work in it. No work at all. No keys. No locking-up."

"Me, I'm going to keep on fighting. Soldiering anyway," Blackbeard said.

"Come off it, mac. The war's over."

"That's what you think. The war's never over. But this war I know what I'm fighting for. I'm fighting for me."

Marriner laughed.

"Don't we all?" he asked lightly.

Blackbeard looked at him sourly.

"No we don't, cully. That's where you make the big mistake. Last war they got me in. They said, you got to fight for your wife and your family and your girl and your house and your job. Fight for your loved ones, they said, and they beat a drum. And all them loved ones stood on the footpath and cheered when we went away. But come to the end and you look back: What did you fight for? Your wife ran off with the loved one that got your job while you were away. And all you did was give her the opportunity. You fought to put Germany down the drain. Did you do it? Did you hell! You fought for God and the right, and all you got was crab-lice and a hangover and a free civilian suit that some fat dodo made to fall to pieces for a quick profit. You fought for seven bob a day and your chances. You fought to make a world for heroes—you know what they say when you come back?"

He reached into a shirt pocket and took out a flat leather wallet. The others watched him, as though they had watched this a thousand times before and knew what was coming. Blackbeard extracted a newspaper clipping, thin, yellow and worn. He looked up at Marriner as he spread it out.

"Police-court news," he said. "Some poor devil up for vagrancy." He cleared his throat and began to read:

" 'The accused,' said Sergeant Maddick, 'had been keeping the company of thieves, prostitutes and returned soldiers.' "

He stopped reading.

"There you are. A world for heroes, long as they're not returned soldiers. Or thieves. Or prostitutes. Or all them other kinds of cobbers Christ used to have. Who won the war?"

Marriner was still looking at him, and said nothing. Blackbeard shook his head.

"Listen, cully. I asked you a question. Who won the bloody war? I'll tell you who won it. The men that started it; they won it. And who lost it? The men that stopped it. There was winners on both sides, see? And losers."

He wasn't worked up. He was talking quite normally, as though in sorrow, but there was no stopping him.

"You want to know who won? You won, cully. You got a

market for your lean cattle—good enough for soldiers to eat. You got top prices for your hides to get worn out in the desert; and there was many a pair of boots never got the chance to wear out. More profit. You sold your tallow for munitions."

"But I never started it," Marriner defended himself.

Blackbeard smiled.

"No, cully. You didn't start it. Nobody did, I suppose. But you did nothing to stop it. You're there, see; where you're standing. And them bottles behind you, they're yours. And the building. And the land. And everything as far as you can see. And us? I got a good hack in exchange for a plug I lifted from a character who's got so many he won't miss it. Now you wouldn't say that I won and you lost, would you? And me, I did my best to stop the war. And you. You took the profit from the tallow on the cartridges I fired. No hard feelings, mate. I'm just making the point. You won the war. We lost. And I'll make another point: I'd sooner be me than you."

"You reckon you wouldn't have taken the profit, just like I did?"

"Well, I didn't, did I? I didn't stop here to take a profit. I went out to stop the war the only way I knew; shooting somebody. Only thing was, I didn't know the right target. I shot other poor blokes like myself. There was them on both sides could have done with shooting; but they were a long way from where we were. If I'd been here, you say, I'd have taken your profit. But I was a long long way from the profits; and I was there of my own free will. I'll tell you, cully, I made more than I lost. I lost a wife, and by God I can do without her. Now look, d'you reckon we've come to the end of the quid you mentioned?"

Marriner grinned, and pushed the end of the bottle over. He reached out a new one from the store and a clean glass and came and joined the three on the steps of the verandah.

"Doing nothing, one way or the other, wasn't good enough, you reckon?" he asked.

"I don't know," Blackbeard said. "Were you right or was I? You won. I lost. All I know is you've got to fight to stay in the one place. And it's your fault where you go."

He stared at the new bottle.

"Thanks, anyway, for the bottle," he said. "You're a gentleman, as the saying goes."

"I was wondering when you were going to come to your senses," Lantern-jaw commented. He lifted his glass.

"Here's luck. Good hunting."

They were typical of the disillusioned wanderers, the veterans who no longer fitted their own communities. The desert saw a lot of them; they were searching, but they did not know what for. A few of them, a very few, found themselves in that country; the others passed through and went on, or returned whence they came.

Another type of man appeared at this stage; a countryman, dressed in a business suit, driving one of the noisy reliable automobiles of the period—usually a Model-T Ford. They were the cattle buyers, up from the south. Expanding markets caused the great grazing and fattening concerns in the South and East to look closely to new sources of supply; sources where cattle were cheap and available. Mission Mo came on what he thought was a last visit to Bloodwood. He had worked out his claim, made his stake, and was going South to spend it. One afternoon he saw Marriner sitting on the stockyard rail with one of these buyers, and waited a little way away until their conversation was finished.

"Who was that fellow?" he asked.

"A buyer. He's buying for Ramsey."

"Syd Ramsey?" The name was that of one of the greatest cattle kings of them all.

"The same."

"Syd for Short, they call him. Short of tucker, short of money, short of good looks. Watch him."

"He's made me a pretty good offer."

"He would. Big mob, or just a few?"

"Just a few, as a matter of fact. He wants a hundred. Just for a beginning like. He's bought cattle up north and these will join them when they come through. He's giving me a price on station. That may be the best way to sell in the future, that's what I'm thinking. Droving costs more every year."

"Davy, you've got a lot to learn yet. Now don't mind me. We've been partners a long time back. But if you haven't closed the deal don't go on with it."

"I've closed."

"Well . . . bad luck. But watch him just the same."

"It seems a good bargain."

"Yes. As bargains go. But it's an old trick of Syd for Short. Here's the drill. This buyer's gone through, bought a hundred cattle from each of fifteen stations, and those fifteen stations will all be on the route. Now he sends a drover, and the drover has paper to show he's to pick up cattle of fifteen brands, a hundred head of each. No, the number will be different for every station; but say a hundred. All right. Now every mob of cattle that drover will go through will be carrying one of them fifteen brands. So if a few cattle drift in from each of the stations, who's to say they're not the ones that were bought? That drover will finish up with three thousand head, instead of the fifteen hundred he paid for."

"And then where does the drover get off? They're Ramsey cattle."

"Oh, he'll get off all right. Syd for Short's not so tight as all that. He knows when to put his hand in his pocket."

"You mean, he just sends out a drover with orders to lift cattle along the way?"

"Not on your life. Syd's a pillar of the church. That would

make him a thief, wouldn't it? He's never asked a man to break the law in all his life. He's against thieving. No, all he'll do, he'll say, 'Now, me man. I'm not as a rule a betting man. But I'll bet you twenty pounds you're not so good a drover you can deliver without any loss. I'll bet a hundred to a pound of tea there's not a thirty per cent natural increase,' or 'There's not an increase worth looking at.' And he'll be the judge of what's worth looking at.

"So the drover risks his neck and packs in as many as he can, and Syd's never said a word out of place. He won't say a word either, when they're delivered. He'll just make his tally and off he'll go, happy as a sandboy, waiting for the next mob down the trail."

"Is this fair dinkum?"

"Why else would a man buy a hundred head from each of fifteen stations? To make his books fat? Now, I don't know of my own experience, but I've heard the boys talk, and Syd will put his hand in his pocket when it's advisable. They wouldn't talk in front of you, but an old hatter like me, sitting out in the hills with his gold, they don't figure I'm interested in anything they say. I've heard plenty. You watch this fellow."

It was the last deal of the sort Marriner ever made.

When the mixed mob came down the trail that year, at the beginning of the north-west monsoon, the boss drover rode ahead to meet him.

"I picked up seven of your cows coming through," he said. "Couldn't help it. They were in the scrub, and I never saw them till I was up on them. You want to draft them out, or count them as some of the mob you're putting in?"

It was an honest approach, and Marriner felt some remorse for his suspicions. The following day, when the drover went on with his augmented herd, he watched him go quite contentedly. They had had a good night together. But late that afternoon Henry rode in.

"That fellow's doing more mustering than droving," he said. "I picked up the tracks of a shod horse. It turned a little mob of cattle back to the drove, maybe eight or nine. One of them looked like a good stud bull."

He caught a fresh horse, and with Marriner rode through the night. They passed the cattle camp and kept a good mile and a half away from the twinkling fires. By daylight they were camped across the stock route, past the last of Marriner's waters. There would be small chance of finding EGE cattle further to the south.

In midmorning the mob caught up with them.

"Just thought we'd give our mob another tally," Marriner explained.

"You're going to have your work cut out, mister."

"I don't think so," Marriner said. "We tally them here. If we have to ride on with you instead, I won't be complaining just about the extra tally."

The drover gave in with a bad grace. If Marriner had a complaint, any station owner on the route ahead would side with him against a drover, and bring his hands to the tallying as well. And reports would go to other station owners on the route behind him.

He brought up the herd and funnelled the animals between riders, keeping a check himself. The process might have been more difficult except that the neck-branded EGE cattle stood out from the others. There were a hundred and thirty-seven.

"You can draft out the thirty-seven; or you can give me a paper saying you took delivery of the extra on behalf of Ramsey, whatever you like. Either way you can make a special note of the stud. You better draft him out. His price comes high."

"I don't know how I got them cattle," the drover said. "They must have come up out of the river bank when I was going through the trees."

"Next time you come through I'll lend you a couple of riders," Marriner promised. He and Henry tailed the extra cattle back to the last water hole.

"That was good work, Henry," Marriner said. "You're a good lad. You keep your eyes open."

It was his sorrow that their daily association always ended round about sundown, except when they were in camp. There was no possibility that Monica would ever welcome him to the new house. For that matter, Marriner himself spent little of his waking time there.

It was fine and roomy, and for another man it would have been comfortable, but he was seldom at ease in it. In his dress he liked the rough confinement of his narrow-legged denims, his elastic-sided, high-heeled boots and leather gaiters, and the reassuring pressure of the spur straps across his insteps; and he felt uncomfortable in the soft clothes that Monica provided for him to change into in the evenings.

The rowel-marks of his spurs on the painted and polished cement floors got him into constant hot water; the spiked wheels tangled in the throw rugs and carpets. His appearance provided another bone of contention. Monica envisaged the great landowner, full of wealth and good deeds, sitting at his ease in an atmosphere of simple luxury; but her imagination did not go much further. Instead, she had this working-man, smelling of horses and cattle, and infrequently shaved; a man who as often as not when he was home came in late for his evening meal, ate it alone in the kitchen, and disappeared to the store in search of male company.

However disappointing, this was an arrangement that suited the women well enough. Monica was increasingly involved in her domestic affairs. Her second child came two years after the first; the third a little less than two years later.

She was a good mother. She breast-fed her babies, showered them with attention, spent all her time clothing them and thinking up distractions for them, and, as they reached four or five years of age, teaching them the rudiments of schooling. She was a good teacher too; so good that Marriner devoutly wished she had seen fit to spend a little time on the native children, and especially upon his own.

From the very beginning of her residence in the new house, too, she had begun to keep a garden; and Marriner was amazed at her success. She had ample water for irrigation; and there were three elderly natives constantly at work under her direction. They made plenty of mistakes, and these drove her to distraction, but as the garden grew a little older its production was remarkable.

Especially was this so with the citrus fruits. Pomelos, grape-fruit, three kinds of oranges, limes, lemons and kumquats flourished with amazing vigour; they carried substantial crops at four or five years of age. Mulberries rioted. Papaws set heavy crops in a few months. Strawberries and peanuts both made substantial returns; only a hundred yards away date-palms offered promise. There were passion-fruits and grenadillas. There were pineapples and bananas too, but these did not do so well. Some of the visitors suggested there was not enough iron in the soil. Monica persisted with them, however. In the garden she was an indefatigable experimentalist; she only asked that she be freed of the heavier work entailed.

So her garden was a year-round delight. In season a wealth of grapes dripped from the arbors. The massed flowers of tropical bushes—hibiscus, poinsettia, frangipani, cascara, oleander—gave her a scented privacy. Ginger lilies, cannas, strelitzias, the green-flowered giant lilies all spread their vivid colours; begonias, allamandas and the pink corallita vines ran rampant.

But, like any woman, Monica devoted her most tender care to the poor little scrubs of English flowers which here languished, clinging to life with a pathetic determination, but unable to reproduce more than a pallid echo of their true beauties.

The vegetable garden was as prolific. It produced a series of gluts, one vegetable after another, so that in one week there would be a hundredweight of radishes, and none the next. But the natives could cope with any overproduction, and the hunters grew fat in inactivity.

There were at all times about a dozen grown men in the native camp. There were twice as many girls—too many; and in the case of one or two their sources of income were questionable. Then there were the old people and the children.

Marriner could have employed all the men who offered. He preferred to take those who were more than willing; there were some in the camp whom he had employed before, and would not again. Then there was always, too, a little drifting population, resting between jobs. The promise of constant employment was not, after all, enticing. There was a limit to the attainable desires of a native; more than the simplest things would be denied him no matter how hard he worked. Lazy, he would be as well fed as though he were working; and he liked, as well as any man, a change of occupation.

After an absence of several years, Activity returned again. This time he brought with him a small herd of camels; seven of the creaking, complaining beasts, with packsaddles or riding-saddles for five of them. He was extremely proud of this plant.

"What will you do with them?" Marriner asked.

Activity rubbed his hand slowly up and down his thigh.

"Someday they come in handy," he said.

"Going into the transport business?"

"Might be."

"You going to keep them here?"

Activity looked at Marriner questioningly, but otherwise didn't answer. Marriner nodded.

"All right, Activity. As long as they're not a nuisance."

Monica was at first intrigued, then amused by the sight of the camel herd. Afterwards she became annoyed.

"There are so many things we need. You let him have camels. He'll be wasting his time looking after them. We haven't even got dairy cows."

"Maybe I could do something about that." The household had been sporadically supplied with milk since the birth of James, but the type of cows they milked was so hard to handle and the results so poor that the effort seemed misplaced.

"You should have done something about it years ago. If that pack of natives wanted something you'd give it to them fast enough. They're too lazy even to want."

"I should have done something. We could keep goats."

"We should have goats. And poultry—this eternal beef. Hens and ducks and geese and turkeys."

"Well, why not?" Marriner said. He wondered why they had been so long about it. "I'll speak to Cummings. He can order up some stock."

When the goats arrived, the natives took them to their hearts. They learned to herd them and to milk them. They took the kids to bed with them against the cold nights. Both goats and natives prospered, and there was still less reason to hunt.

Bloodwood was now marked upon the Territory maps. There was a sufficient nucleus of population for the Administration to set up a police post. Marriner relinquished twenty acres not far from the store, and the Administration sent up carpenters. In a little while a constable arrived; a neatly booted man in khaki uniform and blue shirt. He brought a string of good horses and a black-tracker, a villainous-looking, sophisticated native with a broken nose and cauliflower ears; a man who had taken more batterings than he could remember.

13

It was a perversity of fate that Dallas should have been murdered in the month that the policeman took up his duties, and that the policeman himself, making his first official visit as a matter of routine to the Dallas homestead, should have been the one to find the body. It was a black-fellow murder. Dallas had been speared, several times, in the yard near to the hut in which he lived. His stores had been ransacked. He had kept nothing of value on the place, but his belongings, food and some clothes, had been rifled. It was significant that his saddles and harness were untouched. There was very little disturbance.

For Nick Perrin, the policeman, the murder had a special significance, in that it was his first. It also forecast the first important police action in which he was executive. Besides that, it tapped a deep well of fear in him; for he was a young man and, in spite of his training, unused to violence.

He was a well-developed young man, however; big, bluff, callous, a man without finer feelings—something of the type Dallas himself must have been in his youth. He loved the uniform, the power and authority it gave him, and the fact that it enabled him to separate himself from his fellows while remaining in their company. So much had been evident in the brief time he had been at Bloodwood Plains.

From the moment of discovery of the body he might have been at a loss how to proceed but for Quart-pot, his black-tracker, camp servant and general factotum. As soon as he recognized the crumpled heap for what it was, Quart-pot slipped from his horse, motioning his master to keep back, and approached carefully, setting his feet with delicacy on the undisturbed ground and looking for tracks. From a distance of about five yards he circled the body. He moved slowly, sometimes retreating a few steps.

"How old are those tracks?" the constable asked.

"Yesterday, boss. They kill him yesterday. Three fellow."

He made a wider cast.

"Two feller came out, talk along this man," he pointed to the corpse. "One fellow, good way off, throw spear. That this broken spear. Hit'im long side, he turn, other two man club him, spear him some more. No fight, boss. Kill'im quick. Oh, quick."

"What was it for?"

Quart-pot, looking at the ground, did not reply.

He got a complete picture of the scene from the footprints. Although he had never seen them before he would thereafter be able to make a complete and reliable identification of the owners of those footprints, as clearly individual to him as their faces. So he took his time about proceedings; before he went near the shanty that Dallas had called "home" he made a wide cast of the area and established the point at which the raiders had taken their departure with their spoils. That was a trail he would take up later.

In the meantime, Perrin had dismounted by the body. It had stiffened into death so that he had difficulty turning it over, and when he did it groaned of the impetus of its displaced gases. Decomposition was so slight that Quart-pot's estimate of the time of the murder must have been accurate. There was little else to discover from the corpse. The skull had been battered, and he had been speared, in all, seven times. Only one broken spear remained in the body; and the half of this had been carried away.

They had already noted, before finding the body at all, that no natives remained in the near-by encampment. Quart-pot now went thither, walking first round the area, then closely examining the ground between the rough shelters. Perrin came up, but did not disturb him until he had apparently come to a conclusion. There were thousands of prints there in the dusty soil, prints of men and women and children; prints of the hungry, ever-busy dogs that accompanied them, dingoes most of them, not a generation removed from the wild, captured as puppies in some hollow tree, some cave among the rocks, and brought up to help in the hunt.

"Everybody lit out when Dallas was killed, eh?" Perrin suggested, but Quart-pot shook his head.

"No more, boss," he said with decision. "They been gone two, three weeks. Everybody. Fresh prints—them fellers that speared this dead one. Besides them—nothing."

"They were gone, then, before Dallas was killed?"

"That right."

Perrin thought awhile.

"Have a look at the house. Dallas had a gin here, I bet. See where she went. Did she go with the murderers?"

Quart-pot could answer that without investigation.

"No more. Three men only together."

But at the house he looked long and carefully, covering the same ground over and over till Perrin's patience wore thin. The earth floor was covered with prints.

"He got a gin here, all right." Quart-pot pointed to women's clothes hanging on a nail. "She been gone long time too. That Dallas, he been here plenty. Them three, they come in, quick, look round." The spilt flour, sugar and tea would have told Perrin that, anyway. "That gin, she been here. Two weeks ago, three weeks. Same like those people." He pointed with his chin towards the encampment.

"The gin left with the tribe?"

"Maybe."

"What do you mean, 'maybe'? That was what you said, wasn't it?"

"Maybe she been gone longer."

He found good prints of the girl in a corner where, apparently, she had been in the habit of squatting, perhaps while Dallas ate. While she waited for him, anyway. Quart-pot demonstrated the way she had sat to make the prints. He went out again to scour the country round about. Perrin went back to the horses, and led them to water.

After half an hour Quart-pot called him. He went over. The black had found, at a considerable distance from the hut, the old tracks made when the people had left in a body.

"They just go walkabout," he said. "They not hurried. They go away. Some other water hole. Out there." He indicated the west.

"Did the gin go with them?"

"No more." He was still searching, print after print.

"Could you swear to that?"

"No more." After a pause he said, "I don't see her."

"Well, which way did the murderers go?"

Quart-pot immediately indicated the east, back in the direction of Bloodwood.

"All right. When you're finished we'll eat. Then we'll follow them."

"All right, boss."

Quart-pot spent another twenty minutes, crystallizing his impressions. Then he set a fire, boiled a billy, and laid out a meal as though it were just another day.

The trail of the murderers led back consistently to the east without any attempt at concealment. They were able to follow it for the most part at a run, a smart canter sometimes. Quart-pot, from every vantage-point, gauged the direction the men would have taken; and sometimes, on horseback, they cut corners through a patch of ground a man on foot would avoid. At the next vantage-point he would check the tracks with one brief glance. It was a time-saving way of proceeding; had the tracks led off in an unsuspected direction so that they missed them, they had only to go back to the last point of contact and start again. But these murderers had made no attempt, yet, at concealment. Either they had no fear of pursuit, or they had some more elaborate plan in mind.

After two hours' riding they saw, ahead of them, but a little to the left of their track, a man travelling alone. He was a native on foot, and headed in their general direction. Perrin put his horse to the gallop and, followed at a little interval by Quart-pot, rode to head the fellow off. At the end of a quarter-mile Quart-pot rode back to their original line of march, to check the tracks he had been following.

Perrin, however, headed the man, pulled his hack to a sudden stop, tied it to a bush, and walked back the twenty yards or so to where the man now stood. He was a naked savage. In his right hand he carried a woomera for throwing his spears; in his left hand, butts foremost, five slender spears and a couple of boomerang-shaped throwing sticks. As Perrin approached he quickly stooped, turned the spears in his hand and caught them up again, so that they were now point foremost.

Immediately, Perrin pulled his service revolver out of its holster and shot him in the chest. The man gave a high, thin, wavering cry, and as he fell Perrin put three more bullets into him. Quart-pot, spurring his horse, rode over. He looked down at the scene, his face impassive.

"This one of them?" Perrin asked.

Quart-pot dismounted and looked at the man's tracks.

"No more, boss," he said. "Some other fellow."

"Well, he threatened me. He pulled out his spears and threatened me." Quart-pot said nothing, and after a moment Perrin said, "He asked for it."

It was almost as though he had broken a chain of good fortune when he killed the man. They left him lying there, on the red earth; and at the next range they lost the trail.

They lost it, naturally enough, upon a shelf of rock. It should have been comparatively easy to pick it up again beyond, but there was nothing. And at a little distance there was a hillside studded with boulders, naked boulders where bare and careful feet could pass without trace.

They cast all round the hill, and found nothing. They worked until dark, then camped. On the following day they rode at speed for Bloodwood.

There was, as it happened, a considerable gathering at the store. It was a Sunday, and the miners conscientiously kept their seventh day free from work; though they lent it no other religious significance. So there were about eight of them, with one or two of the station men and Marriner himself, when the constable rode over. He brought Quart-pot with him, and the black man stood solitary in the black dark, a little way from the gathering.

Perrin broke his news without preamble.

"Dallas is murdered," he said. "The blacks got him."

The circle of conversation was stilled. Then a voice asked, "How?"

"He wasn't expecting it. They clubbed and speared him out in the open. In front of his house."

"What for?"

"How would I know? They took his rations. Maybe that was what for."

"Them Wailbri. You can't trust them."

"You can't trust any of the murdering bastards. Who are the Wailbri?" the policeman asked.

"Round here, they're Dallas's mob."

"Then it wasn't the Wailbri. They're not there. Haven't been there in a week."

"They were there just over two weeks ago. This is Sunday. Two weeks last Thursday I was there and the blacks were in camp." That was from Hanrahan. "His lubra wasn't, though. Dallas said she'd cleared out on him. It was funny, because her clothes were there. The only clothes I ever saw on her."

"That's nothing. She'll have gone walkabout. If she didn't leave her clothes she'd leave them, anyway, under the first rock she passed," someone else said.

"All right," Marriner said. "What about this? We've never had trouble here. You say it isn't Wailbri?"

"They pulled out two weeks ago. Dallas got his the day before yesterday. The tracks came this way," the policeman said. "We lost them forty miles back; but they were heading this way. I want some help. I want to clean this up, because there's trouble brewing."

"Dallas asked for trouble all these years," Hanrahan said, and Marriner silently agreed. "He's been kicking them round for years. It doesn't pay when you live by yourself."

"Apart from that, there's trouble brewing," the policeman said. "I had trouble myself on the way. And the time to hit it is now, before it works up any more."

"Trouble? What kind of trouble?"

"I had to shoot a coon back there, on my way over. I got off my horse to question him. It looked like he was one of the killers. He wasn't; but he threatened me with a spear. He had a big handful of hooks, and he swung them round and threatened me. So I shot him. He's one good nigger now."

"Just a minute," Marriner put in. "How do you mean he threatened you? Did he put the spear in the woomera?"

"I know when a nigger threatens me. He was carrying the spear butt-first. When I got down he swung it round, carried it point-first. That's threat enough for me. And he meant it. There's something been stirred up here. We've got to get to the bottom of it. And I want some men."

"He was giving you the peace sign," Marriner said. "When a native carries his spears butt-first he's carrying them at the ready. He carries them in the left hand, butt-first, and then he can swing the sockets round into the

woomera at his right shoulder in a second. When he wants
to make a sign of peace and show he's harmless, he swings
them round point-first."

Perrin stared at him for a second.

"Is that so?" he sneered. "Well, I suppose they were
giving Dallas the peace sign as well? Some of you nigger-
lovers want to get it in your heads there's trouble and you
can't afford to let it get away. If you don't stop it straightaway you'll have something on your hands like they had at
Copper Creek, up on the Daly. They wiped out more whites
than you've got here. Now look. I'm going after these coons
tomorrow, and I'm not going to come back till I get them.
And I want some men."

"I've got half-a-dozen good trackers," Marriner offered,
but the policeman gestured the offer away.

"To hell with them," he said. "If they're better than
Quart-pot they'll be damn good. And how would I know
they're not the murderers themselves?"

"They've been out at the stock camp for the last week.
When did this happen?"

"I told you. Two days ago. But even if they've got alibis,
it could be their brothers. What's the name of this tribe
here?"

"Eiliuwarra."

"Well, it's Eiliuwarra work, I'll bet any money. They
headed straight back for here."

Marriner stood up.

"These people have never given any trouble. You want to
make sure of your facts first."

"I'll be sure. And a dead man's evidence enough for me."

Marriner felt sick. The miners were, he knew, siding with
the policeman. That was to be expected. They lived lonely
lives, and were themselves open to attack. None of them had
experienced the companionship of the dark people in the way
that the stockmen had. They had no bond in their interest in

growing things, in movement, in the observation of nature. Marriner could feel the temper of their thoughts.

"Poor old Bluey," someone said.

"I guess I knew him longer than anyone else here," Marriner said. "And saw more of him. It's a hell of a thing to have happen. But I'm not going to talk about it now. I'll see you all in the morning."

In the morning, before any of them had moved, the natives had fled from the settlement. The old people were there, and the younger children. But the able-bodied men had gone; and with them had gone a good many of the younger women. They had gone on foot, and the traces were hard to find because the goat herd and the horse herd had been moved back and forth over the prints; and the fugitives had struck out for the open country in ones and twos.

"This makes you think, eh?" Perrin said to Marriner. "Now we know. The murderers came from here."

"Now, why would they?" Marriner asked. "Would they kill Dallas for rations? They get more and better rations here."

"Why did they run?" the policeman asked. "You know why."

Quart-pot was casting round for the tracks of the fugitives. The miners, mounted and with rifles as usual in the saddle holsters, were waiting. Now and then one cracked a grim joke.

"Where'd you get that coon, Sarge?" someone asked. "He must be the ugliest bastard in the country. I never see a bloke with his face so scarred up."

"He was a handsome colt like you when we got him," Perrin said. "That's what the service did to him. We used to send him into the pubs to buy grog, and if he could get it we'd charge the pubkeeper with supplying natives. It got so every shanty owner in the Territory would beat him up on sight, after they got to know him. Then if he played up on

us, we used to send him over to Big Mickey Shannigan for a
bottle of wine, because we knew that Mickey would give him
the father of a hiding. And Mickey had the law on his side—
he could use force to throw him off licensed premises. So it
kept Quart-pot in order. He's a good boy now. Have you
seen his hands?"

The black fingers were twisted and scarred; and held
stiffly, as though they could not close.

"That came from the time he tapped on Mickey's window
one night," the policeman said. "There was a table just
inside the window, and Mickey put two bottles of wine on it,
wide apart. 'Grab them quick when I open the window,' he
said, and he raised the sash. Silly, here, put in both hands,
and quick as a flash, Mick slammed the window down on his
arms. Then he jumped up on the table with his big boots
and, still holding the sash down, he danced on Quart-pot's
hands till every finger was busted out, with Quart-pot
screaming and yelling outside. We could hear him, but
didn't know what was going on. So we let him be. Well,
he's never got them right since, but he's awful easy to
handle."

After a while, Perrin rode over to Marriner.

"You better stay behind," he said. "I've got a job for
you. You round up all your stockmen, everybody you can
give an alibi for; and keep them from going off, joining these
runaways. That might save them a lot of trouble. But you
better be sure they've got alibis. I'll check them through
later."

Marriner was in two minds. In the first place, he had no
reason to take orders, and he resented the preparations for
the manhunt. But, in the second place, he realized that by
this action he could keep the pick of his men out of trouble.
He did not seriously believe the murderers came from the
Eiliuwarra people at all. Those of them who were not busy
were the ones with little initiative. But he had no real taste

for riding with the policeman, and this was the deciding factor.

"All right," he agreed, and rode off.

From a little distance he saw the riders set out, gather in behind Quart-pot and become committed to the pursuit. They went north. His own way lay east, towards Argadala. Activity was waiting with a saddled horse by the yards, and Marriner called to him.

"You ride with me," he said.

They rode hard towards Argadala, with no thought for the horses.

"What made them all run away?" Marriner asked.

Activity looked solemn.

"Big yabber," he said. "Talk, talk, talk. Plenty fright. This policeman shoot first, shoot old man. Shoot him dead. No questions. Bang, bang, bang, and he's dead. So last night they thought any fellow, a young fellow, like, that could have walked over, killed Dallas, walked back—well, he'd be shot dead too. And they thought maybe if they got to Bluebush Hill they'd stop there for a while. Hard to find."

"The fools," Marriner said. "They should never have run." He thought that over, and amended it. "They should have taken horses." And a third time he said, "They have a chance."

Bluebush Hill was, indeed, a likely citadel. At no point could its walls be negotiated by horses. The heights were pocked with caves. At the top of the many-branched hill was a level plateau, and from a few vantage-points a wide-awake band could easily forecast the direction of pursuit and establish themselves, if necessary, at any other point, equally difficult of access. There were certain water holes, some of only a few gallons' capacity, that could keep the natives indefinitely. The pursuers would have to bring their own unless by great good fortune they stumbled across a native well. The observation of birds would not help them here

—the wells were by habit guarded even against these. Sticks and debris that would float were laid across the surface.

"Policeman will shoot," Activity said.

"There's a danger of that," Marriner admitted. "But I don't think so."

They ride in silence for an hour and a half before Marriner asked the next question.

"What time did they leave?"

"Too late."

"What? You think they won't make it?"

Activity pursed his lips. "This Quart-pot, he's good."

"Who all went? Any of the stockmen?"

Activity looked at him.

"That boy Henry."

"What?" Marriner pulled his horse to a shuddering stop. "Henry? Why on earth Henry?"

"Long time now he's chasing that girl Judy. Judy went along with her daddy."

"But why wasn't Henry out at the camp?"

"He rode in. Long time now he's been like a big calf, a big mickey. Sometimes he rides in, sees that Judy girl."

Marriner tried to remember Judy. He could place her vaguely, as one of the children round the camp. Now that he had put his mind to it he realized that she was woman-sized, a big, happy girl, slim and slow moving.

"I never even knew that Henry had a girl," Marriner said.

"He's got a girl, sure enough. That boy's in love."

"He'll start a fight. If they catch up with him, he'll fight," Marriner realized, thinking aloud.

He turned his horse, and headed for where he thought Blue-bush lay. In a few yards, Activity was alongside him, changing the direction subtly.

"Why didn't you tell me? Why in God's name didn't you tell me?" Marriner asked, but Activity didn't reply.

In the silence it came to Marriner that in some way he had
been prepared to abandon the people; that the presence of
Henry with them made a difference he would not have been
willing to admit. They were his people; it was his place to
be with the policeman when he came upon them. It was his
duty to stand by them; but it was a duty he had not envisaged,
nor would have, except for the presence of his son.

The fool, he thought, as he galloped. The young fool.
But that was wrong, too. For the dark people were Henry's
people; he belonged to the tribe; he was rejected of Marriner's house.

"Who else is with them? Who else?"

Activity recited the names, seventeen names. They were
all names that Marriner knew; a few were good friends.
Some were women; there were one or two older children.
All who were able-bodied and unemployed were among the
fugitives. Why? Was it the upsurge of an old instinct? The
panic counsel of fear?

Marriner rode with an urgency amounting to desperation.
He tried to keep himself calm: there was no need for alarm;
the policeman simply sought an arrest; at least Henry would
have the sense to submit; at least Henry would have the protection of his lighter colour; the people may have had time
to reach the safety of Bluebush Hill.

But when they came to the bodies lying on the plain, he
knew that Henry's would be among them. They were dead,
all eighteen of them. Unarmed, they had been shot, a half-
dozen in a group, then a pathetic straggle, fanned out where
they had made their futile bids for safety. Here was the body
of a thirteen-year-old girl with buds of breasts: it was Jacob's
daughter. Here was a lad who had broken in his first horse
a month before. Marriner had sat on the stockyard rails
with the men and laughed at the boy's juvenile discomfitures
before he found himself shouting with excitement at the
eventual success. There was a mother in early pregnancy.

Once she had been in the little crowd of Henry's contemporaries, the group that played together. Reuben and Walter. Walter had gone away, like Activity, with the camel men, and sometimes, for a little while after that, he had kneeled to Mecca. And Henry. All that joy and quick response, that swift reasoning, that identification with burgeoning nature spilled out with his blood on nature's earth.

This was the end of all those years. The eighteen bodies dotted the plain like the corpses of a herd of cows that had grazed the poisonous gastrolobium; scattered as though the wind had tossed them, a reiterated statement of vengeance. It should have been a savage statement, a statement screaming to the skies; but the bodies lay dumb, testifying to no passions, to no truths save the passivity of death.

Dismounted, Marriner stood a long time looking at Henry. The impulse came to him to drop to his knees and take his dead son in his arms; but he did not. He did not touch him. He looked at him a long time. Then he trudged through the sand from one heap of flesh to the next, his mind dull, his emotions so tense that he hardly knew what he did. Behind him, Activity took the reins of his horse, and just stood. Both horses were nervous; they quieted in Activity's presence.

Cummings, who almost never handled a horse, rode out to meet them coming in, a half-mile from the homestead.

Apart from the stockmen and Roberts, he was the only one who understood the feelings Marriner entertained for Henry. He said nothing whatever when he rode up. It was obvious that he knew of the killings; and that he now knew that Marriner knew. He rode in close and held out his hand. His eyes were swimming, but they were also furious. The first words he spoke made no reference to the murders.

"I sent them home," he said. "I got them out of here. I closed the store."

After a while he said, "They wanted to get drunk."

With these two in his company, Marriner rode through the homestead buildings, and on to where the new police station stood in its fenced twenty acres. The battered, broken face of Quart-pot appeared briefly at the door and disappeared. Almost immediately Perrin came out. He had had a few drinks.

"You murderer," Marriner said. "You bloody murderer."

"Take it easy. Take it easy," the policeman reasoned. "I didn't know he was your son. That didn't come out till it was all over. He just looked like another nigger. If it's any help to you, I'm sorry."

"He didn't even look black," Marriner said. "And if he did? Why did you shoot them? Why? You're a rotten killer, that's why."

"Now, just a minute. You saw us go. You knew what we were doing—we were hunting murderers. Remember Bluey Dallas? Remember he was murdered?"

"You shot them down just for the hell of killing. Little girls. Women. Like a mob of 'roos. With your mouth watering."

"Listen, get this straight," Perrin said, his voice hardening. "I'm sorry for you. But we were hunting murderers. And from now on it will be safe to live in this country. A man won't run the risk of being speared at his camp-fire for a couple of pounds of tea."

"Murderers? Little girls? Twenty years I've lived with these people. There's never been a murderer among them. Dallas was our only murderer. Yes, Dallas. There's never been murderers among the blacks."

"I've got news for you. They were murderers all right. Quart-pot found the tracks. All three. I've got their names. Wallace, Didgery, Jack. All murderers, and all dead. And the rest were accomplices, before and after. And 'while armed resisted arrest.' Now get that straight. This yeller-feller of yours among them. I'm sorry he got killed. I said

that. But you can't make a difference between one nigger
and another at the gallop."

"He didn't even look like a nigger," Marriner repeated.

"Well, he was one. It's in the ordinance. 'Any person of
mixed blood living in a native encampment, or with natives,
or in native fashion shall be deemed to be a native.' If you
want special treatment for your yellow kids, why don't
you see that they live with you? You didn't do much for
him anyway."

"That's enough. . . ." Cummings rode forward. He was
flushed and shaking. Marriner stopped him.

"All right, Cres," he said. "Let's go."

As soon as they had ridden a little way he asked, "What's
that about the Dallas killers?"

"That's what his tracker says. He says the three tracks
were among those of the people on the run. He followed
them all the way. The others identified them, back at the
yards. Wallace, Didgery and Jack."

"Activity?" Marriner asked.

"Yes, Davy?"

"Who killed Dallas?"

Activity said nothing, ready to speak but forming his words,
and producing no sound. He was trying to say the right thing.

"All right. Wallace killed Dallas?"

"That man Didgery throw the spear. Wallace, Jack, they
killed Dallas."

"That's true, then?"

"True."

"Why? Why did they do it?"

Activity rode a little way further before he found the word.

"Pay-back."

"What pay-back?"

"You remember this fellow Mary? She walked all the
time with that Trubbidy? Dallas shoot her. Those old men,
all the time they talked pay-back."

"But good Lord! That was twenty years ago. Why now?"

Activity seemed reluctant to talk.

"That Dallas live along Wailbri country."

"Would that have mattered?"

"They say: Plenty time. They say: Wait yet. Then long time after this Dallas shoot some fellow Hatty. You know Hatty?"

Marriner could dimly remember another girl who had gone from his own tribe to Dallas's bed.

"I remember Hatty."

"That one Hatty belongs to Wallace; that Mary belongs to Didgery. Long time they waited. Then those Wailbri go walk-about, Dallas lose one more lubra, stay by himself."

"Henry knew all this?"

"Now I don't know, for sure. Maybe Henry knew. I think maybe he did."

"All right, Activity."

Not for the first time was Marriner taken at a disadvantage by the native's capacity for keeping his own counsel. But that was a minor aspect of this affair. He felt his own responsibility more heavily than he could have imagined. It was a responsibility based, to a far greater extent than he would have anticipated, upon his mental commitment with the laughing girl Mary; and in the sorrow of his bereavement he accused himself continually.

"If only I had . . ."

If he had been true to himself. If he had made Mary his mistress, instead of Trubbidy. If, having accepted Trubbidy, he had prevented Mary, as his inclinations pointed, from going with Dallas. If, having discovered Dallas's Maudie in her final disposition he had been true to his manhood and confronted her murderer. If, having failed to do these things, he had yet refused the association with Dallas that enabled Dallas to work his holdings, sell his stock, obtain his stores—

this simple lack of co-operation might have driven Dallas from the country. He had betrayed his true friends in his every association with Dallas. He knew so little of them, so little about their motives, their laws and their long memories that he had permitted them thus to betray themselves.

He spurred away from his two companions, the black man and the white, but he did not go to the house. He felt he could not. Instead he went to the harness shed and took a blanket-roll. He rode a little way to an old camp, and slept by himself under the stars. He laid down to sleep and he slept a little; but not much.

His thoughts were with the avengers, and the avengers of the avenged; and the bitter, hard and fierce motives of which their savagery was born. He was not bitter, or hard, or fierce; he was a gentle man; yet all this violence had been born of his presence among the people, nurtured in his own development, and intertwined with his destiny.

In the early morning, when Venus rose on the eastern horizon, he thought of Henry getting up to look for the horses; and he sobbed a little into the canvas on which his head was pillowed.

14

Even in the aftermath, Marriner failed his people. It was Cummings who, without consulting him, reported the slaughter of the tribesmen to the Administration; and it was Cummings who threatened to pursue the affair into the courts of the land. But on the arguments that of the fleeing people three at least were known murderers, that the rest were technically accomplices, at least after the fact, and on the maintained submission that this large body had, while armed, resisted arrest, no action was taken.

No official action; but for other, and unstated reasons, Perrin was removed to another sphere. The new policeman, Gerry Shortland, was a light-hearted, humorous kind of a fellow who was as popular with the natives as he was with the miners; at least, after a period. He trained one of Marriner's stockmen as a black assistant, and through him, armed with the retailed gossip of liaisons and quarrels and jealousies, put himself on a basis of intimate familiarity with the Bloodwood people.

Marriner, more and more, devoted his time to the routines of the stock camp. He was the better able to do this as Roberts, a tireless worker, grasped the essentials of stock raising in the Territory. He did nothing without Marriner's consent; but it seemed to Marriner sometimes that his consent was a formality.

It was as a result of Roberts' urging that Bloodwood became one of the first stations to fence—not only to line the boundaries, but to set up a system of internal fencing. The outer boundaries, indeed, remained unfenced long after other sections were enclosed.

But the separation of the bullocks from the breeding stock ensured a better control of breeding and consequently a better class of cattle; and the additional handling reduced the nervousness of the beasts so that they carried more weight. There was, too, a smaller loss from stock wandering, a greater control of the feed available, and a more efficient use of the waters, both natural and bore-supplied. Marriner was sometimes amazed at the lengths to which Robert's organizing ability could go; and the factors which brought it into operation.

At the old camel camps a new kind of grass, a buffel grass, was growing among the spinifex. It spread slowly, but surely; and it carried nutrition through a dry season longer than any of the native feeds with the exception of the shrubs; and these were not available in all places. Buffel was a good grass. It came from the Middle East, and had been brought accidentally in the padding of the camel saddles; the seed working out a little at a time in the normal processes of wear, and being distributed at the camps when the drying of the sweat freed it from camel-hide and saddle padding.

Roberts looked forward to the day when such grasses would be sown; and he even made some experimental plantings, which did not seem, however, to prosper. The fact was that germination was improved by the period of inactivity the seed spent in the camel saddles, a factor which Roberts, in his limited experimentation, was hardly able to take into account. He was too good a manager, though, to sacrifice the work of the present for such experiments; he noted the possibility of large-scale introduction and stored details in his mind against the future.

For his own advancement, Roberts had registered a brand, and now had a tidy herd of cattle as well as a few good horses running on the station. He paid agistment fees for these, but showed a good book profit. He looked after them with the Marriner cattle, and the time of the stockmen was not charged against the herd. In several years Marriner was surprised by the return Roberts showed.

A great deal of this, however, was dissipated in a single season in which Roberts, as a spare time occupation, set up a sawmill. His expenditure on machinery was considerable. But he had no real knowledge of handling timber, and breakdowns and minor accidents were at first frequent. The only good logs available were those of the local carbean. The trees were scattered, and when cut the logs were exceptionally heavy; and when the planks were sawn the wood warped and twisted, no matter what precautions were taken. Again, in this twisted state, they became as hard as iron, so that each nail-hole had to be bored, and with metal-working bits.

The miners, whom Roberts looked upon as his main potential customers, much preferred to pay a high price for the timber that was laboriously hauled over the track from the South. To unload his product, he had to sell at prices that didn't cover his costs, and even then his mill was idle most of the time. When that stage was reached, he had no hope of getting a price for his machinery.

He was able to sell a little of the timber to Marriner; but he was too honest to make much use of the timber on the station; at least in places where it was not a satisfactory medium. In the finish he took his loss and started again, with a considerable book-debt to his employer. However, he had retained his breeding cattle, and he was a cheerful loser.

There was another business in which he might have made a small fortune. He persuaded Marriner to buy a truck. It was the first motor vehicle permanently in those parts; and it made such good profit that within a few months Marriner had bought another truck and a car. His engineer serviced the fleet, in addition to looking after the windmills and the drilling plant. There was no shortage of drivers. The natives were keen to learn the operation of machines that had such clearly visible potentialities for travel, travel being the life of the tribe; and in a remarkably short time in that desert country several of the more intelligent became skilled drivers.

Marriner personally was completely uninterested in this mechanization. He paid the bills and he took the profits; and with the replacement of the long, slow, horse or camel journey to Quorn the profits were considerable.

The car opened up new fields to his womenfolk. The education of his children had previously been entrusted to a governess; Monica now decided that with transport so much more expeditious, their futures would be best assured at boarding-school. It must have been a wrench for her. Her children were the centre of her life. And it was her decision alone. She sought her husband's assent, but, as with her every other desire, her expression of it was sufficient.

For himself, he hardly missed the children. His real connection with them had extended through no more than an hour or two of the longer evenings of the wet season; and only then on evenings when, as it sometimes happened, there was no company at the store. He was unable to play with children; and they, having nothing to which they could respond, treated him as an amiable stranger. He was, indeed, much more of a stranger to them than the very kitchen-girls.

Monica herself accompanied the children when they went south for the first time. She and her mother had been practically marooned at Bloodwood Plains for several years by their distaste for the rigours of the journey, which rigours, in travelling either with horses or camels, were considerable. And while her mother on the first occasion remained at Bloodwood to provide company and chaperonage for the governess and the youngest child, it rapidly became an institutional jaunt for them, twice a year, to accompany the children to school. Their absences grew progressively longer, and on each return they came fortified with amenities that transformed the house into the semblance of an upper-class suburban residence, and emphasized its separation from the remainder of the buildings that constituted the Bloodwood homestead.

Among these innovations—curtains and carpets, and modern furnishings for the kitchen—Marriner felt himself an alien, ill at ease. To a certain extent, too, he resented the machinery which was invading the station elsewhere—the electrical plant, the trucks and the pumping engines.

When Martin, his head driver, who pushed his trucks twenty to thirty hours at a stretch across the desert, aspired to ownership of the fleet, Marriner happily helped him, taking a financial loss to do so. Martin secured a mail contract, charged a contract price to the station for deliveries, carried passengers and goods, and for a time did splendidly. He was an inventive man; the long sandhills in which other drivers were bogged down, sometimes for days, seldom held him up much; he would forecast trouble, let the air out of his tyres, lay down his rolls of coir matting, or spread the sand lightly with leafy twigs, and methodically defeat the obstacle. He was never caught out without the tools that would help him defeat an emergency.

But he was one of the vast army whose members work better under discipline; and he had no understanding whatever of money matters. Three years after he took over the fleet, Marriner had to come to his financial rescue. It was a costly process; but transport was now essential to the working of the station; and he secured Martin's loyalty forever by assuming his debts and putting him back on good wages.

Through these and other operations Marriner gained a reputation for financial impregnability. When a rival store started on the wolfram fields the proprietors took business from Marriner; but they also drummed up new and previously non-existent business; and Marriner took his profit from carting the goods. When he built a hotel—a drinking-shanty with three or four guest-rooms—to replace the old corner of the store, his neighbours forecast disaster. Then the road-workers came, and the telegraph station; and a ready clientele for him. Cummings took over the management of the hotel. He was a rich man in his own right by now; a confirmed bachelor, a tireless worker, and happy in his niche.

Even the years of drought could not pull Marriner down. There came those years, when water hole after water hole shrunk to a muddy morass, and finally to a stretch of dry and dusty sand. The cattle that had been centred on such a hole would find, or be driven to another one that lasted a little longer. The numbers of cattle round each surviving water hole increased; and when only a few holes were left, they had eaten everything edible for three to five miles from the water. Further than that they could not graze daily and return for their evening drink.

So they weakened daily, dying of starvation, their range still further limited by their weakness; and beyond its peri-meter the desert almost lush with food. Certainly in the droughts the grasses were scarce, but the shrubs and the spinifex carried the wherewithal for survival. The problem of drought was not that there was no feed; it was that the feed and the water were too far apart.

For Marriner, it was much less a problem than for his neighbours. In the first place his plentiful bore-waters did not fail; the concentrations on his surface waters were con-sequently less acute; and at no time did he have to cope with the desperate herds such as thronged the last watering places on other drought-struck stations. And Roberts, with his fences, was able, early in each crisis, to make the best dis-posal of such accumulations of stock as did exist. Again, they were ruthless, shooting old and weakened cows before they could die in the water and foul it; and shooting too, in orgies of slaughter, the concentrations of kangaroos that were driven in from the drier parts back in the hills.

They were also prodigal in slashing and breaking such edible shrubs, close to water, as had grown too tall for the cattle to graze. They worked like Trojans through the drought, and, while their losses were considerable, they came out of it very well. Three weeks after the first rain fell—that is to say, after an interval of twenty completely dry months—they were selling store cattle at enhanced prices to station owners who were forced to buy to build up their depleted herds.

When others bought, Marriner was selling, to rest his land after the beating the drought had given it. When others sold, he bought. He bought in the years of depression markets and low prices; it was at these times that he bought quality cattle to improve his herds. It could not be said that he thrived in the evil times that ruined his neighbours; but he came to little harm.

For this he had to thank his investments, and the wealth of which he himself did not know the boundaries. He also had to thank the men who worked for him. But there was a peculiar quality of acceptance in his own make-up. The wealth came without his asking; the men stayed with him. But he remained unmoved; as he would have remained unmoved by the dispersal of his fortunes and the defection of his men.

In drought-time, after the skies had blazed unbrokenly blue for month after month, and the first few cirrus clouds appeared in the north, he could admire them for their evening beauty; and when the others said, "Rain tomorrow," feel genuinely surprised. On the morrow the clouds would be a little thicker, ride a little further south. Day after day they would form and disappear, but at their height always a little stronger until the day came when they made a thick quilting across the northern half of the sky. Then, a week, perhaps, or a fortnight after the first appearance of the small cloud, the sky would darken completely, and the rain would fall, a thick, lashing rain, heavy and cold, that left the natives huddled shivering in their inadequate shelters, nursing their small fires and waiting for the dawn and the sunshine.

Or perhaps it would fall in the distance, still on the Marriner lands; and Roberts, laughing and singing from sheer relief, would set about making his dispositions for the transfer of cattle. For within a week one of the native grasses would have sprung to its full development; in another twelve days it would have disappeared, its place taken by another of more permanent habit. Within a couple of days of the first downpour the standing grasses would have become more palatable. The effect of rain was immediate.

Marriner, too, was happy after rain; but his thoughts were not wrapped up in the circumstance. Sometimes when it rained in the upper reaches of the river, and the water came tumbling down over the sand of the dry watercourse, he would watch the tangle of debris it carried, look for the snakes and lizards swimming in the water, without a thought for the water holes the flood would fill. Like his own natives he had substituted acceptance for seeking. Like them he was an exploiter, now tied to the purposes of conservation. Like them, his enjoyment was of the day; the future was with the past in being beyond his control.

Had Marriner been a failure; had he been a poor man eking out a miserable existence on a poverty-stricken holding; or a man, say, working for one of his fellows, this attitude would certainly have condemned him. He would have been reckoned reckless, irresponsible, even a "hatter." But, linked with Marriner's Midas touch, the attitude moved beyond the understanding of his fellows. It was thought to be the mask of a man who knew all the answers, who had all the eventualities covered; acceptance was misread as imperturbability, carelessness as strength; he was seen to be courageous, independent, well informed, secure, impregnable.

His appearance in these days of his middle age cemented these impressions. In repose he was very still. He spoke little, was never agitated. He was a great deal in his own company even when he was in the presence of others. His was the last opinion given on any subject, the first sought. It usually ratified the opinion of the man who knew the subject best—Martin, Cummings, Roberts, each in his own field. On local matters he was well informed, for the natives told him a great deal; far more than they confided in other whites. His subterfuges—"We'll see," or "We'll come out of it"—were accepted as the most inspired of prophecies.

His tall figure was a little stooped now, but only a little. He was lean, in spite of his wealth. His face had hardened, its lines firmed, so that his recessed lower jaw now gave no first impression of weakness. His blue eyes seemed to have faded a little with the years, but the crow's feet in which they were nested, the lines that stamp the man who of habit looks into distances, were more impressive than the eyes themselves. His hair was iron-grey and vigorous; it was the hair of a man many years younger than Marriner. His hands looked strong, and above all they were quiet hands, never restless; and this circumstance enhanced the impression of strength that surrounded him.

He seldom found that any situation deteriorated while he thought about it. There was the matter of Casey; Henry's younger sister, Trubbidy's daughter, and his own. She had grown up a little wild girl, with the tribe, but despite his neglect of her, he felt he had some sort of moral responsibility towards her; and he had therefore been disturbed when he first discovered that Roberts had entered into a liaison of sorts with her. He was more than disturbed; he was angered. But on sober reflection he felt that if she were going to enter into any relationship with anyone—and it was too much to hope that she wouldn't—Roberts was easily the best choice she could make. Between Roberts and any of the other white men in the district there was no comparison. The alternative for Casey was a native.

In thought and in upbringing she was native herself. She had a few advantages, because of the extra supplies with which he had kept Trubbidy supplied; but she had no education, no schooling whatsoever. In a wild kind of way she had beauty. She had the lost, the searching eyes of her mother. She had a determined face, slashed across with a wide red gap of a mouth. She had brilliant teeth and a ready smile. Her hair was beautiful, light brown and wavy. She had a good figure, and she was lithe and active.

When he first thought of interrupting the romance, or as he considered it, the liaison, Marriner was stayed, paradoxically, by the thought of his own responsibility. From his own appreciation of Roberts, he realized the rightness of her new devotion. If he should destroy their happiness, for he supposed they had found happiness, with what could he offer to replace it? And on moral grounds, how could he object?

That Casey was indeed happy became more and more apparent. After the affair had gone on for several months he relegated it to the back of his mind. When Casey, throwing caution to the winds, moved into Roberts's isolated hut, Marriner thought again of making a protest, but Roberts took the wind out of his sails.

"You knew about it, didn't you?" he asked. "About Casey?"

"Yes, I knew."

"I'm very fond of her. I'll look after her."

"I know that, boy. Just be careful. I don't know that Mrs. Marriner . . . Well I wouldn't like her to know. She might make something of it—well, there's the children to think of."

"We don't want any trouble."

"She's a good girl, Casey."

"She's clever. I'm teaching her to read and write. She's quick."

"You're what?" Marriner was taken by surprise.

"I'm teaching her. She learns quickly. You wouldn't believe how quickly."

"I'd never have thought it. We'll put her on the pay-roll. Get Cres to find a job for her."

Roberts laughed. "I can see Cres with a woman secretary. You wouldn't get him into the office. Seriously though, I didn't think she had it in her. She learns quicker than I ever did. I wish I could get someone to teach her to sew. She tries; then something stops her and she gives up. She gives up too easily. But it would be different if someone would show her."

Marriner thought uneasily of his womenfolk.

"Keep her at her reading. One thing at a time."

But he was glad when Roberts had spoken to him. He disliked having to pretend to ignorance.

Still another link with the past had turned up again. Three or four years before, Mission Mo had worked out his gold claim. For a pocket it had paid a surprising dividend. Mo had gone off to enjoy a limited prosperity that with care might have lasted him his lifetime. But care was not in Mo's make-up, not, anyway, in regard to financial matters. However Spartan he could be among the ranges, with the scantiest of supplies between him and his eternity, he was prodigal, apparently, in the city with money in his pocket. He came back, anyway, motherless broke, as he said himself.

He didn't ever give much indication of the way in which his money had gone. Horses took their share, and probably women. Surprisingly, while it lasted, his money had taken him through the South Seas, and given him colourful memories of lagoons and tropic moons. In all probability, Marriner thought, he had not gone alone, but he was as secretive about the details of his experiences as he had always been about his earlier life.

In essence, he was unchanged. He wanted nothing but to search for the mother lode once more; the search meant more than the discovery. Marriner happily enough grubstaked him; gave him of the best: new saddles and gear, the pick of the quiet horses.

Both of them were delighted with the renewal of the old relationship. It took Marriner back to the days when he was at Bloodwood; the happy, feckless days without responsibility. It made Mo happy with the peculiar independence it gave him; an independence from the routine of finding his own living. His tie to Marriner was for him a small price to pay for the limitless provision of his daily wants, small as these might be.

The renewal of this partnership was the more rewarding to Marriner for the reason that Bloodwood Plains now bore little resemblance to the insignificant soak where the Eiliuwarra were camped so many years before. Three busy windmills dominated the skyline. There was a road, a frequently busy road, on the other side of which half-a-dozen houses flanked the police station. There was the hotel, the store, the big sheds where the trucks were garaged. And linking all these, small subsidiary roads, metalled with river gravel and kept in good repair.

In contrast was the painted homestead, set in its burgeoning gardens, but to Marriner's eye unbelievably out of place.

The house was a picture; its lawns green and forever cool from the sprinkled water, its boundaries marked with groves of flowering trees, its verandahs cool and restful. The tall columns had long before been brought and installed as a handsome front entrance; the place looked groomed, and was dignified by its outer simplicity.

But Marriner, in the perversity of his fifty years, liked best the other side of the dry river—the scattered collection of

native humpies, even ugly as they were now with their
additions built of rusty discarded iron, the roughly flattened
sides of fuel drums, torn pieces of corrugated roofing, scraps
of wall-board and patches of tin. They were ugly, but they
were familiar, peopled with familiar people. They stretched
a couple of hundred yards along the bank, and then there was
a little space to the whip-pole and the cattle yards. The goats
frequently browsed on the rough herbage beyond the encampment, careless of the children and dogs that sunned
themselves on the ground between the huts.

Activity's camels often grazed there too, or stood for
hours, heads up, oblivious of their surroundings, gazing into
the distances where their abilities were supreme. There was
seldom any work for them, and no one disturbed them.
Activity sometimes spent a little time with them, and sometimes one or two of the bolder small boys; but for the most
part they enjoyed an amiable and solitary retirement. They
were simply monuments to an epoch swiftly vanished.

Monica now disliked the sight of the camels, but she could
ignore them. The morning cry of the whip-pole, however,
still aroused her to anger, whenever she heard it. Its parts,
the bucket on a rope, the long lever, the forked tree that
was its fulcrum, had all been renewed, and several times; but
it seemed never to have lost its noisy protest, the whining,
creaking, groan and splash that accompanied its use. It was
accompanied always by cheerful laughter, noisy badinage,
as the women and children gathered round with bottles and
basins and old chipped enamel jugs, or cans that had once held
oil, and collected their household supply.

"You can run a pipe down to the camp and put a tap on it.
There's no need to go through this every morning," she
scolded Marriner.

"I'll see about it," he said, as he had said before.

"You never will," she told him shrewdly. And, with the
quick change of front which characterizes some women, she

added, "Anyway, I don't want that. If you lay water on there that will make the camp permanent. They should be cleared out of there altogether. Let them go to Argadala."

"They were here before me," said Marriner. It was the one point on which he was really stubborn.

"If that argument was good, you'd never have been here at all," she pointed out, with perfect logic. "Thay can go. They'd be better off at Argadala. They've got water there, all the time."

"This is their place. This is their dreaming-place," he said, in the natives' own idiom, and she made a sound of disbelief, of rejection.

"This place will never look anything while they're there. Not till you clear out all that rusty iron. And have Blood-wood so that it isn't surrounded at all times, by packs of dirty kids. Dirty, ragged, smelly kids."

"You forget this is a cattle station. I have to have stock-men."

"They're working away far more often than they work here. You've got trucks. You can bring them on the job. It's not the stockmen anyway; it's the useless ones I'm talking about. They can live elsewhere."

He walked away without bothering to bring the argument to a conclusion. He was fond of Monica to a certain degree. He gave her everything she wanted; and on her part it could be said that she never wanted anything out of reach. But on the rock of the native encampment they always split.

15

In the year that young James, Monica's eldest son, was sixteen, he announced his intention of leaving school and learning to manage the station. Marriner was taken unawares. He had been hardly more than conscious of the lad's presence when he was home on his occasional vacations; and then thought of him only as a lad who, though he had learned to ride, much preferred playing with the younger members of the family on the green lawns.

James now, however, was nearly six feet tall. He had to wear spectacles and was already slightly stooped. He had a pink and white complexion that was purely of the city. His relations with his father were formal, almost to the point of being distant.

"Go back to school," Marriner advised him. "Learn accountancy. That's what you'll need for running a station in your time. Leave the rest of it to others."

"But you're not an accountant," James demurred.

"No. But Cummings is the next thing to one. This place started with one man and I had time on my hands. Years of time. And I was running it as a station before I knew it. It grew with me. Now it's a business. If you want to make it yours, learn accountancy."

"I'm sure," said Monica, "if Creswell Cummings could learn to run it, James can learn from him."

"Possibly he can." Marriner remembered something a soldier had told him years before. "But it isn't sufficient to stay in one place. He has to be ahead of the game."

"Couldn't he have a year? And if he finds it necessary to

learn accountancy, or anything else, couldn't he go back again
to college?"

Monica was hungry for the companionship of her son, and
Marriner recognized the symptoms.

"All right," he said. "We'll see how it works out."

And perhaps it was the presence of his son, as a trainee in
ownership, that decided him, for the first time since his
marriage, to take a holiday. To his surprise the suggestion
was received favourably by his wife. He wanted to go north,
away from the business commitments which would ensnare
him in Adelaide; away from natives, cattle and deserts. He
decided he would return to his first home.

There was nothing of nostalgia to influence his decision.
He wanted to pick up no relinquished threads, renew no old
acquaintances, freshen no happy memories. But once he was
committed to the journey nostalgia gripped him fast.

Particularly was this so in the early stages. A road now
crossed the country where he had struggled painfully with
Edrington's plant of horses. In a day in the car, without
pushing too hard, he crossed the distance that had taken him
six weeks. The road ran straight, taking no account of
water holes; but here and there it passed landmarks he recognized, or thought he recognized; and the old man who was
Marriner now lived much with the young man whom
Edrington had saved. It was inconceivable at this distance
that he had known so little, been so innocent. But—and
this too, occupied him briefly—how much had he learned?
And how greatly had he changed?

He was being driven by one of the younger natives, and
had nothing but his surroundings to occupy his thoughts. In
places where the desert had once stretched away without
signs of civilized life, now grazed cattle bearing brands
familiar to him. He called at the stations and was made
welcome. The name of Marriner was a sufficient introduction; but he was impatient or dissatisfied with the hospitality

he received. Rather testily he wondered sometimes whether it was Marriner or his EGE brand they entertained. Sometimes, but less often as they went further north, he was personally acquainted with the owner.

Few of these stations displayed anything of the wealth that was evident at Bloodwood Plains. Some were mere huts in the sand, a shelter for a man and his wife, with a windmill and a yard for cattle. Others were more elaborate. But he could see nothing that was lacking at Bloodwood; and his fencing system, his watering troughs, his yards and his machinery were all much more solidly contrived than anything here.

Marriner and his driver took their time to the Queensland border, and here, at the mining town of Mount Isa, he sent the car back and waited for the train.

Mount Isa repelled him. It was a boom town, peopled by hungry shopkeepers who sought only to skim as much as they could from the well-filled pockets of the miners; to make their pile and get out; and to reject whatever associations would not advance these ambitions. By contrast, when, after a three-day rail trip, he reached the sea at Townsville he revelled in the unsolicited hospitality of strangers. In a holiday resort on an island off the coast he stayed nearly two months, swimming in the quiet sea, soaking in the moisture-laden sun.

He was travelling light. He bought his requirements as he needed them. And he had no communication whatever with Bloodwood. He would have stayed on the island forever except that some prickings of conscience urged him to be about his business.

He dutifully visited Brisbane, his home town, as he had intended. The corner store he had once owned was gone; the widening of a highway had taken both it and the house; and at the proximate position was a garage, with new-fangled pumps for the sale of petrol. He spent an afternoon wandering about the neighbourhood, and recognized a couple of names from his youth; but he made no attempt to see anybody he might once have known, nor was he anywhere recognized.

The traffic, the material changes in the city amazed him; but not for long. He was quickly adjusted.

He kept moving—Sydney, Melbourne, round half the coast of Australia to Adelaide. He arrived there a little more than three months after he had departed from Bloodwood. He had thought of looking up his agents, his bankers, and others; but before he could do so, in a chance meeting he ran into Roberts; a different Roberts, a Roberts in city clothes and with the beginnings, already, of a city pallor.

"Good to see you," he said, reluctant to release the younger man's hand. He meant it, too. Roberts brought the aura of the desert.

"But what are you doing here?" he asked.

Roberts forced a wry grin.

"I work here now."

"The hell you do!"

"Yep. That's the way of it. I'm working here."

"You've left me then?"

"The other way round. I got my marching orders."

"They can't do that, boy. Come back with me. What happened? Who fired you?"

"I'm not going back. It was Mrs. Marriner fired me. But I was happy to go. It was over Casey. It all came out. So she told me to get off the station. So I did."

"I told you to be careful."

"It was bad advice. A good father would have told me to get married. But you were never Casey's father, were you? Not really."

Roberts's face, now that Marriner looked more closely, was white and strained. They were standing near the railway station at the edge of the city proper, and there were seats on the sidewalk. Marriner took Roberts by the elbow and led him to one.

"Sit down. I want to know. I want to get this straightened out. I want you back with me, boy. I'll set you up—I'll sell you a thousand miles or so, a good block. You've got cattle, horses."

"That's something you can do. You can buy my stock from me. Give me a price. I'll take your first figure. It'll be fair. I need the money. I need to set myself up."

"Here in the city?"

"Here in the city."

"You can't do it, boy. You couldn't live here."

Roberts was looking at him peculiarly.

"There's Casey. You didn't ask about her. She's with me. We're married."

Marriner was not expecting that. He waited a moment, not saying anything; but Roberts outplayed him, waiting too.

"Well, I'll wish you every happiness, boy. You and the lass."

"Thanks. Anyway, she's the reason I won't be living in the country. Not any more. Not in all my life. Here, I've got a flat, near the sea. You know what happens? The girl in the flat next door drops in; just like that. Just friendly. She teaches Casey housekeeping. They work together and we all go out together, two husbands and their wives. She's shown Casey how to do her hair. Casey's blossomed. You wouldn't recognize her. I'm proud to have her on my arm when we go out."

"Why, that's wonderful."

"Wonderful, you say. Well, it is. And if I go out of town, back to the country, she's just another gin. Can't you hear them, the way they'd talk?—the way they talked at Bloodwood? 'Good-looking stud you've got. How long have you had her? Where did you pick her up?' Not for me. I've found something, and I'm going to keep it."

"I'd like to come and see you both."

"Yes. Well, I wouldn't like you to. In fact, you'll stay away. We've been good friends. You've been a good boss. Good to me. But for Casey you're the old life, and she's found a new one. So stay away. She's developing, and fast. I don't want her put back where she was, not even for the little time you'd see her. And if you want to know something else, it wouldn't be good for you either. You're her father, remember. And if you were to see her the way she is now you'd be thinking for the rest of your life what you could have done for her yourself. That's if you've any kind of feelings in you."

The fire seared through the words. Marriner sat still in the sunshine, staring at the city traffic without seeing it. He spoke after a long time.

"Well, I've wished you luck, boy, and that goes for both of you. About the girl—well, I'm sorry. I've done nothing for her, that's the truth. I've done nothing because there wasn't any time when I could see what to do. I don't know yet, and you don't know, whether she's going to be happy your way, in the long run. But I'm glad she's happy for a time. I'm glad I bumped into you, boy. And sorry that I came out so badly."

"You'd have bumped into me, anyway," Roberts said. "I've been haunting Masterman's, waiting for news of you. They'd have let me know when you came and where you were. I want you to buy those cattle of mine. I'll need the cash. At market prices there's eleven hundred quid in them. The market's dropping. Give us the even thousand and we'll call it square."

"Of course." Marriner pulled out his cheque-book and wrote slowly and carefully. He made the cheque out in the figure of two thousand pounds. When he handed it to Roberts the young man tore it across.

"That's not the one I want," he said, and handed back the

pieces. "There's a thousand pounds, give or take a little. Not two thousand. I can hear them saying, 'There goes Roberts. Old Marriner paid him a fortune to take his yellow daughter off his hands.' It's no good to me."

"A wedding present?" Marriner suggested. He felt battered.

"Eleven hundred pounds, if you like. I earned that. I want no more."

Marriner wrote out the second cheque and they parted. He went straight back to his hotel room, and the following morning, early in the morning before the city was awake, he caught the train to Quorn.

The altered atmosphere at Bloodwood hit him before he got out of the mail-car—his own car, driven by his own employee. For a moment he wondered what was missing. The sunshine was as fierce, the faces were familiar, the buildings were not altered. But the children had gone, the ever-present swarm of thin-legged native urchins did not materialize. He knew at once what must have happened and walked over to check, even before he went to the house.

The native encampment was gone. No trace of it remained. Not even the bones discarded by the native dogs were left on the spot; only the scars of beaten earth where the footsteps had worn paths between the huts. From the look of things, Activity's camels had gone with the people. And the goats. There were half-a-dozen milch nannies feeding quietly together, but the big herd of goats, three hundred or more, had gone.

The untrained eye would never see that this had been a tribal home; the people had gone without trace. But for Marriner it was different. Every suitable tree carried the scars on its trunk where a bark plaque had been cut away to make a coolamon to cradle a baby, or serve as a household dish. The ancient tracks of the hunters centred upon this spot. And in addition he had his knowledge; he remembered the incidents that marked each tree, each clump of bushes, each feature of the land.

The whip-pole was gone. It had been torn down and the hole in the soak beneath filled up with sand. He felt sorry about the whip-pole, and loitered round the place where it had been. Its cranky music had marked his days; it was the first sound that had ever come to him in this place where he had lived his life. He could see it, with the women clustered about it, malicious in domestic gossip, happy in the lightness of their marital servitude, loving with their children.

At the house, Monica welcomed him warmly, perhaps a little warily. She chattered about a number of things in which he took only a superficial interest. James was riding with the muster, and liked it. There was a new policeman. One of the road contractors had brought his wife and was living in the hotel while he built something more permanent. And:

"Roberts has left us," she said.

"I know. I ran into him in Adelaide. We discussed it. I paid him for his stock."

"His stock?" She was vague.

"How about the natives? When did they go?"

She had been waiting for it. She nodded.

"I knew you wouldn't like it. We shifted them right after you left. They're at Argadala; and James tells me they're very happy there. The gardeners are camping on the verandah at the back of the store in the meantime. The house-girls are living in the hut where Roberts used to be. And everybody is much better off. You should have shifted them all years ago."

"This was their place. This was their dreaming. They belonged here."

"Well, they're quite happy where they are. And you've no idea what a relief it is. That whip-pole was wearing me down, screeching and groaning every morning, and the women screeching with it."

"You had to shift that too."

"Well, with the people gone, there was no possible use for it. There never was any real use for it, anyway. Honestly, Dave, you've no idea what an improvement it's been. All those children gone. You know how the filthy little brats were always underfoot. And the view from the garden! It's improved out of sight."

He knew all the arguments before she mentioned them. It was on account of his stubbornness that they had not prevailed before.

Cummings, he found, was also enthusiastic about the change.

"We're a long way better off for it," he said. "Should have done it years ago. And we're going to have a lot less trouble with the girls and the crowd from the pub."

Well, that was true. Miners and road-menders, fortified with rum, debauched the younger girls, or attempted to, on every possible occasion. And it was not as though the people had been shifted to alien soil. Argadala was their country too. Still, even a black man has roots; even a black man has his loves. That was not the argument to produce.

"What about the men? How do we get on with the men based at Argadala?"

"Well, that's been working well, too. We're working the cattle with Argadala as a centre. Roberts started to enlarge the yards there—you know about Bob?"

"I talked with him in Adelaide. I bought his stock by the way—you can look after that. It's all station cattle now."

"I was sorry about that. I didn't know what to do. I couldn't get in touch with you. And there was no way things could be patched up."

"No. I couldn't patch them up myself."

"Well, anyway, we finished the yards to Bob's design;

and now it's just as easy to work the cattle from there, or easier, than it ever was here. It's more central for one thing, for the musters. Then by the time cattle are moving through this way—and they only come on their way to the markets—the men have got their camp outfits with them anyway. If we want men here at other times, we only have to send a truck. It has simplified the work from this end, it really has. And I thought, for the permanent hands here in the garage and the gardens, we'd put up a bit of proper accommodation."

"Do as you like. In the meantime anyway, I want to get hold of Activity. I want to have a look round and I'll take him with me."

"He's around. There's a truck going out in the morning. They can bring him in."

"Don't bother. I'll go out with it. Most of the horses are at Argadala?"

"That's right."

Cummings had a few questions for him. He was surprised, a bit dismayed, that Marriner had not called on Masterman's.

"They've been going to ship us a windmill for the past two months, but there's been no word of it."

"Where are you putting it?"

"Blowfly Creek. Oh, you didn't know. Well, a whirlwind got the mill at Blowfly, twisted it all up. You never saw such a mess. Nothing worth saving. Vanes all ripped from the fan, stanchions twisted over. No chance of repairing it, even if the metal weren't strained. A couple of weeks ago the tank was dry too, and young James shifted all the cattle away from there. Good boy that. He's learning fast."

"Bloodwood doesn't need me. I can see that," Marriner said. He grinned a bit ruefully.

Of them all, he was most pleased to see Activity.

"Run in a couple of good horses," he told him. "And get your swag ready. I'm going to have a look round for a few days."

"Yowai, Davy." Activity grinned from ear to ear.

"How do you like this camp?"

"Don't know, Davy. All right, maybe. Good camp."

But Activity was troubled. Like Marriner he was beginning to show the signs of his age. He was probably older than Marriner; and he carried more weight, was more thickset. A little grey now showed in his straight, fine hair, a little grey on his stubbled chin.

"I've been waiting for you, Davy. I think maybe I'll go walkabout again. I think I'll take my camels and go away."

Marriner shook his head.

"Nobody wants camels any more, Activity. No use for them."

"I got a use for them. I got a real friendly feeling for them, you know that, Davy? I'll take my camels and go away. I thought, I'll wait for Davy. Maybe ride round one last time, like we're doing. And then go. This is my country, but it's different, Davy. Someday I'll come back again. But I'll go now, soon."

They rode out past Bluebush Hill. It was seldom that anyone came this way. Except when, after the rains, the succulents flourished amongst the spinifex, cattle never grazed so far from accessible water. There was game here, emus and kangaroos; but it was never worth while to ride far after game. Marriner chose their route because of an unspoken desire to visit the place where Henry was buried; and Activity, seeming to understand, accompanied him without comment.

The bodies lay at no great depth, all together within the perimeter of a rough oblong, the corners of which were marked with stunted cairns of small stones. Henry lay with the rest. He had chosen to be with them, and Marriner felt it right that he should rest there. He was the one who lay nearest to the northern cairn; it was his memorial.

They did not stay long. They didn't dismount, but sat a little while, leaning forward against the pommels of the stock saddles. Between the stones the earth was indistinguishable from that outside: it carried a thin covering of spinifex, a few thriving bushes of the red-flowered desert fuchsia, one spindly, twisted hakea sapling; and the red earth was marked with the tracks of lizards and birds. It might have lain thus undisturbed a thousand years, except for the evidence of the cairns.

But the grave could never recall the memory of the light-hearted Henry as the country itself recalled it. The weather was the best of winter weather; cloudless, hot, sunny days tempered to sparkling keenness by the south-east breeze, clear cloudless nights, cold enough to make the fire welcome. The land was glorious with colour, thrusting with life.

Bluebush Hill, Lubra's Leap, Love-a-duck, the Pill-box, Fiddler's Soak—they rode from one to the other, tracing the boundaries of the five thousand square miles. The clear air, the unfettered movement, the simple demands of travel eased Marriner, tranquillized his spirit, set him free. As of long custom he made decisions for the future—in the round enclosed valley they called the Pill-box the wild horses had bred up too fast; they must be rounded up and, at the first opportunity, the stallions must be shot.

He felt a pang at the decision. A glorious, well-nourished horse, a bay gleaming like burnished copper, ran a band near the entrance to the Pill-box; racing them away from the unknown menace the strange riders represented, wheeling round behind them slashing the laggards with his teeth, then, stretched flat to the ground, bursting into unbelievable speed to turn the mare in the advance, running briefly beside her for a moment of her loved companionship before he returned to the rear of the mob and his duty there.

"Look at that buck run!" Marriner told Activity, his eyes shining.

238

"I'd like to fork that horse. He's pretty." Activity's understatement was the highest praise.

The days were full of such highlights. One evening, out on the eastern boundary, near the hill they called Diamond Head, they panicked a little mob of cattle; and a young calf, heedless of all the warnings his mother had ever given him, split away from the mob. Activity raced after it, tried to turn it. It beat him and, blatting madly, thrust through scrubby country for the horizon. At that hour its noisy presence was a dinner invitation for the dingoes; and therefore they had to take the mob back to the calf, that being more practical than the reverse. They had a half-hour of hard riding, and finished glowing from their exertions.

They had been away a week before they turned for home, and planned their first stage to take them to Blowfly Creek. They turned the corner of the hill in the blazing heat of an afternoon to come upon the ruined windmill, a monument to the terrific wrenching power of the dust-devils. The thin steel members of the frame were twisted as though they had been softest copper; seventeen of the twenty metal vanes had been stripped from the fan; the tail of the windmill, which kept its angle to the wind, was untouched, and still moved the broken wreck within a circumscribed arc, pointing obliquely to the sky instead of horizontally.

The tank beside the mill was dry; a thick layer of mud in its bottom was cracked into a jigsaw pattern of bricky plaques. The long troughs were empty; the parrots which had thronged this place when the troughs were full had adopted some other meeting place; the yards had the abandoned air of a lost enterprise.

Marriner and Activity had ropes and a bucket in the packs, and they led the horses up the remembered slope of the hill to the obliquely slanting chasm in the rock. They approached the overhanging side of the lip. From here it would be easier to drop the roped bucket into the water.

Marriner held the horses while Activity walked to the edge. He looked over and froze, as though some shock had checked his movements. Marriner dropped the reins he held and walked forward.

For a second he did not know what they were, the three black blobs that floated in the water not far below. Then, in horror, he recognized them. They were the bodies of women, floating, buttocks upward, head down and limbs trailing, the hair streamed out in the water. It was unbelievable. It was not to be denied. The hot sun beat on them, the water, green-tinged, sparkled about them with a lively vigour; they floated, dead, without movement in that windless place.

It was easy, after all, to reconstruct what had happened; the three women, on walkabout from Argadala, coming to this place and the tank dry; but the ancient water hole of Blowfly Creek a constant insurance against their thirst. So they had followed the remembered and never-practised instructions; they had got beeswax and bloodwood sap and spread it on hands and feet. And the first girl had gone down to the water and in the hot sheltered pool she had taken time off to swim; and called to her companions so that they joined her. And then when she had swum enough she had tried to climb that precipitous slope, and the adhesive had washed from her hands, and she could not.

Or perhaps they had not mixed it carefully or well in the first place. Or perhaps they had the wrong ingredients. And certainly they had not scampered up and down that place as children, and learned the poise and balance that supplemented the material recipe.

And there in a torment they had realized their fate. How long the transition? From the moment when, having cast their cares aside with their clothes, the girls had played unthinking in the pool, until the realization they were trapped? How long?

They must have been there many hours, clawing at the impervious rock, struggling and straining; working together and alone; two helping one, gaining a yard or two from the water's edge and falling back, screaming in panic towards the last; living too long; dying of weakness before they drowned.

They were too young to have learned the ancient arts; these were not much taught after the cattle came. These people had become alien to their own lands. The smooth cliffs had been a place of play and happiness to those who learned to live with them; now they had become the instruments of torment, the instruments of death; the cliffs and the placid water, and the serene and lovely loneliness of this ancient well.

Marriner could not take himself away. As vivid as this, its contorted counterpart, he remembered the first time he had seen the chasm in the red-shouldered hill: the two girls, Mary and Trubbidy, seated at the brink, smearing their pink palms with the black adhesive paste; then going lightly over the lip of the flue; the muscles flexing under the naked skin, the pointed buttocks outthrust, the limbs deliberate in co-ordinated rhythm, the long lean thighs that were such delicate columns of strength, the sensitive fingers, the laughing faces, the sounds of laughter and happiness.

And, as clearly as though he could see, he could imagine this later scene: the frantic struggle for the unavailable hold, the moment for reflection, the determined renewal of the assault, the bleeding fingers, the contorted faces, the shrill agony of the useless screams.

And the last one, a companion of death and waiting for death; the last to die, a prisoner waiting. How long did she have to wait, there in the deep water? What did she think? What did she remember? What did she hope for?

Here, and in this place, Marriner saw vividly and for the first time the whole tragedy of the tribe. And in it he was

integral. For the Eiliuwarra people had accepted him, and
that was all. That was their only transgression against their
laws. They had paid for his meat with their services; to his
profit they had lost their land and their inheritance. He had
in no way improved their lives: they paid him back their
wages to buy the clothes they would not have needed had
he not been there. And when he had usurped their time,
when their children learned to play with bottle-tops instead
of miniature weapons, when their men forsook the use of the
spear for that of the rope, he usurped their inheritance. They
had let slip the wisdom that had sustained them through the
vanished ages; they had put little that was useful in its
place.

It was the broken windmill that had brought the tragedy;
the winds of this land had vanquished the windmill as they
could never have vanquished the knowledge, the ability,
the skill he had seen once in the two black girls who climbed
the cliffs like lizards. It was the windmill that the later
women had depended upon; it was the windmill that had
broken, and broken the women with it. Time must defeat a
windmill; man, without possessions, is unconquerable. And
these people of the plains remained unconquerable as long
as they remained fortified with their own wisdom; not subject to destruction, shielded from hunger and thirst, armoured
against the implacable earth. Marriner could see it clearly.

They left the bodies in the pool and rode away. It seemed
right to leave them there, even when they watered the
horses from that place. They could not camp, but rode
through the night and came to Argadala; and on that ride
Marriner came to a decision.

It was the first decision of any moment he had ever made in
this coun'ry; it was the first time he had made a decision and
not followed an indicated course.

"I'm going away," he told Activity. The black man said
nothing. He was silent, as a friend must sometimes be.

"You remember this place the first time I came?" Marriner asked. "You remember how it was?"

Activity nodded.

"I'm going to find another place like that. I'm going to go again, until I come to a place where the people have no horses, no cattle. I'm going to find that place and stay there, like I stayed at Bloodwood. A place like Bloodwood was, and the camp, and the whip-pole; the way it was when I came. And the people hunting."

They rode for a while in the silence, in the moonlight; the hoofs shuffling through sand, chinking sometimes on a rock; the harness jingling when the horses lifted their heads, the leathers creaking a little.

"You know some place like that still, Activity? Is there a place like that still left?"

"Nor'west, Davy. Some fellows out there. It's a long trip. I go with you."

Without reining in, Marriner looked over at him. It was not the first time he had been astonished by Activity's ability to match his wilder thoughts; it was, perhaps, the most significant.

"You know a place?"

"Sure, Davy. They still there."

"You'd come with me? Straightway? We'll get fresh horses and go. Say nothing to anybody. Just go, as though we're riding the boundaries some more."

"Camels, Davy. Too far for horses."

"Camels then." They rode for a little while in silence, then Marriner spoke again.

"What people are they, Activity? Who is it lives there?"

"Pintubi."

Activity had never been more matter-of-fact. He seemed as phlegmatic as though they proposed only to go to the next water hole. Yet he was tense too. He, too, in his own way felt the need for release in action. And perhaps he, too, felt

243

guilty; as guilty as Marriner, or worse; for it was he who had brought Marriner to his tribe; it was he who first of all had overlooked the ancient restrictions; it was he who had turned his face towards the promise of a new kind of life. He was the wanderer, he the adventurer.

But perhaps his need was only the need for the fulfilment of his old friendship with Marriner; perhaps he still looked to the far horizons with no other motive than that provided by his adventuresomeness.

"You can find the way?" asked Marriner.

"Yowai, Davy. I can."

And by that much, by his acceptance of Activity, Marriner's impulse to find a new life for himself, to break all association with the old, was already modified. Yet otherwise he went directly to meet the challenge of his mind; he made no other concessions.

When the camels had been yarded, the harness overhauled, the packs made ready, he set out; and none at Bloodwood knew that he intended never to return.

16

They went out north and west, over the territory of the station where Dallas had been murdered. Gerry Shortland, long retired from the police, was the owner there now. He was heading for prosperity with no side excursions, a Spartan-living man of good humour and a considerable determination. The Wailbri tribe lived close to his station, and admired him.

Beyond his boundaries the travellers headed into the most arid country Marriner had ever seen; but they were well equipped and amply supplied. On their longest stretch they went eight days between water holes. They were lucky, at that, in their season; for rain had not long fallen. In the temper of his mood Marriner would have set out at any season; and thus prematurely condemned himself.

They travelled four hundred miles and came to well-grassed country, with the tree-lined snake of a watercourse splitting the plain. It had been only a week or two since the rains had filled it and made it run; the water holes were deep and looked as though they would hold their contents for a long time.

Two natives came to their night-camp. They advanced slowly in the evening light, drawing attention to their approach, and carrying their spears points forward. After a while they squatted in the sand. They had no English, but Activity could establish some kind of communication with them, and even Marriner, who had a smattering of Eiliuwarra words and phrases, could understand a little from time to time. It was significant that the natives were not afraid of the camels. They had seen such beasts before and treated them, if not with familiarity, at least with the indifference of custom.

In appearance, the two men were striking. They were taller than average, bearded, and their long hair was bound into a tight bundle at the back of the head. They were fully armed with the weapons of the plains; each carried a stone knife tucked into a band that circled the upper part of the left arm; and otherwise they carried spears, a spear thrower, and throwing sticks. They seemed quite at their ease. They sat for perhaps an hour, and then departed.

The following day, at about a mile's distance, Marriner and Activity came to the natives' encampment. Marriner gasped, unable completely to comprehend the truth of what he saw. It was a large encampment. There must have been more than a hundred people; and these were even less equipped with the impedimenta of the white man—his clothes, his knives, his tobacco—than the Eiliuwarra had been at his first meeting so many years before. Their visitors of the previous night met them at a little distance, and accompanied them into the camp.

Near the bank of the creek there was even a whip-pole. It was not working. It had not worked for many years; and apparently in the time that it had a useful function—in the months when the water hole was dried up—the tribe was in the habit of simply going to another place. They had never used it. It was the symbol, and the only symbol, of a brief settlement here by some white wanderer. He had left no other traces.

But to Marriner, its presence seemed significant, setting the seal of approval of some metaphysical authority upon his choice of this land and these people. Marriner was not a religious man; he never had been. What religious thought had come to him from time to time had been confused by his familiarity with the light sincerity of the natives, who believed in a variety of things. But he was easily moved by some pseudo-spiritual experience; and this was one of the rare occasions when he had felt one.

Thus in some degree their arrival was a homecoming for both men. They were more satisfactorily attuned to these wild people than they had been to those who, neither civilized nor primitive, sat around the settlement at Bloodwood. Here was a livelier feeling; necessarily so; for the people had to hunt and keep themselves; the children had to learn; the women by their industry had to guard against the occasional hunting failures of their men.

One of the tribesmen here commanded a considerable respect. He was an old man, thin, but straight, bearing himself well and possessed of great dignity. He seemed to spend a good deal of his time with the two strangers; more than any of the other men in camp; certainly a great deal more than any of the other old men. Activity, too, accorded him more than the usual respect.

"This is one clever old man," he explained. "He knows plenty. He's—what do you call it? He makes the rain."

"A rain maker?"

"True. Suppose they've got no rain a long time, they come to him. He watches. He makes a big thing—a lovely thing. Big." Activity stepped out about fourteen feet. "That big. Makes it all feathers, pretty coloured feathers. It is a wooden thing with feathers stuck on with blood. All paint and feathers. It takes a long time. Then someday he burns it. And the rain comes. It comes for sure."

"A witch doctor, eh?"

"No, I don't know. He's a big man. Very clever."

"A *kurdaitcha* man? Does he point the bone?"

"Maybe he's a *kurdaitcha* man. I don't know."

No native would know. A *kurdaitcha* man could not be seen. A *kurdaitcha* man had magic shoes, made of emu feathers gummed together with blood; and when he put

247

them on he left no tracks. Or if he left a track, it read the same coming as going. He could, with the proper incantations, point a bone towards a man and the man would die; even though he was a hundred miles away in the heart of another tribe.

But the *kurdaitcha* man could not be seen. Nobody could know his identity.

"This fellow's too clever, too strong," Activity said.

"I'd like to see that rain making," Marriner commented.

Activity held a long conversation with the old man. They talked for an hour. Then he reported:

"He can't show this making rain. They got to need it bad. They got to need it like if they don't have rain, everybody will die. But he says he'll show you something. He will show you how he can kill, a long way away."

"Bone-pointing?"

"No, I don't think so. Something else."

He talked again for a while.

"He'll show you. Not here. Not today. Tomorrow. We'll go with him tomorrow."

"All right. Then he can show me. Whatever it is."

Marriner was no more than casually interested. He would see whatever there was to be seen. Some display of legerdemain, or a clever deceit. Whatever it was it could not much affect him, and it would show a polite interest to go. The old man had a great and readily discernible influence. It would be as well to be acceptable to him.

But if it were a deceit he practised, the old magician knew how to make it undetectable. There was no fuss, no fanfare about his operation. He had no claque, no confederates. Marriner, Activity and he simply walked out a mile or two into the desert, to a place where a small ghost gum grew at the edge of a wide expanse of stony emptiness. On the starkly white trunk of the gum, the magician, with a pointed stone, carefully scratched a wide oval, eighteen inches deep, nine wide, at the height of his chest on the trunk. Then all three walked away from the tree.

They walked a long way, but kept the tree always in sight. At a distance of eight or nine hundred yards the magician stopped, and made his preparations. The tree's white trunk stood more or less alone; no one could approach it without their knowledge; and by looking back from time to time, following Activity's lead, Marriner made certain that no one had, indeed, approached it.

The preparations were long. First, the magician put a curved flat stone, an oval plaque, on the ground. It was his churinga, his talisman, the inanimate residence of his spiritual being. He encircled the space in which the stone lay, and then, at great length, he decorated himself with the down of birds, gluing it to his skin with blood extracted from a vein in his arm. These preparations took the best part of two hours during which Marriner and Activity, sitting on the sand, waited patiently. He completed this phase by binding a tight stricture about his right arm, beginning high under the armpit, and working downwards.

These bonds were so tight it seemed impossible he could continue the process to its conclusion. The blood swelled the remainder of his arm, and at its upper end the lashings seemed to cut into the flesh. When the binding had been brought halfway down his forearm he took the churinga in his right hand, the fingers outspread against its surface, and bound the stone tightly to his arm.

Now he was ready. The incantations which had attended the binding of the arm changed their rhythm, and he rose to his feet within the circle. Carefully he aimed as though he were about to throw the bound stone towards the distant ghost gum; and again; again and again and again; the rhythm of his voice accelerating, the stone swinging at the end of his arm, the fingers spread against its surface, bloated and swollen with the pressure of the constricted blood. His face drew to itself an intensity of expression not commonly seen on any face, in any circumstances; his posturing was not the posturing of an actor; but an action series of terrific moment, demanding the fullest output of his muscles.

Each time he assumed the throwing stance it was as though his aim had grown surer, his body more confident. In one unbelievable burst he finally put himself to the test. His arm whirled, it seemed, with the speed of light; his whole body strained at the effort, the blood spurted from the bound fingers.

That was all. His show was finished, except for the final stage. He sat down quickly, and quickly released the binding from his tortured arm. The stone he released first, and set it carefully on the sand, new-marked with his blood.

It was, in truth, as Marriner realized on second thoughts, an exaggeration to say the blood had spurted from his fingers. It had indeed broken the bond of skin and marked the stone; it was only a dribbling of blood, but its presence, and the angle at which it had streaked the stone testified to the amazing effort with which the old man had thrown away nothing; the whole-heartedness with which he had concluded his miming.

The magician motioned that they should walk to the tree, and they did so. To Marriner's amazement he found, in the centre of the oval that the old man had outlined, the deep indentation of a stone. The mark was fresh; the bark and some of the underlying wood new-bruised, the gash the size and shape of one that could have been made with the magician's churinga stone.

And the force with which the blow had been delivered was undoubtedly great. If something had actually flown the half-mile from where the magician stood, and then struck the tree, it must have had the velocity of a heavy-calibre bullet. Or more, indeed. And the missile, if there were a missile, must have been heavy.

"Look for tracks, Activity," Marriner warned.

He could see none himself. It did not seem possible that an accomplice could have crept on the tree; yet one might have, while their attention was wholly captured by the magician's performance. But an accomplice would have stood to deliver the blow; he would have stood in full sight; for such a mighty thump could not have been delivered by a man lying, for instance, on the ground.

And anyone who delivered it must have left tracks. The side of his foot at least must have thrust away the loose earth with that energetic movement, to such a depth that a later covering would have been conspicuous.

"No tracks," Activity said.

He pointed out the undisturbed marks the magician's feet had made while he traced the oval on the bark; nothing had covered them. He identified his own boots and Marriner's. There were no additional marks anywhere, though he traced a wide circle.

That was all. The magician claimed he could strike at a distance. He had.

He now seemed to have some further rites in hand, for he made no attempt to come up on Marriner and Activity, or to look at the tree. He continued to sit away off in the desert; and after they had waited a little while for him, the two men went back to the camp.

Neither spoke of what they had seen, simply because speaking seemed superfluous; but Marriner knew that he was glad. The old world still had its powers, and he was glad of it. With these people the secrets had been handed on, the old abilities were not lost. Not yet would they drown in available drinking water; not yet would they lose the power to live close to their country, their beloved country, the country of their dreaming; a country of which the spirit was allied with their own spirits, of which the soil was rich with the blood of their ancestors.

In his happiness, Marriner also dreamed his dreams. He was renewed; a youth again without the faults of youth; he had his second chance. And in his phoenix joy he could see clearly the enormities of the sins he felt were now forgiven him. These people were strong people, happy, well nourished, independent; as the Eiliuwarra, too, had been; they differed enormously from the people he had left at the Argadala encampment. For those, after a few years of the white man's leadership, were fitted neither to the desert nor the new world; they were as incongruous to either as their bodies to the ill-fitting scraps of European clothing with which they now hid their new-found nakedness.

Neither nature nor man now balanced their diet. Their lives were committed inevitably to the casual needs of the white people—not there could the embryo artist become an artist, nor could he continue to waste his life playing with ochre on sheets of bark; not there could the engineer or the scientist be developed; and the hunter had no more time to practise his skills. The magician was shamed before his people there; yet he could never be a leader in the new religions.

Suddenly it was all very clear to Marriner. His was the culpability of the bystander; but he was no less to be condemned. The man who watches the rape of the virgin is himself a monster; his culpability is no less than that of a participant. Yet the worst of men may redeem himself. Of his own volition Marriner had discovered the way of redemption.

These thoughts had no more real definition than the quality of a new-found happiness; but it was real happiness. The sound that ruptured his calm, in that early evening, was the tinny, distant tinkle of a horse-bell.

Alert, he and Activity waited for the cavalcade. It was a small one, of four horses. The traveller was Mission Mo.

"Which way did you come?" the little miner asked.

"Straight through," said Marriner.

"With camels?"

"That's right."

"Then that explains it. I came right round, in here from the west. Davy, my boy, I've really made our fortunes this time. You're a wealthy man. If you didn't have a penny, you'd be wealthy now. And so am I. It's the mother lode, Davy. If it isn't, it's as close to the mother lode as man ever saw. It's rich. And it's big."

"Gold?" asked Marriner, and his heart sank. It could not have been anything else.

"Of course it's gold."

"Where?"

"About seven miles, I'd say. No more. This is the nearest good water, though there's enough over there for now."

He sat back.

"Look at it. A Godforsaken wilderness. There'll be a city here. Right here where we are."

"A city?"

"A fair dinkum city. You want to see this strike. Have a look at it. Ride over tomorrow. It's rich, I'm telling you. I'll show you samples."

"No. Never mind."

The little man looked at him.

"You never had much interest, did you, Davy? You never thought I'd make it. Yet you never complained. I've cost you a packet over the years. Well, you're going to get it all back now. A hundred times, by Christ. A hundred times over."

Marriner could see it: not a city, but a drab mining town, drab because its publicans and shopkeepers would be interested only in taking the most money in the shortest time; a town peopled with quicksilver citizens whose eye was to the main chance; a town where the dogs would prosper and the natives would scavenge; a city of temporary iron and false fronts and rusty dumps and harsh voices.

And he would bring it about. He and his agent, Mission Mo. It had been waiting here for him to come to. He had discovered this place with the inevitability of the fore-ordained.

In the morning Mission Mo rode away. His samples were dishearteningly rich, and he as jubilant. When he had gone, Marriner turned to Activity.

"Is there some other place, Activity? Some place further on? Can we keep going?"

And Activity did not fail him.

"Yowai, Davy. Plenty more. We can find them."

And Activity was right. For there is always a place beyond; and there is always someone or something to point the way.

And so the camel tracks, when they led off from that place, had direction. They moved with surety into the desert, the great animals passive to the direction of the men. The Pintubi people watched the strangers go, without comment and without warning.

The desert is too wide. To this day no one has crossed it; no one knows what lies within. There is a point, there must be a point, at which the tracks of the camels come to an end; and surely a man would be dreaming who entertained the idea that at that point sparkling waters lie in the tree-dappled sun, and children are at play. It is not impossible, but it remains a dream.

For Activity, too, was divorced from his inheritance; his judgment debauched by his association with men not of his kind.

The trail led all the long way from Bloodwood Plains to a dream. Its making was the first venture on which Marriner embarked of his own volition in the country of his adoption. Surely, it could only have led him to disaster.